Håkan Nesser

Münster's Case

Håkan Nesser was awarded the 1993 Swedish Crime
Writers' Academy Prize for new authors for *Mind's
Eye* (published in Sweden as *Det Grovmaskiga Nätet*);
he received the Best Novel Award in 1994 for *Borkmann's Point* and in 1996 for *Woman with Birthmark*.
In 1999 he was awarded the Crime Writers of Scan-
dinavia's Glass Key Award for the best crime novel of
the year for *Carambole*, and in 2010 he won the pres-
tigious European Crime Fiction Star Award. Nesser
lives in Sweden and London.

ALSO BY HÅKAN NESSER

Borkmann's Point
The Return
Mind's Eye
Woman with Birthmark
The Inspector and Silence

Münster's Case

Münster's Case

An Inspector Van Veeteren Mystery

Håkan Nesser

Translated from the Swedish by Laurie Thompson

VINTAGE CRIME / BLACK LIZARD
Vintage Books
A Division of Random House, Inc.
New York

FIRST VINTAGE CRIME/BLACK LIZARD EDITION, JUNE 2013

Translation copyright © 2012 by Laurie Thompson

The Library of Congress has cataloged the Pantheon edition as follows:
Nesser, Håkan.
[Münsters fall. English]
Münster's case : an Inspector Van Veeteren mystery / Håkan Nesser ;
translated from the Swedish by Laurie Thompson.
p. cm.
1. Van Veeteren, Inspector (Fictitious character)—Fiction. 2. Murder—
Investigation—Fiction. 3. Sweden—Fiction. I. Thompson, Laurie. II. Title.
PT9876.24.E76M8613 2012
839.73'74—dc23 2012005613

Vintage ISBN: 978-0-307-94641-6

www.weeklylizard.com

Printed in the United States of America
10 9 8 7 6 5 4 3 2 1

For the man in the street, the most important thing is to realize that deeds have consequences.
For a detective, they have causes.

—*Erwin Baasteuwel, Detective Inspector*

I

I

The last day of Waldemar Leverkuhn's life could hardly have begun any better.

After a windy night of nonstop rain, mild autumn sunshine was now creeping in through the kitchen window. From the balcony overlooking the courtyard he could hear the characteristic soft cooing of lovelorn pigeons, and the fading echo of his wife's footsteps on the stairs as she set off for the market. The *Neuwe Blatt* was spread out on the table in front of him, and he had just laced his morning coffee with a couple of drops of gin when Wauters rang.

"We won," Wauters said.

"Won?" said Leverkuhn.

"Christ yes, we won!" said Wauters. "They said so on the radio."

"On the radio?"

"Fuck me if we haven't won twenty thousand! Five each—and not a day too soon!"

"The lottery?"

"The lottery, yes. What else? What did I tell you? There was something special in the air when I bought the ticket. My God, yes! Mrs. Milkerson in the corner shop sort of *coaxed* it out! As if she really was picking out the right one. Two, five, five. One, six, five, five! It was the fives that won it for us, of course. I've had a feeling this was going to happen all week!"

"How much did you say?"

"Twenty thousand, for God's sake! Five each. I'll have to ring the others. Let's get together at Freddy's this evening—dammit, a party in Capernaum is called for!"

"Five thousand . . . ?" said Leverkuhn, but Wauters had already hung up.

He remained standing for a while with the receiver in his hand, feeling dizzy. Five thousand guilders? He blinked carefully a few times, and when his eyes started to focus again they turned automatically to look at the wedding photograph on the bureau. The one in the gold frame. They settled gradually on Marie-Louise's round, milk-fresh face. Her dimples and corkscrew curls. A warm wind in her hair. Glitter in her eyes.

That was then, he thought. She was a stunner in those days. Nineteen forty-eight. As tasty as a cream cake! He took out his handkerchief and blew his nose. Scratched himself a little tentatively in the crotch. It was different nowadays . . . but that's the way it is with women . . . early blossoming, childbirth, breast-feeding, weight gain . . . reluctance. It was sort of in the nature of things. Different with men, so very different.

He sighed and went out of the bedroom. Continued his train of thought, even though he didn't really want to. That seemed to happen often nowadays. Men, oh yes, they were still up for it much longer, that was the big difference . . . that damned big difference. Mind you, it evened itself out toward the end. Now, well into the autumn of his life, he rarely got the urge anymore, it had to be admitted. That applied to both of them.

But what else could you expect? Seventy-two and sixty-nine. He'd heard about people who could keep going for longer than that, but as far as he was concerned it was probably all over and done with, he'd just have to make the best of it.

There was the odd little twitch now and then, though, which he preferred to do without. A vague reminder of days long past, no more than a memory, a sad recollection.

But that's the way it was. A little twitch that he could have done without. He flopped down over the kitchen table again.

Five thousand!

My God! He tried to think. Five thousand guilders!

But it was hard to pin down those butterflies fluttering in his stomach. What the hell could he do with that amount of money?

A car? Hardly. It would probably be enough for a pretty decent secondhand model, and he had a driver's license; but it was ten years since he'd sat at the wheel, and he hadn't had any pressing desire to get out and see the world for a long time now.

Nor did he prefer an expensive vacation. It was like Palinski used to say: he'd seen most things and more besides.

A better television set?

No point. The one they had was only a couple of years old, and in any case, he used it only as something to sit in front of and fall asleep.

A new suit?

For his own funeral?

No, the first thing to stick its head over the parapet inside his mind was that there was nothing he really needed. Which no doubt said a lot about what a miserable old grump he'd become. Couldn't even work out how to spend his own money any longer. Couldn't be bothered. What a joke!

Leverkuhn slid the newspaper to one side and poured himself another cup of coffee with a dash of gin.

That was surely something he could allow himself? Another cup? He listened to the pigeons as he sipped his coffee. Maybe that was how he should deal with the situation? Allow himself a few things? Buy an extra round or two at Freddy's. More expensive wines. A decent bite to eat at Keefer's or Kraus.

Why not? Live a bit of the good life for a year or two.

Now the phone rang again.

Palinski, of course.

"Dammit, a party in Capernaum is called for tonight!"

The very same words as Wauters. How odd that he wasn't even capable of thinking up his own swearwords. After his opening remark he roared with laughter on the phone for half a minute, then finished off by yelling something about how the wine would be flowing at Freddy's.

"... half past six! White shirt and new tie, you old devil!"

And he hung up. Leverkuhn observed his newlywed wife again for a while, then returned to the kitchen. Drank up the rest of the coffee and belched. Then smiled.

He smiled at last. After all, five thousand was five thousand.

Bonger, Wauters, Leverkuhn, and Palinski.

They were a long-standing, ancient quartet. He had known Bonger and Palinski since he was a boy. Since they were at school together at the Magdeburgska, and the wartime winters in the cellars on Zuiderslaan and Merdwick. They had drifted apart for a few decades in the middle of their lives, naturally, but their paths had crossed once again in their late middle age.

Wauters had joined them later, much later. One of the lone gents who hung out at Freddy's, Herr Wauters. Moved there from Hamburg and Frigge and God only knows where else. He had never been married (the only one of the quartet who had managed to avoid that, he liked to point out—although he now shared the bachelor state with both Bonger and Palinski)—and he was probably the loneliest old man you could possibly imagine. Or at least, that's what Bonger used to confide in them, strictly between friends of course. It was Bonger who had gotten to know him first, and introduced him into their circle. A bit of a gambler as well, this Wauters, if you could believe the rumors he spread somewhat discriminately about himself, that is. But now he restricted himself to the soccer pools and the lottery. The horses nowadays were nothing but drugged-up donkeys, he used to maintain with a sigh, and the jockeys were all greedy pricks. And as for cards? Well, if you'd lost nearly twelve hundred on a full house, huh, let's face it—it was about bloody time you took things easy in your old age!

According to Benjamin Wauters.

Bonger, Wauters, Leverkuhn, and Palinski.

The other evening Palinski had worked out that their combined age came to 292, and so if they could hang on for another couple of years, they could look forward to celebrating their three hundredth anniversary at the turn of the century. Christ Almighty, that wasn't something to be sneered at!

Palinski had patted Fröken Gautiers's generously proportioned bum and informed her of that fact as well, but Fröken Gautiers had merely snorted and stated that she would have guessed four hundred.

But in reality these round figures had no significance at all, because this Saturday was the last day of Waldemar Leverkuhn's life. As already said.

Marie-Louise arrived with the bags of groceries just as he was on his way out.

"Where are you going?"

"Out."

"Why?"

"To buy a tie."

There was a clicking noise from her false teeth, twice, as always happened when she was irritated by something. *Tick, tock.*

"A tie?"

"Yes."

"Why are you going to buy a tie? You already have fifty."

"I've grown tired of them."

She shook her head and pushed her way past him with the bags. The smell of kidney floated into his nostrils.

"You don't need to cook a meal tonight."

"Eh? What do you mean by that?"

"I'm eating out."

She put the bags on the table.

"I've bought some kidney."

"So I've noticed."

"Why have you suddenly decided to eat out? I thought we were going to have an early meal—I'm going to Emmeline's this evening, and you're supposed to be going—"

"To Freddy's, yes. But I'm going to have a bite to eat out as well. You can put it in the freezer. The kidney, that is."

She screwed up her eyes and stared at him.

"Has something happened?"

He buttoned up his overcoat.

"Not that I know of. Like what?"

"Have you taken your medicine?"

He didn't reply.

"Put a scarf on. It's windy out there."

He shrugged and went out.

Five thousand, he thought. I could spend a few nights in a hotel.

Wauters and Palinski were also wearing new ties, but not Bonger.

Bonger never wore a tie, had probably never owned one in his life, but at least his shirt was fairly clean. His wife had died eight years ago, and nowadays it was a matter of getting by as best he could—with regard to shirts and everything else.

Wauters had reserved a table in the restaurant area, and they started with champagne and caviar as recommended by Palinski, apart from Bonger, who declined the caviar and ordered lobster tails in a sauternes sauce.

"What's got into you old devils this evening?" Fröken Gautiers wondered incredulously. "Don't tell me you've sold your prostates to some research institute."

But she took their orders without more ado, and when Palinski patted her bottom as usual she almost forgot to fend off his rheumatic hand.

"Your very good health, my friends!" proposed Wauters at regular intervals.

"Let the party in Capernaum commence!" Palinski urged at even more regular intervals.

For Christ's sake, I'm sick and fed up with these idiots, Leverkuhn thought.

By about eleven Wauters had told them eight or nine times how he had bought the lottery ticket. Palinski had begun to sing "Oh, those sinful days of youth" about as frequently, breaking off after a line and a half because he couldn't remember the words. Bonger's stomach had started acting up. For his part, Waldemar Leverkuhn established that he was probably even more drunk than he'd been at the Oktoberfest in Grünwald fifteen years ago. Or was it sixteen?

Whatever, it was about time to head home.

If only he could find his shoes, that is. He'd been sitting in his stockinged feet for the last half hour or so. He had realized this, somewhat to his surprise, when he had made his way to the bathroom to pee; but no matter how much he fished around for them under the table with his feet, he didn't get a bite.

This was a damned nuisance. He could smell that Bonger's stomach had spoken once more, and when Palinski started singing yet again, he realized that his search needed to be more systematic.

He coughed by way of creating a diversion, then ducked down discreetly, but unfortunately caught the edge of the tablecloth as he collapsed onto the floor. The chaos that ensued made him reluctant to leave his temporary exile under the table. Especially as he could see no sign of his shoes.

"Leave me alone, damn you!" he growled threateningly. "Fuck off and leave me in peace!"

He rolled over onto his back and pulled down the rest of the tablecloth and all the glasses and crockery. From the surrounding tables came a mixed chorus of roars of masculine laughter and horrified feminine shrieks. Wauters and Palinski offered well-meaning advice, and Bongers weighed in with another stink bomb.

Then Fröken Gautiers and Herr Van der Valk and Freddy himself made an appearance; and ten minutes later Waldemar

Leverkuhn was standing on the sidewalk outside, in the rain, complete with both overcoat and shoes. Palinski and Wauters went off in a taxi, and Bonger asked right away if Leverkuhn might like to share one with him.

Most certainly not, you bloody skunk! Leverkuhn thought; and he must have said so as well because Bonger's fist hovered threateningly under his nose for a worrying second: but then both the hand and its owner set off along Langgracht.

Touchy as usual, Leverkuhn thought as he started walking in more or less the same direction. The rain was getting heavier. But it didn't worry him, not in the least. Despite being drunk, he felt on top of the world and could walk in a more or less straight line. It was only when he turned onto the slope leading to the Wagner Bridge that he slipped and fell over. Two women who happened to be passing, probably whores from the Zwille, helped him to his feet and made sure he was on steadier ground in Zuyderstraat.

The rest of the walk home was no problem, and he reached his apartment just as the clock in the Keymer church struck a quarter to twelve.

But his wife wasn't at home yet. Waldemar Leverkuhn closed the door without locking it, left his shoes, overcoat, and jacket in the hall, and crept into bed.

Two minutes later he was asleep on his back with his mouth wide open; and when a little later his rasping snores were silenced by a carving knife stabbing twenty-eight times through his neck and torso, it is not clear if he knew anything about it.

2

The woman was as gray as dawn.

With her shoulders hunched in her shabby coat, she sat opposite Intendent Münster, looking at the floor. Showed no sign of touching either the mug of tea or the sandwiches Fröken Katz had brought in. There was an aura of weary resignation surrounding her, and Münster wondered for a moment if it might be best to summon the doctor and give her an injection. Get her into bed for some rest instead of sitting here and being tortured. Krause had already conducted a preliminary interrogation after all.

But as Van Veeteren used to say: The first few hours are the most important. And the first quarter of an hour is worth as much as the whole of the third week.

Assuming it was going to be a long drawn-out business, of course. But you never knew.

He glanced at the clock. Six forty-five. All right, he thought. Just a quarter of an hour.

"I'll have to review the details one more time," he said. "Then you can get some sleep."

She shook her head. "I don't need to sleep."

Münster read quickly through Krause's notes.

"So you got home at about two o'clock, is that right?"

"Yes, about five past. There had been a power outage, and we'd been stuck in the train for over an hour. Just outside Voigtshuuis."

"Where had you been?"

"Bossingen. Visiting a friend. We generally meet on a Saturday. . . . Not every week, but now and then. I've already told an officer this."

"Yes, I know," said Münster. "What time was it when you set off from Bossingen?"

"I took the twelve o'clock train. It leaves at eleven fifty-nine, and is supposed to arrive at a quarter to one. But it was nearly two."

"And then what?"

"Then I went home and found him."

She shrugged and fell silent. She still hadn't raised her eyes. For a brief second Münster recalled a kitten that had been run over; he'd found it when he was ten or eleven. It was lying there, stuck to the asphalt in a pool of blood as he came cycling past, and it hadn't raised its eyes either. It simply lay there, staring into the tall grass at the side of the road, waiting to die.

He wondered why that particular image had come back to him on this gloomy morning. It wasn't Fru Leverkuhn who was dying after all, it was her husband who was dead.

Murdered. Seventy-two years of age and he had met his killer, a killer who had found it safest to stab his knife into him between twenty and thirty times, making sure he would never again be able to get out of bed.

At some time between half past twelve and half past two, according to the preliminary forensic report, which had been delivered shortly before Münster arrived at the police station.

A bit over the top, to be sure. One or two stabs would presumably have been enough. The loss of blood had been so great that for once it was justified to talk about bathing in his own blood. Apparently there was more on the bed and on the floor than in the man's body.

He eyed Marie-Louise Leverkuhn and waited for a few seconds.

"And so you phoned the police straight away?"

"Yes . . . er, no: I went outside for a bit first."

"Went outside? What on earth for?"

She shrugged once again.

"I don't know. I must have been in some sort of shock, I suppose. . . . I think I was intending to walk to Entwick Plejn."

"Why did you want to go to Entwick Plejn?"

"The police station. I was going to report it there . . . but then it dawned on me that it would be better to phone. I mean, it was late, and I supposed they would only be open there during office hours. Is that the case?"

"I think so," said Münster. "What time did you get back?"

She thought for a moment.

"Just after half past two, I suppose."

Münster thumbed through his papers. That seemed to be right. The call had been recorded at 02:43.

"I see here it says that the door wasn't locked when you got home."

"No."

"Had somebody broken in?"

"No. He sometimes forgot to lock it . . . or just didn't bother."

"He seemed to have been drinking quite heavily."

She made no reply. Münster hesitated for a few moments.

"Fru Leverkuhn," he said eventually, leaning forward over the desk and trying to fish her gaze up from the floor. "There is no doubt at all that your husband was murdered. Have you any idea of who might have done it?"

"No."

"Not the slightest suspicion? Somebody he might have fallen out with, or something of the sort?"

She shook her head ever so slightly.

"Was anything missing from the apartment? Besides the knife, that is."

"I don't think so."

"No trace of the killer?"

"No."

"Was there anything at all that you noticed, that you think might be of significance?"

A shudder ran through her body, and she raised her eyes at last.

"No, everything was the same as usual, everything. . . . Oh, what am I saying? I mean . . ."

"It's okay, I understand," said Münster. "It's as you said, you've had a nasty shock. We'll have a break now. I think it would be best if you have a lie down for a while. I'll send for a lady officer to look after you."

He closed his notebook and stood up. Beckoned Fru Leverkuhn to accompany him and opened the door for her. As she passed by close to him, he noticed her smell for the first time.

Mothballs, unless he was much mistaken.

Rooth looked very much like how Münster felt.

"Have you been at it for long?"

Rooth stirred his coffee with a pencil.

"You can say that again," he said. "When I was a kid we used to have something called Sunday mornings. Where have they gone to?"

"No idea," said Münster. "You've been there, I take it?"

"For three hours," said Rooth. "I got there shortly after Krause. Spent an hour looking at the bloodbath, two hours interviewing the neighbors. Krause looked after the wife."

"So I heard," said Münster. "What did the neighbors have to say?"

"Unanimous information," Rooth explained as he dug a sandwich out of a plastic bag on his deck. "Would you like one?"

Münster shook his head.

"Unanimous information? What the hell does that mean?"

Rooth blew his nose.

"There are only six apartments in the house. One is empty. Three—including the Leverkuhns'—are occupied by retirees. Sixty-five and up. A fat woman in her forties lives in the fourth, and a young couple in the last one. They were all at home last night and they all heard the same thing."

"You don't say. What?"

"The young couple screwing away. The sound insulation seems to be bad, and they don't have the best bed in the world, apparently."

"Three hours?" said Münster.

Rooth took a bite at his sandwich and frowned.

"Yes, and they admit it. The stallion isn't exactly a bloody athlete either, by the looks of him. But then, he's black, of course. It sometimes makes you wonder. . . ."

"Are you telling me that these old folk were lying awake listening to sexual gymnastics the entire time between eleven and two?"

"Not all the time; they dozed off now and again. There's only one couple, by the way. Van Ecks on the ground floor. The others are on their own . . . Herr Engel and Fröken Mathisen."

"I see," said Münster, thinking that information over. "But nobody heard anything from the Leverkuhns' apartment?"

"Not even a fly's fart," said Rooth, taking another bite. "Nobody noticed any visitors entering the premises, and nobody heard any suspicious sounds, apart from the screwing. But it seems that getting into the building is no problem. According to Van Eck you can open the outside door with a toothpick."

Münster said nothing while Rooth finished off his sandwich.

"What do you think?" he asked.

Rooth yawned.

"Not a bloody thing," he said. "I'm a bit too tired to think. I assume somebody got in, stabbed the poor bastard to death, then left. Or was sitting waiting for him when he came home. Take your pick."

"Twenty to thirty stabs?" said Münster.

"Two would have been enough," said Rooth. "A madman, I assume."

Münster stood up and walked over to the window. Forced apart a couple of slats in the venetian blinds and peered out over the mist-covered town. It was nearly half past eight, but it was obvious that it was going to be one of those gray, rainy Sundays when it never became really light. One of those damp waiting rooms.

He let go of the blinds and turned around.

"Why?" he said. "Who the hell would want to stab to death a seventy-year-old man like this?"

Rooth said nothing.

"What about the weapon?"

Rooth looked up from his coffee cup.

"The only thing missing from the apartment—according to the wife, at least—is a carving knife. Meusse says it could have been the one the killer used. The length seems to be about right, so that's the assumption he's making."

"Hmm," said Münster. "What are you thinking of doing now, then?"

Rooth scratched his chin.

"Going home and lying down for a bit. You're taking over as I understand it. I'll be back on duty tomorrow if I'm still alive. There are a few people that need to be informed, by the way. I saved that for you. I hope you'll forgive me, but you're better at that kind of thing than I am. Besides, you can't make phone calls like that at any old time in the morning."

"Thank you," said Münster. "Who needs to be informed?"

Rooth took a scrap of paper from his inside pocket.

"A son and a daughter," he said. "Neither of them live here in Maardam. There is another daughter, but she's in a psychiatric hospital somewhere or other, so I suppose that can wait."

"All right," said Münster, accepting the addresses. "Go home and go to bed, I'll solve this little problem."

"Good," said Rooth. "If you've cracked it by tomorrow morning you'll get a bar of chocolate."

"Stingy old bastard," said Münster, lifting up the receiver.

There was no reply from either of the numbers, and he wondered if he ought to hand the job over to Krause or one of the others. In any case, it was obvious that old Fru Leverkuhn did not feel she was in a fit state to call her children. To call and tell them that somebody had just killed their father, that is, by stabbing him twenty to thirty times with the knife they had given him as a Christmas present fifteen years ago.

He could appreciate her point of view. He folded the scrap of paper and decided that this was one of those tasks he couldn't simply delegate to somebody else. Duties, as they used to be called.

Instead he rang Synn. He explained that he would probably have to work all day, and he could hear the disappointment in her silence and the words she didn't speak. His own disappointment was no less heartfelt, and they hung up after less than a minute.

There were few things Intendent Münster liked better than spending a day in a damp sitting room with Synn. And their children. An unplanned, rainy Sunday.

He closed his eyes and leaned back in his desk chair.

Why, he thought listlessly.

Why did somebody have to go and kill an old man in this bestial fashion?

And why did he have to have a job that so often required him to spend rainy Sundays digging out answers to questions like this, instead of being with his beloved family?

Why?

He sighed and looked at the clock. The morning had barely started.

3

He walked to Freddy's. A gray mist hung over the canals and the deserted Sunday streets, but at least it had stopped raining for the moment. The little restaurant was in Weiskerstraat, on the corner of Langgraacht, and the entrance doors were not yet open. SUNDAYS NOON TO MIDNIGHT, it said on a yellowed piece of paper taped to the door, but he knocked on the wet glass, and after a long pause, he was allowed in. The door was opened by a powerfully built woman in her forties. She was almost as tall as he was, dressed in jeans and a flannel shirt, with a slightly grubby red shawl over her head. She was evidently busy transforming the premises into a reasonably presentable state.

Sprucing up the place.

"Elizabeth Gautiers?"

She nodded and put a pile of plastic-laminated menus down on the bar counter. Münster looked around. The lighting was very low-key—he assumed this was connected with the level of cleanliness aimed at. Otherwise it looked much the same as any other similar establishment. Dark wooden panels, drab furnishings in brown, green, and red. A cigarette machine and a television set. Another room at the back had tables with white cloths and was a bit more generously lit: a slightly more posh dining area. Voices and the clattering of pots and pans could be heard from the kitchen. It was half past ten and they were starting to prepare for lunch.

"Was it you who rang?"

Münster produced his ID and looked for a convenient place to sit.

"We can sit through there. Would you like anything?"

She pointed toward the white tablecloths and led the way through the saloon doors.

"Coffee, please," said Münster, ignoring the fact that he had promised Synn to reduce his intake to four cups per day. This would be his third. "If it's not too much trouble."

It wasn't. They sat down under the branches of a weeping fig made of cloth and plastic, and he took out his notebook.

"As I said, it's about that group of diners you had here last night." He checked the names. "Palinski, Bonger, Wauters, and Leverkuhn. All of them regulars, I believe? It appears Leverkuhn has been murdered."

This was evidently news to her; her jaw dropped so far that he could hear a slight clicking noise. Münster wondered if she could possibly have false teeth—she couldn't be more than forty-five, surely? His own age, more or less.

"Murdered?"

"No doubt about it," said Münster, and paused.

"Er . . . but why?"

"We don't know yet."

She sat absolutely still for a few seconds. Then she removed the shawl and revealed a head of hair almost exactly the same shade of red. But not quite as grubby. A rather beautiful woman, Münster decided, somewhat to his surprise. Large, but beautiful. A good catch for the right man. She lit a cigarette.

"Robbery, I expect?"

Münster made no reply.

"Was he attacked on the way home?"

"Not exactly. Can you tell me what time he left here?"

Elizabeth Gautiers thought for a moment.

"Eleven," she said. "Maybe a few minutes past. It had been a special occasion," she added after a while.

"Special?"

"They got drunk. Leverkuhn fell under the table."

"Under the table?"

She laughed.

"Yes, he really did. He dragged the tablecloth down with him, and there was a bit of a palaver. Still, we managed to stand them up and set them on their way. . . . You mean he was killed on the way home?"

"No," said Münster. "In his bed. Did they have an argument, these gentlemen, or anything of the sort?"

"No more than usual."

"Did you see how they set off for home? Did you phone for a taxi, perhaps?"

"That's never necessary," said Gautiers. "There are always plenty of taxis just round the corner, in Megsje Plejn. Let me see, I think two of them took a taxi—I was watching through the window. But Leverkuhn and Bonger started walking."

Münster nodded and made a note.

"You know them pretty well, I take it?"

"I certainly do. They sit here two evenings a week, at least. Bonger and Wauters more than that—four or five times. But they are usually in the bar. . . ."

"How long have they been coming here?"

"Ever since I've been working here; that's eight years now."

"But yesterday they were in the restaurant?"

She stubbed out her cigarette and thought about that.

"Yes, there was something special about last night, as I said. They seemed to be celebrating something. I think they had won some money."

Münster wrote that down.

"What makes you think that? How would they have won some money?"

"I don't know. Soccer pools or the lottery, I expect—they usually sit here filling in coupons on Wednesday nights. They try to keep it secret for some silly reason; they don't speak aloud about it, but you catch on even so."

"Are you certain about this?"

She thought it over again.

"No, not certain," she said. "But it can hardly have been anything else. They were dressed up as well. They ordered expensive wines and cognac. And they ate à la carte. . . . But for God's sake, why would they want to kill Leverkuhn? Poor old guy. Was he robbed?"

Münster shook his head.

"No. Murdered. Somebody stabbed him to death with a knife."

She stared at him in astonishment.

"But who? I mean . . . why?"

The worst interrogations, Münster thought as he went out into the street, are the ones when the person being interviewed has nothing to say apart from repeating and confirming the questions you ask. As in this case.

"But who?"

"Why?"

Money had cropped up, and even if it was several years since Intendent Münster had flirted with Marxism, he still had the feeling that there was a crass financial side to practically everything. Especially when it had to do with his own specialty, of course. The shadowy side.

Cui bono, then? Nothing about sudden winnings had emerged from the conversation with the wife. Maybe this was a lead to be followed, although on reflection he realized that these gentlemen— or Leverkuhn at least—might well have preferred to keep quiet about such a stroke of luck, to make sure the money didn't disappear into the housekeeping accounts or some other bottomless pit.

If they had in fact been lucky enough to pull off a win, that is. Of course it wasn't out of the question—people did win money now and again. It had never happened to him, but no doubt that was not entirely unconnected with the fact that he very rarely gambled.

He checked his watch and decided to walk back to the police station. The clouds of mist had begun to let through some spots of rain, but it felt mild and pleasant, and after all, he was wearing an overcoat and gloves.

He wasn't sure of what he would actually do when he got back to the station. Apart from trying to get hold of the son and daughter, of course. With a bit of luck, reports ought to have come in by now from the pathologist, Meusse, and the crime scene boys, which would no doubt provide other things that needed doing.

Moreover it was possible that Jung and Moreno had managed to get their claws into the other old gentlemen, although it was probably best not to invest too much hope in that. Both of them had looked more than acceptably weary when he had sent them out.

The best-case scenario, needless to say, would be a note on his desk to the effect that one of the oldies had broken down and confessed. Or that somebody else had, anybody. And in that case there would be nothing to stop him from going home to Synn and the kids and spending the rest of the day with the family.

A lovely, gray Sunday, just right for sitting indoors. There was certainly something to be said for postponing a key interrogation until Monday morning. A softening-up day in the cells was usually enough to make most criminals confess to more or less anything you wanted them to.

He'd had plenty of experience of that in the past.

As for the chances of such a confession having been made . . . well, Intendent Münster thought it best not to think in any detail about that. It was better to allow himself to hope for a while. You never know. And if there was one thing about this damned job that you could be certain about, this was it.

That you can never know.

He turned up his collar to keep the rain out, put his hands into his pockets, and allowed himself to feel some cautious optimism.

4

Jung had a headache.

There were reasons for that, but without saying a word about it to his colleagues he took the streetcar to Armastenplejn, where Palinski lived. Today was one of those days when there was no point in hurrying, he told himself, stressing that fact with pedagogical insistence.

The streetcar was practically empty at this ungodly hour on Sunday morning, and as he sat swaying from side to side on the vandalized seat he took the opportunity of slipping two effervescent tablets into the can of Coca-Cola he had bought in the canteen. The result was an astounding amount of froth, and he found himself needing to slurp down the foaming drink as quickly as he could. Even so, his jacket and trousers were covered in a mass of stains, and he realized that his goings-on found little in the way of tolerant understanding in the four prudish female eyes staring at him from a few rows farther back. On their way to church, no doubt, to receive well-earned tolerant understanding of their own foibles. These stout-hearted ladies.

So what? Jung thought. He stared back at them and wiped away the mess as best he could with his scarf.

His head was still aching when he got off. He found the right building, and noticed a café next door that was open. After a few seconds' hesitation, he went into the café and ordered a cup of black coffee.

Keep off the booze when you're on standby! That was a sensible rule, tried and tested; but it had been Maureen's birthday, and you sometimes need to reorganize your priorities.

Besides, they had had the apartment to themselves for once—in fact, it was the first time since they had moved in together at the end of August. Sophie was sleeping over in the home of one of her girlfriends. Or possibly boyfriends—she would soon be seventeen, after all.

They had spent a few hours eating and drinking. Shared a rather expensive Rioja in front of the television for a couple more hours. Then made love for an hour and a half. At least. He remembered looking at the clock and noting that it was twenty-five minutes to four.

The duty officer had rung at a quarter to six.

I'm a wreck today, Jung thought. *But a quite young and happy wreck.*

He emptied his cup of coffee and ordered another.

Palinski also looked like a wreck, but forty years older. His white shirt might possibly have been clean the previous evening, but after being exposed to a night of sweaty alcoholic fumes it was no longer particularly impressive. A pair of disconsolate, thin legs stuck out from underneath it, crisscrossed with varicose veins and wearing a pair of sagging socks. His head was balanced precariously on a fragile stick insect of a neck, and seemed to be on the point of cracking at any moment. His hands were trembling like the wings of a skylark, and his lower jaw was apparently disconnected from its anchorage.

Oh my God, Jung thought as he waved his ID in front of Palinski's nose. *I'm standing here face-to-face with my own future.*

"Police," he said. "Let me in."

Palinski started coughing. Then closed his eyes.

Headache, was Jung's diagnosis. He gritted his teeth and forced his way in.

"What do you want? I'm not well."

"You're hungover," said Jung. "Stop lying."

"No . . . er," said Palinski. "What do you mean?"

"Are you saying you don't know what a hangover is?"

Palinski did not reply, but coughed up some more phlegm and swallowed it. Jung looked around for a spittoon, and took a deep breath. The air in the apartment was heavy with the reek of old man. Tobacco. Unwashed clothes. Unscrubbed floors. He found his way into the kitchen and managed to open a window. Sat down at the rickety table and gestured to his host to follow suit.

"I must take a pill first," croaked Palinski, and he staggered into what must presumably be the bathroom.

It took five minutes. Then Palinski reappeared in a frayed dressing gown and with a newly scrubbed face. He was evidently a little more cocksure.

"What the devil do you want, then?" he said, sitting down opposite Jung.

"Leverkuhn is dead," said Jung. "What can you tell me about that?"

Palinski lost control of his jaw and his cockiness simultaneously. "What?"

"Murdered," said Jung. "Well?"

Palinski stared at him, his mouth half open, and began trembling again.

"What . . . what the devil are you saying?"

"I'm saying that somebody murdered Waldemar Leverkuhn in his home last night. You are one of the last people to see him alive, and I want to hear what you have to say for yourself."

It looked as if Palinski was about to faint. *I'm probably coming down too heavily on him*, Jung thought.

"You and he were out together last night," he said, trying to calm things down. "Is that right?"

"Yes . . . yes, we were."

"At Freddy's in Weiskerstraat?"

"Yes."

"Together with two other gents?"

"Yes."

Palinski closed his mouth and clung to the tabletop.

"Are you all right?" Jung asked tentatively.

"Ill," said Palinski. "I'm ill. Are you saying he's dead?"

"As dead as a doornail," said Jung. "Somebody stabbed him at least twenty times."

"Stabbed him?" Palinski squeaked. "I don't understand."

"Neither do we," said Jung. "Maybe you could make us a cup of tea or coffee, so that we can talk it through in peace and quiet?"

"Yes. . . . Of course," said Palinski. "Fucking hell! Who could have done a thing like that?"

"We don't know," said Jung.

Palinski stood up with considerable difficulty.

"The way of all flesh," he said out of the blue. "I think I need a few drops of something strong. Fucking hell!"

"Give me a couple as well," said Jung.

He left Palinski an hour later with a fairly clear head and fairly clear information. Yes, they had been at Freddy's as always on a Saturday night. From about half past six until eleven o'clock, or thereabouts. They'd eaten and drunk and chatted. About politics, and women, and all things in heaven and earth.

As usual. Maybe they'd been a bit merry. Leverkuhn had fallen under the table, but it was nothing serious.

Then Palinski and Wauters had shared a taxi. He'd gotten home at about twenty past eleven and gone straight to bed. Bonger and Leverkuhn had walked home, he thought, but he wasn't sure. They'd been standing outside Freddy's, arguing about something or other, he thought, when he and Wauters went off in their taxi.

Had the gentlemen been quarrelling? Good Lord no! They were the best of friends. That's why they kept meeting at Freddy's every Wednesday and Saturday. And sometimes more often than that.

Any other enemies? Of Leverkuhn, that is.

No . . . Palinski shook his aching head cautiously. Enemies? How the devil could he have had any enemies? You didn't have enemies when you were their age, for Christ's sake. People with enemies lived to be only half their age.

And Leverkuhn didn't show any signs of behaving oddly as the evening wore on.

Palinski frowned and thought that over.

No, nothing at all.

It was raining when Jung came out into the street again, but nevertheless he decided to walk to the canals, where he had his next appointment.

Bonger.

Apparently, he had a houseboat on the Bertrandgraacht, and as Jung walked slowly along Palitzerlaan and Keymerstraat, he thought about how often he himself had considered that way of living. In the old days, that is. Before Maureen. There was something especially attractive about living on a boat. The gentle rocking of the dark canal waters. The independence. The freedom—or the illusion of freedom in any case—yes, it had its appeal.

When he came to the address he had been given, he realized that it had its negative sides as well.

Bonger's home was an old, flat-bottomed, wooden tub barely thirty feet long; it was lying suspiciously deep in the water, and the need of paint and maintenance was obvious. The deck was full of cans and drums, ropes, and old trash, and the living area in the cabin seemed to be mainly below water level.

Ugh! Jung thought and shuddered involuntarily in the rain. *What a dump!*

There was a narrow, slippery gangplank between the quay and the rail, but Jung didn't use it. Instead he pulled at the end of a rope running from the canal railing, over a tree root and to a bell fixed to the chimney. It rang twice, not very loudly, and it aroused no reaction. He had the distinct impression that there was nobody at home. He tugged at the rope again.

"He's not in!"

Jung turned around. The hoarse voice came from a heavily muffled-up woman who was chaining a bicycle to a tree some thirty feet farther down the canal.

"No smoke, no lanterns on," she explained. "That means he's not at home. He's very careful about always having a lantern on."

"I see," said Jung. "I take it you're his neighbor."

The woman picked up her two grocery bags and heaved them over the railings onto another houseboat that seemed to be in rather better condition than Bonger's—with red striped curtains in the windows and plants growing in a little greenhouse on the cabin roof. Tomatoes, by the look of them.

"Yes, I am," she said, climbing on board with surprising agility. "Assuming it's Felix Bonger you're looking for."

"Exactly," said Jung. "You don't happen to know where he is, do you?"

She shook her head.

"He ought to be at home, but I rang shortly before I left to go shopping. I usually get a few items for him from the Kleinmarckt on Sundays. But he wasn't in."

"Are you absolutely certain?" Jung asked.

"Climb aboard and take a look for yourself!" snorted the woman. "Nobody locks doors around here."

Jung did just that, walked down a few steps and peered in through the door. It was a rectangular room with a sofa bed, a table with two chairs, an electric cooker, a refrigerator, and a television set. Clothes were hanging from coat hangers along the walls, and books and magazines were strewn about haphazardly. Hanging from the ceiling were an electric bulb without a shade and a stuffed parrot on a perch. A broken concertina was lying on top of a low cupboard.

The strongest impression, however, was the smell of dirt and ingrained damp. And of old man.

No, Jung thought. *This looks even worse than it did from the canal bank.*

When he came back up on deck the woman had disappeared into her own cabin. Jung hesitated; there was probably a question or two he ought to ask her, but as he felt his way cautiously across the gangplank again, he decided that the urge to eat could not be resisted much longer.

And he was starting to feel cold. If he took a slightly longer route back to the police station, he guessed he would be able to stop by Kurmann's for a steak with fried potatoes and gravy. Nothing could be simpler.

And a beer.

It was nearly twelve o'clock. There was no time for dillydallying.

5

Marie-Louise Leverkuhn left the police station with Münster's blessing shortly after one o'clock on Sunday. She was accompanied by Emmeline von Post, the friend with whom she had spent Saturday evening and who had been informed of the awful happening a few hours previously.

She immediately offered that the newly widowed Marie-Louise was welcome to stay in her terraced house in Bossingen.

For the time being. Until things had calmed down a bit. In other words, for as long as it might be thought necessary.

After all, they had known each other for fifty years. And been colleagues for twenty-five.

Münster escorted the two ladies to the car park, and before they bundled themselves into Fröken von Post's red Renault, he stressed once more how important it was to contact him the moment she recalled anything at all, no matter how insignificant, that might possibly be of interest to the police in their work.

Their work being to capture her husband's murderer.

"In any case we shall be in touch with you in a day or so," he added. "Thank you for volunteering to take care of her, Fröken von Post."

"We humans have to help each other in our hour of need," said Marie-Louise's short and plump friend, squeezing herself into the driver's seat. "Where would we be if we didn't?"

Yes, where would we be indeed? Münster thought as he returned to his office on the third floor.

Up the creek without a paddle, presumably. But wasn't that where we were all heading for anyway?

The forensic reports were ready half an hour later. While he sat chewing two plain sandwiches from the automatic machine in the canteen, Münster worked his way through the reports.

It was not especially uplifting reading.

Waldemar Leverkuhn had been killed by several deep knife wounds to his trunk and neck. The exact number of blows had been established at twenty-eight, but when the last ten or twelve were made he was most likely already dead.

There had been no resistance, and the probable time of death was now narrowed down to between 1:15 and 2:15 a.m. But taking into account the widow's evidence, that could be narrowed down further to 1:15 to 2:00, since she had arrived home soon after two.

At the moment of death Leverkuhn had been wearing a white shirt, tie, underpants, trousers, and one sock, and the alcohol content in his blood had been 1.76.

No weapon had been recovered, but there was no doubt that it must have been a large knife with a blade about eight inches long—possibly identical with the carving knife reported missing by Fru Leverkuhn.

No fingerprints or any other clues had been found at the scene of the crime, but chemical analysis of textile fibers and other particles had yet to be carried out.

All this was carefully noted on two densely typed pages, and Münster read through it twice.

He phoned Synn and spoke to her for ten minutes.

He put his feet up on his desk.

Then he closed his eyes and tried to work out what Van Veeteren would have done in a situation like this.

That did not take very long to work out. He called the duty officer and announced that he would like to see Inspector Jung and Inspector Moreno in his office at four o'clock.

Then he took the elevator down to the basement and spent the next two hours in the sauna.

"Nice weather today," said Jung.

"We had sun yesterday," Münster pointed out.

"I'm serious," said Jung. "I like these curtains of rain. The gray sort of makes you want to look inside yourself instead. At the essentials of life, if you follow me . . . the internal landscape."

Ewa Moreno frowned.

"You know," she said, "sometimes an unassuming colleague can say things that are very sensible. Have you been taking a course?"

"The university of life," said Jung. "Who's going to kick off?"

"Ladies first," said Münster. "I agree with you. There's something special about black, wet tree trunks. . . . But perhaps we ought to discuss that another day."

Moreno opened her notebook and started.

"Benjamin Wauters," she said. "Born 1925 in Frigge. Lived in Maardam since 1980. All over the place before that. He's worked on the railways all his life until he retired. Confirmed bachelor. No relations at all—not any that he wants to acknowledge, at least. Suffers from verbal diarrhea, to be honest. Loquacious and lonely. The other old farts he meets at Freddy's are the only company he keeps, apart from his cat. Half angora, I think. I don't think I've ever seen anything so well groomed. I had the impression that they take their meals together. A very neat and tidy apartment as well. Flowers on the window ledges and all that."

"What about last night?" interpolated Münster.

"He didn't have much to say about that," said Moreno. "Apparently they had a decent meal for once—they usually spend their time in the bar. They got a bit drunk, he admitted. Leverkuhn fell under the table, and so they thought they ought to accept a walkover—that's the way he put it. He's a sports junkie, and a gambler, he made no attempt to conceal it. Anyway, that's about it, though it took two hours over coffee and all his dirty jokes."

"No insights about the murder?"

"None that he'd thought through," said Moreno. "He was sure it must have been a madman and pure coincidence. Nobody had any reason to bump Leverkuhn off, he maintained. A good friend and a solid guy, even if he could be a bit cranky at times. To tell you the truth I agree with him. At any rate it seems out of the question that any of these men could have had anything to do with the murder."

"I agree," said Jung, and recapitulated his meeting with Palinski and his visit to Bonger's canal boat.

Münster sighed.

"A complete blank, then," he said. "Well, I suppose that was to be expected."

"Were the doors unlocked, then?" Jung asked. "At the Leverkuhns', I mean."

"Apparently."

"So we only need some junkie as high as a kite to go past, sneak inside, and find a poor old guy fast asleep that he can take his revenge on. Then sneak out the same way as he came in. Dead easy, don't you think?"

"Good thinking," said Moreno. "But how are we going to find him?"

Münster thought for a moment.

"If that's the answer," he said, "we'll never find him."

"Unless he starts talking out of turn," said Jung. "And somebody is kind enough to tip us off."

Münster sat in silence for a few seconds again, eyeing his colleagues one after the other.

"Do you really think this is what happened?"

Jung shrugged and yawned. Moreno looked doubtful.

"It's very possible," she said. "Considering we don't have the slightest hint of a motive, that could well be the answer. And nothing had been stolen from the place apart from that knife."

"You don't need to have a motive for killing anyone nowadays," said Jung. "All that's needed is for you to feel a bit annoyed, or to think you've been slighted for one reason or another, and that gives you the green light to go ahead and snuff someone out. Would you like a few examples?"

"No thank you," said Münster. "Motives are beginning to be a bit old-fashioned."

He leaned back and folded his hands behind his head. Moreno's digital wristwatch produced a mournful chirping sound.

"Five o'clock," she said. "Was there anything else?"

Münster leafed through the documents on his desk.

"I don't think so. . . . Hang on. Did any of the old boys say anything about having won some money?"

Moreno looked at Jung and shook her head.

"No," said Jung. "Why?"

"Well, the people at Freddy's had the impression that they were celebrating something last night, but I suppose they were just guessing. This fourth character . . . Bonger. We'd better make sure we find him, no matter what?"

Jung nodded.

"I'll check in on him again on the way home. Otherwise it'll be tomorrow. He doesn't have a telephone, we'd have to contact him via his neighbor. I can't believe there are still people like that about."

"What do you mean?" asked Moreno.

"People without a telephone. In this day and age."

Münster stood up.

"All right," he said. "Thank you for coming in on a Sunday. Let's cross our fingers and hope that somebody confesses tomorrow morning."

"Yes, let's hope," said Jung. "But I doubt somebody who bumps off a poor old man in that manner is going to start being bothered by pangs of conscience. Let's face it, this is not a very pleasant story."

"Very nasty," said Moreno. "As usual."

On the way home Münster called in at the scene of the crime in Kolderweg. As he was the one in charge of the investigation, for the moment at least, it was of course about time he did so. He stayed for ten minutes and wandered around the little three-roomed flat. It looked more or less as he had imagined it. Quite run-down, but comparatively neat and tidy. A hodgepodge of bad taste on the walls, furniture of the cheap fifties and sixties style. Separate bedrooms, bookcases with no books, and an awful lot of dried blood in and around Leverkuhn's sagging bed. The body had been taken away, as had the bed linen: Münster was grateful for that. It would have been more than enough to examine the photographs during the course of the morning.

And of course, what Moreno had said described the scene of the crime exactly.

Very nasty.

When he finally came home he could see that Synn had been crying.

"What's the matter?" he asked, hugging her as gently as if she were made of dreams.

"I don't know," she said. "I just don't want life to be like this. We get up in the mornings and get ready for work, and send the children off to school. We see each other again after it's dark, we eat, and we go to sleep. It's the same all week long. . . . I know it has to be like this right now, but what if we were to drop dead in a month? Or six months? It shouldn't be like this. There ought to be time to live as well."

"Just live?" Münster said.

"Just live," said Synn. "Okay, I know there are people who are worse off than we are. . . . Ninety-five percent of humanity, to be exact."

"Ninety-eight," said Münster.

He stroked her tenderly over the nape of her neck and down her back.

"Should we go and watch the children sleep?"

"They're not asleep yet," said Synn.

"Then we'll just have to be patient," said Münster.

6

It was only when he entered the police station on Monday morning that Münster remembered he hadn't yet contacted the Leverkuhns' children. One and a half days had passed since the murder; there was no further time to be lost. Luckily the media had not published any names in their restrained coverage of the case, so he hoped that he would still be the first to break it to them.

It was bad enough to have to be the bearer of bad news. Even worse if the bereaved had already been informed—a position Münster had found himself in several times before.

In order to avoid any further delay he instructed Krause to make preliminary contact—not to pass on the message itself, but to prepare the way so that Münster himself could give them the gloomy facts.

After all, he had already accepted the fact that it was his duty to do so.

Half an hour later he had the first of them on the line. Ruth Leverkuhn. Forty-four years old, lives up north in Wernice, more than sixty miles from Maardam. Despite the distance involved, as soon as Münster had explained that her father had been the victim of an accident, they arranged a private meeting: Ruth Leverkuhn preferred not to discuss serious matters on the telephone.

But she was told that Waldemar Leverkuhn was dead, of course.

And that Münster was a CID officer.

So, the Rote Moor Café in Salutorget it was. Since, for whatever reason, she preferred such a location rather than the police station.

And at twelve noon. Since, for some other unknown reason, she preferred to talk to the police before visiting her mother in Bossingen.

The son, Mauritz Leverkuhn, born 1958, rang barely ten minutes later. He lived even farther north—in Frigge—and Münster didn't beat around the bush. He got straight to the point.

Your father is dead.

During the night between Saturday and Sunday. In his bed. Murdered, it seemed. Stabbed with a knife.

It "seemed," Münster thought as he listened to the silence at the other end of the line. Talk about cautious prognoses. . . .

Then he heard—or at least, thought he could hear—the usual muted signs of shock in Mauritz Leverkuhn's confused questions.

"What time, did you say?"

"Where is my mother?"

"Where's the body now?"

"What was he wearing?"

Münster filled him in on these points and more besides. And made sure he had Emmeline von Post's telephone number so that he could contact his mother. Eventually he expressed his condolences and arranged a meeting on Tuesday morning.

The son's intention was to set off as soon as possible—no later than this evening—in order to be by his mother's side.

As far as the eldest daughter, Irene Leverkuhn, was concerned, Münster had already spoken to the Gellner Home, where she had been a resident for the last four years. A confidence-inspiring welfare officer had listened and understood, and assured Münster that she personally would inform her patient about her father's untimely death.

In the most appropriate way, and as considerately as possible.

Irene Leverkuhn was in a frail state.

Münster decided to postpone a conversation with this daughter indefinitely. The welfare officer had indicated that in all probability it would not be productive, and there were things to do that were no doubt more important.

He sat for a while wondering about what they might be. What more important things? There was still half an hour to go before the update meeting, and for want of anything better to do he took another look at the forensic crime scene report, to which a few more pages had been added during the night. He also phoned and spoke to the pathologists Meusse and Mulder at the lab, but neither of them was able to cast much light on the darkness. None at all, to be more precise.

But there were still a few analyses left to do, so there was hope.

It would be silly to throw in the towel too soon, Mulder pointed out, as was his wont. These things take time.

Jung did not have a headache this Monday morning.

But he was tired. Sophie had come home quite late on Sunday evening after being away for nearly two whole days. Over tea and sandwiches and a bit of intimate small talk in the kitchen, it emerged that she had taken the opportunity of making her sexual debut on Saturday night.

About time, too: she was sixteen, well on the way to seventeen, and most of her girlfriends were way ahead of her in that respect. The unfortunate part was that she was not especially interested in the young boy in question—a certain Fritz Kümmerle, a promising central midfielder with a shot like Beckenbauer's and a future staked out on soccer pitches all over Europe and indeed the world—and that they had made no attempt to take precautions.

Plus, she had been somewhat intoxicated at the time. Due to red wine and other substances as well.

Obviously it was mainly up to Maureen to look after her sobbing daughter, but even so Jung was aware—with a dubious feeling of satisfaction as well as of being an outsider—of the trust displayed in him simply by the fact that he was allowed to be present during these discussions. To be sure, he had known Sophie for four or five years by now, but nevertheless, he was no more than a plastic father.

Perhaps it was not irrelevant that her real father was a piece of shit.

Anyhow, neither Jung nor Maureen nor the unhappy debutante had gone to bed before half past one.

So he was a little on the tired side.

Bonger's boat didn't seem to be in any better condition. Just as run-down as it had looked the previous day, Jung decided. He tugged at the bell rope several times without success, and looked around to see if there was any sign of life elsewhere on the dark canal. The woman on the boat next door seemed to be at home: a thin, gray wisp of smoke was floating up out of the chimney, and the bicycle was locked to the railings under the lime tree, in the same place that she had parked it yesterday. Jung walked over to her boat, announced his presence with a cough, and tapped his bunch of keys on the black-painted rail that ran around the whole boat. After a few seconds she appeared in the narrow doorway. She was wearing a thick wool sweater that reached down as far as her knees, high rubber boots, and a beret. In one hand she was holding the gutted body of an animal—a hare, as far as Jung could tell. In her other hand, a carving knife.

"Sorry to disturb you," said Jung.

"Huh," said the woman. "It's you again."

"Yes," said Jung. "Perhaps I should explain myself. . . . I'm a police officer. Detective Inspector Jung. I'm looking for Herr Bonger, as I said."

She nodded grumpily, and suddenly seemed to become aware of what she was holding in her hands.

"Stew," she explained. "Andres bumped it off yesterday. . . . My son, that is."

She held up the carcass, and Jung tried to give the impression of looking at it with the eye of a connoisseur.

"Very nice," he said. "We all end up like that eventually. . . . But this Bonger—you don't happen to have seen him, I suppose?"

She shook her head.

"Not since Saturday."

"He didn't come home last night, then?"

"I doubt it."

She came up on deck and peered at Bonger's boat.

"No lights, no smoke," she said. "That means he's not in, as I explained yesterday. Anything else you want to know?"

"Does he go away often?"

She shrugged.

"No," she said. "No, he isn't away often for more than an hour or two. Why do you want to find him?"

"Routine inquiries," said Jung.

"And what the hell is that supposed to mean?" said the woman. "I'm not an idiot, you know."

"We just want to ask him a few questions."

"What about?"

"You don't seem to be too fond of the police," said Jung.

"Too right I'm not," said the woman.

Jung thought for a moment.

"It's about a death," he explained. "One of Bonger's friends has been murdered. We think Bonger might have some information that could be useful for us."

"Murder?" said the woman.

"Yes," said Jung. "Pretty brutal. With something like that." He pointed at the carving knife. The woman frowned ever so slightly.

"What's your name, by the way?" Jung asked, taking a notebook out of his pocket.

"Jümpers," said the woman reluctantly. "Elizabeth Jümpers. And when is this murder supposed to have taken place?"

"On Saturday night," said Jung. "In fact Herr Bonger is one of the last people to have seen the victim. Waldemar Leverkuhn. Perhaps you know him?"

"Leverkuhn? No . . . I've never heard of him."

"Do you know of any relatives or friends he might be staying with? Bonger, that is."

She thought for a moment, then shook her head slowly.

"No, I don't think so. He's a pretty solitary character."

"Does he ever have visitors on his boat?"

"Never. At least, I've never seen any."

Jung sighed.

"Ah well," he said. "I expect he'll turn up. If you see him, could you please tell him we've been looking for him. It would be good if he could contact us as soon as possible. He can ring at any time."

He handed her a business card. The woman put the knife down, took the card, and put it in her back pocket.

"Anyway, thank you for your help," said Jung.

"You're welcome," said the woman. "I'll tell him."

Jung hesitated.

"Is it a good life, living on a boat like this?" he asked.

The woman snorted.

"Is it a good life, being a detective inspector like you?" she asked.

Jung gave her a quarter of a smile and took his leave.

"Good luck with the stew!" he shouted as he passed by Bonger's boat, but she had already gone inside.

Not an easy person to make contact with, he thought as he clambered into his car.

But with a heart of gold under that rough exterior, perhaps?

Being a detective inspector like you?

A good question, no doubt about that. He decided not to consider it in any detail. Checked his watch instead, and realized he would be hard-pressed to get to the update meeting in time.

7

It was in fact true that Emmeline von Post had been a colleague of Marie-Louise Leverkuhn's for twenty-five years.

And it was also true that they had known each other for nearly fifty. That they had never really lost contact since they left Boring's Commercial and Office College at the end of the 1940s. Despite getting married, having children, moving house, and all the other things.

But it was hardly true to say that Fru von Post counted Fru Leverkuhn among her very best friends—something the latter might well have claimed, had she been asked. What was true is that since Edward von Post died of cancer four years ago, the two women had socialized much more than they had previously done: they met two Saturdays every month, alternating between Kolderweg in the town center, and the terraced house out in Bossingen— but in reality, well . . . something vital was missing. And Emmeline von Post knew exactly what it was. That important little ingredient, that dimension of trust, open-heartedness, and jokey exchanges; that simple and yet difficult element that she so eagerly and painlessly developed when she was with two or three other close friends, all of them in the prime of life it has to be said. But this . . . this dimension was simply never present when she was together with Marie-Louise Leverkuhn.

That was simply the way it was. Unfortunately and regrettably.

It was difficult to say why, but there was no doubt that there was a limit to their closeness—she had thought about it many times—an invisible line that they were careful not to cross. On the few occasions when she happened to cross it even so, she could immediately see the effect by her friend's reaction. A reserved shaking of the head. Pursed lips, raised shoulders . . . even a negative silence. When she thought about it she realized that it had been that way from the very beginning. It was not something that had developed over the years, and perhaps the fact of the matter was (Emmeline used to think in moments of philosophical perspicacity) that the relationship between people was established and written in stone during the very first contacts, the earliest meetings, and there was not much one could do about it afterward.

Just as it said in that American detective novel she had received from her book club a year or so ago.

Not that she herself was especially keen to pass on intimate details about her husband and children and their private life, of course not; but nevertheless, most people seemed to be rather more willing than Marie-Louise Leverkuhn to lift the veil of secrecy, even if only a tiny little bit.

However, that's the way it was. Marie-Louise simply wasn't the confiding type, and of course there were other worthwhile aspects of life: they had no difficulty in talking about their aches and pains, their medication, and their recipes for rhubarb pie. About colleagues, television personalities, and the price of vegetables; but their private lives remained exactly that: private.

The fact that Emmeline von Post had rushed over to help out in a catastrophic situation like this was naturally due to the fact that there was no one else. She knew that. To Marie-Louise Leverkuhn, just as she had explained to the police, she was the faithful friend who would do whatever she could to help, no matter what the weather.

The loyal and only friend.

So there was no need to hesitate.

. . .

Not much was said during the drive to the Sunday-sleepy suburb. Marie-Louise Leverkuhn sat hunched, her handbag on her knees, staring out through the side windows at the pouring rain, and seeming to be in a state of shock. Her shoulders were raised—as if to shield her from a hard and far too intrusive outside world— and all Emmeline's questions were answered with at best a slight movement of the head or a monosyllabic yes or no.

"Have you slept at all?"

"No."

"Are you going to be okay?"

"Yes."

"Do you want to phone your children?"

No answer.

Oh dear, Emmeline thought. *She's not well at all.*

Hardly surprising. Murdered? Waldemar Leverkuhn murdered? Emmeline shuddered. Who on earth could have imagined such a thing? An old fart like that.

For a few minutes she said nothing, concentrating on her driving and trying to imagine what it must feel like to come home and find your husband butchered like that. Dead. Murdered and bathing in his own blood, as they had said on the radio. A carving knife!

After a while she gave up the attempt to imagine it. It was simply too much to ask.

Much too much. Emmeline peered cautiously from the side at her motionless friend. *Poor Marie-Louise,* she thought, *I promise to take care of you! You're bound to be in shock and confused, the main thing is to get a few tablets down you and then tuck you up in bed. I hope I have the strength.*

When the police rang that morning, her first and immediate reaction had been to rush and do what she could for her friend; but it was only now, as she sat here with the silent widow beside her in the car, that she began to realize what was involved.

Anyway, it's no doubt best not to let silence reign, she thought. *I'd better say something.*

It wasn't a difficult decision to make: if there was anything Emmeline von Post had difficulty in coping with, it was silence.

"You can sleep in Mark's room," she said. "Then you won't be disturbed by all the traffic noise. Will that be okay?"

"Yes."

"I've got a bit of that lamb cutlet left in the freezer. We can eat that, don't you think? You thought it was very good. Then we won't need to go shopping."

"Yes."

"For God's sake! Here am I chattering on about food—you must be absolutely washed out."

No answer.

"Waldemar was such a lovely man."

One thing at a time, Emmeline thought, putting her hand on her friend's arm. *We'll sort it out eventually.*

"What miserable weather," she said. "It was lovely yesterday."

Marie-Louise Leverkuhn went to bed in what used to be the boy's room in Geldenerstraat 24 at half past two on Sunday afternoon and didn't get up until about eight on Monday morning. Emmeline came in to check on her several times during the afternoon and evening, and before going to bed herself she left a tray with juice and some sandwiches on the bedside table. For the sake of nourishment and to get some vitamins into her. And out of consideration for her welfare. Although what her old friend needed above all else, as anybody could see, was of course some peace and quiet.

And that is exactly what she got. Even if it was on the silent side.

For her part Emmeline had quite a frustrating afternoon and evening. The lamb cutlet went into and out of the oven several times—until she finally put it in the refrigerator and decided it would serve as Monday's evening meal. She drank at least five cups of tea and watered the flowers twice. It felt especially odd to have her old friend lying in Mark's room—Mark who had eventually flown the nest eight years ago, but still came back to visit and sleep in his old unchanged boy's room at regular intervals, especially when his all-too-young wife had done something silly again. Of course, it had been high time he found somebody: thirty-five was no age at which to be still living at home with Mommy. There's a time for everything, after all.

But now it was Marie-Louise Leverkuhn lying in his bed, because her husband had been murdered. As Emmeline tiptoed carefully about the house so as not to disturb or wake her guest, it occurred to her how fortunate it was that Edward—her own Edward—had had the good taste to die of cancer, instead of being stabbed to death with a carving knife.

Murdered! It was terrible. Her lower arm broke out in goose bumps whenever she thought of that word—and by Jove, there were not many minutes when she managed to think of anything else.

Eventually, when it was already dark outside and in corners of the house, she also began to think about who could have done the deed, which didn't make things any better. There was a murderer on the loose!

Then she started thinking about Marie-Louise, their meeting last Saturday evening, playing whist and drinking port (perhaps at the very moment Waldemar was being murdered!), and how remarkably reserved she had been during the car ride and the half hour before she went to bed, and then . . . well, then she suddenly felt very weary. And a little dizzy.

There was something very strange about it all.

Obviously you couldn't expect a person to behave normally in circumstances like these, but even so? *There was something else,* Emmeline thought. *Some other thing gnawing away deep down inside her friend, forcing her to keep silent. God only knows what.*

Then she shook her head and told herself it was just the silence inside the house and the darkness growing out of the corners and her thoughts about that blood-soaked body in the bed that sent her imagination spinning. . . . But nevertheless, there was no denying that she didn't know very much about Marie-Louise and her life after all these years. Not much at all.

And about her husband? Absolutely nothing.

But then, perhaps she didn't know any more than that about anybody else? A human being is a riddle, Edward—her Edward—occasionally used to say. An unsolvable riddle (for he was not afraid to throw in an expletive occasionally)!

Having got thus far in her speculations, she went into the kitchen and poured herself a substantial whiskey. Drank it while standing up, established that she still had goose bumps on her lower arm, and poured herself another one.

It was quite simply one of those evenings.

The children rang on Monday morning.

Ruth and Mauritz, one after the other, with less than fifteen minutes between the calls. Marie-Louise shut herself into the bedroom while she was speaking to them, and Emmeline couldn't hear a word—although she would have liked to.

But not a lot seemed to have been said. Both calls took less than five minutes—as if Marie-Louise had been worried about the telephone bill, even though she was not the one who had phoned.

"You must talk about it," Emmeline urged her friend when she came back to the breakfast table after speaking to her son. "It's not good to bottle it all up."

Marie-Louise looked at her with tired, vacant eyes.

"What on earth is there for me to say?" she said.

Three seconds passed before she suddenly burst into tears.

At last, Emmeline thought as she put an arm tenderly round Marie-Louise's hunched shoulders. At last.

8

"Any comments?" said Münster, spreading the photographs out over the table so that all present could study them to their heart's content.

The variations were insignificant: Waldemar Leverkuhn's mutilated body from a dozen different angles and distances. Blood. Crumpled bedclothes. Wounds in close-up. Pale skin covered in moles. An absurdly colorful tie sticking out from under the pillow. Blood. And more blood.

Moreno shook her head. Intendent Heinemann took off his glasses and began rubbing them clean with the aid of his own much more discreet tie. Rooth stopped chewing away at a chocolate cookie and turned his back demonstratively on the table. Only young Krause continued perusing the macabre details, dutifully and with furrowed brow.

"Take them away!" said Rooth. "My digestive system demands an ounce of respect. And in any case, I was there and saw it all live."

Live? Münster thought. *Does he call this live? It's a long time since I've seen anything so stone-cold dead.* He sighed, then gathered up the photographs, leaving two of them lying there as a reminder of the subject of their discussions.

"Let's take the forensics to start with," he said. "Where's Jung, by the way?"

"He was going to speak to that Bonger character," said Moreno. "He'll turn up shortly, no doubt."

"The forensics," said Münster again. "No further news, I'm afraid, just confirmation of what we know already. Waldemar Leverkuhn was killed by twenty-eight deep knife wounds to his stomach, chest, and neck. Mainly to his stomach. Pretty accurate, it seems. But if you stab somebody that many times, accuracy is neither here nor there. Well, what does that suggest?"

"A hot-headed type," said Krause with restrained enthusiasm. "Must be out of his mind—or was when he did it, at least."

"As high as a kite," said Rooth, swallowing the last of the chocolate cookie. "A junkie coming off a bad trip. There's no limit to what they can do, dammit. What does Meusse have to say about the stab wounds?"

Münster agreed. "Yes, you could well be right. The wounds vary a lot. Some of them are deep—five or six inches—others superficial. Some caused not much more than scratches. The killer was right-handed, by the way—no doubt about that."

"Great," said Moreno. "A right-handed drug addict. We've got only about three thousand of those in town. Can't we hit upon some more interesting theory? If there's anything I hate about this glamorous job of ours, it's having to spend time grubbing around the drug addicts."

Münster folded his hands and rested his chin on his knuckles.

"We can't always set the agenda," he said. "Unfortunately. But if we put off speculations until we've finished going through the facts, we can see where we've got to. . . . Knowledge is the mother of speculation, as Reinhart says. We don't know a lot, but we do know a bit."

"Let's hear it, then," said Rooth. "But screw poetry for the time being."

"The weapon . . . ," said Münster, refusing to react, "the weapon seems to have been a pretty substantial knife. The blade was at least eight inches long. Sharp—presumably a carving knife pretty similar to the one Fru Leverkuhn described, and which, according to the same source, disappeared from its place in the kitchen at some point on the evening of the murder. . . ."

"And which now," said Rooth, "is almost certainly lying at the bottom of one of the canals. I may be wrong, but a quick calculation suggests that we have about three miles to choose from."

"Hmm," said Heinemann. "Interesting. Purely from the point of view of probability, that is. Three thousand drug addicts times five thousand meters of canal. . . . That means that if we're going to find both the killer and the murder weapon, the chances are . . . one in about nine million."

He leaned back in his chair and smoothed down his tie over his stomach.

"How nice to see that we're all so optimistic," said Moreno as Jung appeared in the doorway.

"Sorry I'm late," he said. "But I was on official—"

"Excellent," said Rooth. "Sit down!"

Münster cleared his throat. *If only I could give all these comedy shows a miss,* he thought. *I'm not sufficiently arrogant yet, but no doubt that'll come.*

"Regarding the time," he said, "we can assume that Leverkuhn was murdered at some time between a quarter past one and a quarter past two. When I pressed Meusse a bit, he leaned toward the later half hour, in other words between a quarter to and a quarter past two."

"Hmm," said Heinemann. "What time did his wife get home?"

"Three or four minutes past," said Moreno.

"That narrows things down, then," said Krause. "Assuming Meusse is right, that is."

"Meusse hasn't gotten anything wrong for the past fifteen years," said Rooth. "So, between a quarter to two and two. She must have been pretty damned close to bumping into him. Have we checked if she noticed anybody?"

"Yes," said Krause. "Negative."

"She could have been the one who did it, of course," Heine-mann pointed out. "Perhaps we shouldn't exclude that possibility. Sixty percent of all men are murdered by their wives."

"What the hell are you saying?" wondered Rooth. "Thank God I'm not married."

"What I mean is . . . ," said Heinemann.

"We know what you mean," said Münster with a sigh. "We can discuss Fru Leverkuhn's credibility later, but we'll take the report from the lab first."

He fished the relevant papers out of the folder.

"There was a hell of a lot of blood," he continued, "both in the bed and on the floor. But they haven't found any leads. No fingerprints apart from the victim's and a couple of old ones of the wife's—and the only mark on the floor was also from her: a footprint she made when she went in and found him. They had separate bedrooms, as I said earlier."

"What about the rest of the flat?" Moreno asked.

"Only her fingerprints there as well."

"Sorry," Heinemann interrupted. "But did she really go right up to the bed? Surely that wasn't necessary. She must have seen that he was dead before she entered the room. We'd better look into whether she really needed to rummage around at the scene of the crime like that—"

Krause interrupted him.

"It was dark when she went in, she claims. Then she realized something was wrong and went back to switch on the light."

"Aha," said Heinemann.

"That fits in with the footprints in the blood," explained Mün-ster. "You might think it seems odd that the murderer could leave the scene without leaving any trace, but Meusse says that would not be anything remarkable. There was an awful lot of blood, but it wasn't spurting out: most of it apparently ran out when the at-tack was over and done with. Evidently it depends on which sort of artery you happen to hit first."

"An old man's blood," said Rooth. "Viscous."

"That's right," said Münster. "It's not even certain that the murderer would get any blood on his hands. Not very much, in any case."

"Great," said Jung. "So we haven't got a single goddamn clue from the forensic boys. . . . Is that what you're saying?"

"Hmm," said Münster. "I'm afraid that's the way it looks, yes."

"Good," said Rooth. "In that case we'd better all have a cup of coffee. Otherwise we'll get depressed."

He looked benevolently round the table.

We could do with a chief inspector here, thought Münster as he rose to his feet.

But that's the way it was . . . Münster leaned back in his chair and raised his arms toward the ceiling while Rooth and Fröken Katz passed around the mugs.

Exactly the way it was. For just over a year now their notorious chief inspector had been on leave, devoting himself to antiquarian books rather than to police work—and there were indications that he had no intention of returning to police duties at all.

A lot of indications, in fact. It was Chief of Police Hiller who had insisted on what he called leave of absence. Van Veeteren himself—as Münster understood it at least—had been prepared to resign once and for all. To burn all bridges.

Münster couldn't help envying him just a little. The last time he had popped into Krantze's—a cloudy afternoon in the middle of September—he had found Van Veeteren lounging in a worn leather armchair, at the rear of the shop under overloaded bookshelves, with an old folio volume on his knee and a glass of red wine on the armrest. The peaceful expression on his face had made him look not unlike a Tibetan lama.

So there was good reason to assume that Van Veeteren had drawn a line under his police career.

And Reinhart! Münster thought. Detective Intendent Reinhart had spent the last three weeks at home babbling away to his

eight-month-old daughter. Rumor had it that he intended to continue doing so until Christmas. An intention that—it was said—
made Chief of Police Hiller froth at the mouth and turn cross-eyed
in frustration. Temporarily, at least.

There had been no question of appointing replacements, not
for either of these two heavyweights. If there was an opportunity
to cut down on expenses, that is of course what was done. No matter what the cost.

The times they are a-changin', Münster thought, taking a Danish
pastry.

"The wife's a bit odd though, don't you think?" suggested Krause.
"Or at least, her behavior is."

"I agree," said Münster. "We must talk to her again . . . today
or tomorrow. But, of course, it's hardly surprising if she seems a
bit confused."

"In what way has she seemed confused?" asked Heinemann.

"Well," said Munster, "the times she gave are obviously correct.
She did travel on the train she said she was on, and there really was
a power failure last Saturday night. They didn't get to Central Station until a quarter to two, an hour late, so she should have been
at home roughly when she claims. One of the neighbors thinks he
heard her as well. So, she finds her husband dead a few minutes
past two, but she doesn't ring the police until two forty-three. During that time she was out—she says she was going to report the
incident at Entwick Plejn police station. But she goes back home
when she discovers it's closed. . . . I suppose one could have various
views about that. Does anybody wish to comment?"

A few seconds passed.

"Confused," said Rooth eventually. "Excessively confused."

"I suppose so," said Moreno. "But wouldn't it be more abnor-
mal to behave normally in a situation like this? Mind you, she'd
have had plenty of time to get rid of the knife—half an hour, at
least."

"Did anybody see her while she was taking that walk?" Heine-mann wondered.

Münster shook his head.

"Nobody has reported having done so yet, in any case. How's the door-to-door going?"

Krause stretched.

"We'll be finished by this evening," he said. "But everything she says is unverified so far. And it's likely to stay that way—the streets were pretty deserted, and there's not much reason to stand gaping out of the window at that time either. But she ought to have passed Dusar's Café, where there were a few customers. We'll check there this evening. But it was raining. . . ."

Münster turned over a page.

"The relatives," he said. "Three children. Between forty and fifty or thereabouts. Two of them are traveling here today and to-morrow, I've arranged to meet them. The eldest daughter is in a psychiatric home somewhere, and I don't think we have any rea-son to disturb her. . . . No, I don't suppose any of us thinks it's a family affair, do we?"

"Does anybody think anything at all?" muttered Moreno, gaz-ing down into her empty coffee mug.

"Me," said Rooth. "My theory is that Leverkuhn was murdered. Shall we proceed to the old geezers?"

Moreno and Jung reported on their visits to Wauters and Palin-ski, and the failed attempts to contact Bonger. Meanwhile Münster contemplated Moreno's knees and thought about Synn. Rooth ate two more Danish pastries and Heinemann polished his thumb-nails with his tie. Münster wondered vaguely if there really was a mood of despondency and a lack of active interest hanging over the whole group, or if it was just himself who was affected. It was hard to say, and he made no effort to answer the question.

"So he's disappeared, has he?" said Rooth when Moreno and Jung had finished. "Bonger, I mean."

Jung shrugged.

"He hasn't been home since last Saturday night."

Krause cleared his throat to show signs of enthusiasm.

"For Christ's sake," he said. "Four old farts, and two of them have gone. There must be a connection, surely. If they've all managed to hang on until they are past seventy, it's surely pretty unlikely that one of them would disappear naturally the same night as another of them is murdered!"

"'Disappear naturally'?" said Jung. "What does that mean?"

"What's it to do with their age?" Heinemann asked, frowning. "I've always been under the impression that your chances of dying are greater, the older you get. Isn't that the case? Statistically, I mean. . . ."

He looked around the table. Nobody seemed to be inclined to answer. Münster avoided his gaze and looked out the window instead. Noted that it had started raining again. *How old is Heinemann?* he asked himself.

"Anyway," said Rooth, "it's possible that there's a connection here. Do the other oldies know whether or not Bonger returned home on Saturday?"

Jung and Moreno looked at each other.

"No," said Jung. "Not as far as they've told us. Should we give 'em a grilling?"

"Let's wait for a bit with that," said Münster. "Tomorrow morning . . . If Bonger hasn't turned up by then, then something funny's going on. He isn't normally away from his boat for more than a few hours at a time, isn't that what you said?"

"That's right," said Jung.

Silence again. Rooth scraped up a few crumbs from the empty plate where the pastries had been, and Heinemann returned to cleaning his glasses. Krause looked at the clock.

"Anything else?" he wondered. "What do we do now? Speculate?"

Nobody seemed especially enthusiastic about that either, but eventually Rooth said:

"A madman, I'll bet two cocktail sausages on it. An unplanned murder, the only motive we'll ever find will be a junkie as high as a kite—or somebody on anabolics, of course. Did he need to be strong, by the way? What does Meusse have to say about that?"

"No," said Münster. "He said . . . he maintained that with well-hung meat and a sharp knife you don't need a lot of strength."

"Ugh, for Christ's sake," said Rooth.

Münster looked around for any further comments, but as none were offered he realized that it was time to draw the meeting to a close.

"You're probably right," he said, turning to Rooth. "For as long as we don't find a motive, that's the most likely solution. Should we send out a feeler in the direction of the drug squad?"

"Do that," said Moreno. "A feeler, but not one of us."

"I'll see what I can do," Münster promised.

Moreno stayed behind for a while after the others had left, and only then did Münster discover that he'd forgotten a detail.

"Oh, shit! There was another thing," he said. "That story about having won some money—can there be anything in it?"

Moreno looked up from the photograph she was studying with reluctance.

"What do you mean?" she asked.

Münster hesitated.

"Four men club together and win some money," he said. "Two of them kill off the other two, and presto! They've won twice as much."

Moreno said nothing for a few moments.

"Really?" she said eventually. "You think that's what happened?"

Münster shook his head.

"No," he said. "It's just that Fröken Gautiers down at Freddy's said something about a win, and she admits herself that she's only guessing. . . . But I suppose we ought to look into it."

"Rather that than drugs," said Moreno. "I'll take it on."

Münster was about to ask why she was so strongly opposed to the murky narcotics scene, but then he recalled another detail.

Inspector Moreno had a younger sister.

Had had, rather. He thought for a moment. Maybe that was what was depressing her, he thought. But then he noted her hunched shoulders and tousled hair and realized there must be something else as well. Something different. Apart from Synn, Inspector Moreno was the most beautiful woman he had ever had the pleasure of coming into contact with. But right now she looked distinctly human.

"What's the matter?" he asked.

She sighed deeply twice before replying.

"I feel so awful."

"I can see that," Münster said. "Personal problems?"

What an idiotic question, he thought. *I sound like an emasculated social worker.*

But she merely shrugged and twisted her mouth into an ironic smile.

"What else?"

"I tell you what," said Münster, playing the man of cunning and checking his watch. "You go and check up on the old dogs and I'll talk to Ruth Leverkuhn—and then we'll have lunch at Adenaar's. One o'clock. Okay?"

Moreno gave him a searching look.

"Okay," she said. "But I won't be very good company."

"So what?" said Münster. "We can always concentrate on the food."

9

"And what's so strange about that?"

The powerfully built woman glared threateningly at Rooth from behind her bangs, and it occurred to him that he wouldn't have a chance against her if it came to hand-to-hand fighting. He would need a gun.

"My dear Fru Van Eck," he said, taking a sip of the insipid coffee her husband had made in response to her explicit command. "Surely you can understand? An unknown person gets into the building, up the stairs, into the Leverkuhns' flat. He—or she—stabs Herr Leverkuhn twenty-eight times and kills him. It happens up there . . ."

He gestured toward the ceiling.

". . . roughly twenty feet from this kitchen table. The murderer then saunters out again through the door, down the stairs, and disappears. And you don't notice anything at all. That's what I call strange!"

Now she'll thump me, he thought, bracing himself against the edge of the table so that he would be able to get quickly to his feet; but his aggressive tone of voice seemed to throw her off balance.

"Jeez, Constable—"

"Inspector," insisted Rooth, "Detective Inspector Rooth."

"Really? Anyway, we didn't notice a thing, neither me nor Arnold. The only thing we heard that night were those screwing machines, that nigger and his mistress. . . . Isn't that right, Arnold?"

"Er, yes," said Arnold, scratching his wrists nervously.

"We've already explained this, both to you and that other flat-foot, whatever his name is. Why can't you find whoever did it instead of snooping around here? We're honest people."

I don't doubt that for a second, Rooth thought. *Not for a single second*. He decided to change track.

"The front door?" he said. "What about that? It's usually left unlocked, I gather?"

"No," said Fru Van Eck. "It could very well have been locked—but it's a crap lock."

"You can open it by peeing on it," squeaked Arnold Van Eck somewhat surprisingly, and he started giggling.

"Hold your goddamn tongue!" said his wife. "Pour some more coffee instead! Yes, it's a crap lock, but I assume the door was probably open so that Mussolini could get in."

"Mussolini?" said Rooth.

"Yes, he'd probably gone out for a screw as usual—I don't understand why she doesn't castrate the stupid thing."

"It's a cat," explained Arnold.

"He'll have gathered that, for Christ's sake!" snorted Fru Van Eck. "Anyway, she probably propped it open with that brick like she usually does."

"I see," said Rooth, and started to draw a cat in his notebook while trying to recall if he had ever come across such an uncouth woman before. He didn't think so. In the earlier interrogation, conducted by Constable Krause, it had emerged that she had worked for most of her life as a teacher in a school for girls, so there was considerable food for thought.

"What do you think about it?" he asked.

"About what?" asked Fru Van Eck.

"The murder," said Rooth. "Who do you think did it?"

She opened her mouth wide and tossed in two or three small cookies. Her husband cleared his throat but didn't get as far as spitting.

"Immigrants," she said curtly, and washed down the cookies

with a swig of coffee. Slammed her cup down with a bang. "Yes, if you take my advice you'll start interrogating the immigrants."

"Why?" asked Rooth.

"For Christ's sake, don't you see? It's sheer madness! Or it could be some young gangsters. Yes, that's where you'll find your murderer. Take your pick, it's up to you."

Rooth thought for a while.

"Do you have any children yourselves?" he asked.

"Of course we don't," said Fru Van Eck, starting to look threatening again.

Good, Rooth thought. *Genetic self-cleansing.*

"Thank you," he said. "I won't disturb you any longer."

Mussolini was lying on his back on the radiator, snoring.

Rooth had never seen a fatter cat, and purposely sat as far away on the sofa as possible.

"I've spoken to the Van Ecks," he said.

Leonore Mathisen smiled.

"You mean you've spoken to Fru Van Eck?"

"Hmm," said Rooth. "Perhaps that is what I mean. Anyway, we need to clarify a few things. To ask if you've remembered anything else about the night of the murder now that a little time has passed."

"I understand."

"One thing that puzzles us is the fact that nobody heard anything. For example, your bedroom, Fröken Mathisen, is directly above the Leverkuhns' but you fell asleep at . . ."

He rummaged through his notebook and pretended to be looking for the time.

"Half past twelve, roughly."

"That's right," he confirmed. Leonore Mathisen was not much smaller than Fru Van Eck, but the raw material seemed to be completely different. Like a . . . a bit like a currant bush as opposed to a block of granite. To take the comparison further, the bush was wearing cheerful home-dyed clothes in red, yellow, and violet, and a braided hair ribbon in the same colors. The block of granite had been grayish-brown all over and at least a quarter of a century older.

"I heard when he came home, as I said. Shortly before midnight, I think. Then I switched on the clock radio and listened to music until . . . well, I suppose I dozed off after about half an hour."

"Was he alone when he came in?" Rooth asked.

She shrugged.

"No idea. I'm not even sure it was him. I just heard somebody coming up the stairs, and a door opening and closing. But it was their door, of course—I'm sure about that."

"No voices?"

"No."

Rooth turned over a page of his notebook.

"What was he like?" he asked. "Leverkuhn, I mean."

She started fiddling with one of the thin wooden beads she was wearing in clusters around her neck while weighing her words.

"I don't really know," she said. "Very courteous, I'd say. He was always friendly and acknowledged me; rather dapper and correct; occasionally drank one glass too many when he was out with his friends—but never drank so much that he became unpleasant. I suppose I saw him only when he was on his way in and out, come to think about it."

"How long have you been living here?"

She counted.

"Eleven years," she said. "I suppose the Leverkuhns have been living here twice as long as that."

"What about his relationship with his wife?"

She shrugged again.

"As it usually is, I suppose. Old people who've been living together all their lives. . . . She tended to wear the pants, but my dad had a much rougher time."

She laughed.

"Are you married, Inspector?"

"No," Rooth admitted. "I'm single."

She suddenly burst out laughing. Her heavy breasts bobbed up and down, and Mussolini woke up with a start. It struck Rooth that he had never made love to a woman as big as she was, and for a few moments—while her salvo of laughter ebbed away and Mussolini slunk off in the direction of the hall—he sat there trying to imagine what it would be like.

Then he returned to the job at hand.

"Did they have much of a social life?" he asked.

She shook her head.

"Frequent visitors?"

"No, hardly ever. Not that I noticed. They live directly below me, and I have to say that for the most part it's as quiet as a grave, even when they're both at home. The only sounds you ever hear in this building come from the young couple, who live—"

"I know," said Rooth. "And they were at it as usual that night, were they?"

"Yes, they were at it as usual that night," she repeated, stroking her index finger along her bare lower arm, deep in thought.

Then she smiled, revealing twenty-four perfect teeth. At least.

My God, Rooth thought, feeling himself blush. She wants me. Now.

I'd better do a runner before I take the bait!

He stood up, thanked her, and took the same route as Mussolini.

The screwing machines—Tobose Menakdise and Filippa de Booning, according to the handwritten note taped above the letter box—didn't answer when he rang their doorbell, and when he pressed his ear against the wooden door he couldn't hear the faintest sound from inside the flat. He concluded that they were not at home, and wrote a question mark in his notebook. Went back upstairs to the second floor instead, to talk to Herr Engel.

Ruben Engel was about sixty-five, and his dominant feature was a large, fleshy, red nose so striking that in profile he reminded

Rooth of the parrot he'd had as a textile portrait over his bed when he was a young boy. He was not sure whether the appearance—of Engel, not the parrot—was due to an excessive intake of alcohol, or whether there was some other medical cause; but in any case, he was promptly invited to sit down at the kitchen table and partake in a drop or two of mulled wine.

It was so damned cold in the flat, Engel explained, that he always began the day with one or two warm drinks.

In order to keep healthy, of course.

The place looked reasonably clean and tidy, Rooth thought benevolently. More or less like his own flat. Only a few days' worth of dirty dishes, a few weeks' worth of newspapers, and a layer of dust about a month thick on the window ledges and television set.

"Anyway, I'm here in connection with Herr Leverkuhn," he began, and took a swig of the steaming drink. "You said last Saturday night that you knew him a little. That you socialized occasionally."

Engel nodded.

"Only to the extent that we were good neighbors," he said. "I mean, we've been living in the same building for more than twenty years. We went to a football match occasionally. Had a drink together from time to time."

"I see," said Rooth. "How often?"

"Football once a year," said Engel. "Old age is creeping up on us. There are so many hooligans. A drink now and then. I usually drink at Gambrinus just down the road, but then I always have Faludi with me."

"Who is Faludi?"

"An old colleague of mine. An Arab, but a great Arab. He lives a bit farther up the block. Cheers."

"Cheers," said Rooth.

"Aren't you on duty, by the way?"

"Never when I take a drink," said Rooth. "Have you thought back again to last Saturday night, as I asked?"

"Eh? . . . Oh yes, of course," said Engel, licking his lips. "But I don't remember any more than I told you last time."

"So you didn't hear or notice anything unusual?"

"Nope. I came home at around about half past eleven and went to bed like a shot. Listened to our pair of lovers for a while, then fell asleep at midnight, or thereabouts. It's not bad good-night music for an old fart like me, I can tell you! Hee-hee."

He raised his eyes to heaven and lit a cigarette. Rooth sighed.

"Nothing else to add?"

"Not a jot, as I've already said."

"Who do you think did it?" Rooth asked.

That was an old Van Veeteren ploy. Always ask people what they think! They tend to pull themselves together when they are trusted to use their own judgment; and then there's a good chance that if three out of five think the same thing, they're right.

In some cases two out of five.

Engel inhaled and thought it over. Scratched his nose and drank a little more mulled wine.

"It's not anybody living in this building," he said in the end. "And not one of his friends. So it has to be some madman from the outside."

Rooth scratched at the back of his neck.

"Do you know if he had any enemies, people who didn't wish him well?"

"Of course he didn't," said Engel. "Leverkuhn was a good man."

"What about his wife?"

"A good woman," said Engel laconically. "She moans a bit, but that's the way they are. Are you married, Inspector?"

"No," said Rooth, emptying his glass. "I never got around to it."

"Neither did I," said Engel. "I've never managed to hang on to a woman for more than three hours."

Rooth suspected he was dealing with a kindred spirit, but he refrained from exploiting the connection.

"Okay," he said instead. "Many thanks. We'll probably be in touch again, but it's not certain."

"I hope you can solve it," said Engel. "There are too many murderers on the loose nowadays."

"We shall see," said Rooth.

Nobody seems to be taking this especially hard, he thought as he emerged into the stairwell again. If they really were looking for a madman—a lunatic dropout—one might have expected to find traces of fear and uncertainty. But not in this case, it seemed. Unless of course he chose to interpret Herr Engel's parting words literally.

Perhaps people in general have grown just as accustomed over the years to violent deaths and perversities as he had himself. *That wouldn't surprise me,* Rooth thought somberly.

He had hardly walked out the front door when he was accosted by a bearded man about thirty-five years old with a notebook and pen in his hand.

"Bejman, *Neuwe Blatt,*" he explained. "Have you got a moment?"

"No," said Rooth.

"Just a couple of questions?"

"No."

"Why not?"

"We've already told you all we know."

"But you must know something else by now, surely?"

"Hmm," said Rooth, looking around furtively. "Not officially."

Bejman leaned forward to hear better.

"We're looking for a redheaded dwarf."

"A redheaded . . . ?"

"Yes, but don't write anything about that, for God's sake. We're not really sure yet."

He observed the reporter's furrowed brow for two seconds, then hurried over the street and jumped into his car.

I shouldn't have said that, he thought.

10

The Rote Moor was characterized by stucco work, uninspiring cut-glass chandeliers, and self-assured women. Münster sat down behind an oak-paneled wing and hoped the pianist didn't work mornings. As he sat there waiting, gazing out of the crackled windowpane overlooking Salutorget and the bustling shoppers, he began to feel for the first time that he was able to concentrate on the case.

As usual. It always took some time before the initial feeling of distaste faded, a day or two before he managed to shake off his immediate reactions—protesting and distancing himself from the violent killing that was always the starting point, the starting gun, the opening move in every new case. Every new task.

And the disgust. The disgust that was always there. At the start of his career—when he spent nearly all his working time in freezing cold cars on stakeouts during the night, or thanklessly shadowing suspects, or making door-to-door inquiries—he had believed the disgust would go away once he had learned how to face up to all the unpleasantness; but as the years passed he realized that this was not the case. On the contrary, the older he became the more important it seemed to have to protect himself and to keep things at arm's length. It was only when the initial waves of disgust had begun to ebb that it made any sense to start digging deeper into the case. To become closely acquainted with the nature of the crime. Its probable background. Causes and motives.

The very essence, as Van Veeteren used to put it.

The pattern.

No doubt the chief inspector had taught him some of these strategies, but not all. During the last few years—the last few cases—Van Veeteren's disgust had been even greater than his own, he was certain of that. But perhaps that was a right that came with increased age. Age and wisdom.

Hard to say. There was a sort of pattern in the chief inspector's last years as well. And in his current environment among all those books. That unfathomable concept known as *the determinant* that Münster had never really come to grips with. Never understood what it actually meant. But perhaps it would dawn on him one of these days: time and inertia were not only the province of oblivion, but sometimes also of gradual realization. It was a fact.

But Waldemar Leverkuhn. Forget everything else! Münster rested his head on his hands.

A seventy-two-year-old retiree killed in his sleep. Brutally murdered by a hair-raisingly large number of stab wounds—excessive violence, as it was called. A dodgy term of course, but perhaps it was appropriate in this case.

Why?

For Christ's sake, why so many stab wounds?

A waitress in a white hat coughed discreetly, but Münster asked her to wait until his companion arrived, and she withdrew. He turned his back on the premises and instead watched two pigeons strutting back and forth on the broad window ledge while he tried to conjure up an image of Leverkuhn's mutilated body in his mind's eye.

Twenty-eight stabs. What did that suggest?

It was hardly an insoluble puzzle. Fury, of course. Raging fury. The person who had put an end to this old man had been totally out of self-control. There had been no reason to continue after four or five stabs if the aim had been simply to kill the victim. Meusse had been crystal clear on that point. The last thirty seconds—the last fifteen or twenty stabs—were an expression of something other than the urge to kill.

Frenzy? Insanity? Revenge and retribution, perhaps? An implacable and long-standing hatred finally erupting and resolving itself?

The latter possibility was mere speculation; but it was logical, and there was nothing to rule it out.

The possibility that there might be a deep-seated motive, in other words.

Münster tapped on the windowpane and the pigeons flew off, their wings numb with cold.

But of course there was nothing to rule out Rooth's theory either—a crazy drug addict. Nothing at all.

You pay your money and make your choice, Münster thought.

Still, even if Chief of Police Hiller cuts our resources to the bone, I'm going to have a stab at resolving this case.

Good grief! What am I saying? Münster thought with a shudder. It sometimes seemed as if words acquired a life of their own, and lay in wait ready to ambush him.

Ruth Leverkuhn turned up at ten minutes past twelve: ten minutes late, a fact to which she devoted several explanations. She had been a bit late setting off. Lots of traffic, and then she couldn't find a parking space, neither in the square nor down at Zwille; she finally found one in Anckers Steeg and had only put money in the meter for half an hour. She hoped that would be enough.

In view of what they had to talk about, Münster received these trivial bits of information with suppressed surprise. Observed in silence as she hung her brown coat over the back of the empty chair at their table, she made quite a show of digging cigarettes and a lighter out of her handbag, adjusted her glasses and the artificial flowers on the table.

She was about his own age, he surmised, but a bit overweight and the worse for wear. Her brown-tinted shoulder-length hair hung like shabby and unwashed curtains around her pale face. Restlessness and insecurity surrounded her almost like body odor, and it was only when she lit a cigarette that there was a pause in her nervous chattering.

"Have you been in touch with your mother?" Münster asked.

"Yes." She nodded, inhaled deeply, and examined her fingernails. "Yes, I've heard what happened. I phoned her after I'd spoken to you. It's awful, I don't understand, it felt as if it were a dream when I got into the car and drove here . . . a nightmare, rather. But is it really true? That somebody killed him? Murdered him? Is it true?"

"As far as we can tell," said Münster.

"But that's absolutely . . . awful," she said again, taking another drag at her cigarette. "Why?"

"We don't know," said Münster. "I'd like to ask you a few questions, if you don't mind."

She nodded and took another drag. The waitress appeared again and took their order: café au lait for Fröken Leverkuhn, black coffee for the intendent. He took out his notebook and put it on the table in front of him.

"Did you have a good relationship with your father?" he asked. She gave a start.

"What do you mean by that?"

"Exactly what I said," said Münster. "Did you have a good relationship with him?"

"Well, yes. . . . He was my father after all."

"It does happen that children sometimes have bad relationships with their fathers," Münster pointed out.

She hesitated. Scratched herself quickly on the outside of her left breast and took another drag.

"We haven't had all that much contact lately."

"Lately?"

"Since I grew up, I suppose you could say."

"Twenty, twenty-five years?" Münster asked.

She made no reply.

"Why?" Münster asked.

"It just turned out that way."

"Did the same apply to your brother and sister?"

"More or less."

"How often did you meet your mother and father?"

"Just occasionally."

"Once a month?"

"Once a year, more like."

"Once a year?"

"Yes. . . . At Christmas. But not always. You might think it sounds bad, but they didn't take any initiatives either. We simply didn't socialize. Why should we have to observe social conventions when nobody concerned was bothered?

"I'm a lesbian," she added, out of the blue.

"Really," said Münster. "What has that to do with it?"

"I don't know," said Ruth Leverkuhn. "But people talk."

Münster watched the pigeons, which had returned, for a while. Ruth put two spoonfuls of sugar into her cup and stirred.

"When did you last see your father?"

She stubbed out her cigarette and started fumbling for another one while she thought it over.

"That would be nearly two years ago," she said.

"And your mother?"

"The same. We were there for Christmas. Two years ago."

Münster noted it down.

"Have you any idea what might have happened?" he asked. "Did your father have any enemies? People who have known him for a long time, who didn't like him?"

"No . . ." She moved her tongue up behind her upper lip and tried to look thoughtful. "No, I have no idea at all. Not the slightest."

"Any other relatives?"

"Only Uncle Franz. He died a few years ago."

Münster nodded.

"And how were things between your mother and father?"

She shrugged.

"They stuck together."

"Evidently," said Münster. "Did they have much of a social life?"

"No . . . no, hardly any at all, I should think."

Münster thought for a moment.

"Do you intend to visit your mother now?"

"Yes," she said. "Of course. What did you think?"

The last convention, Münster thought.

"What do you do for work?"

"I'm a shop assistant."

"In Wernice?"

"Yes."

"What were you doing last Saturday evening?"

"What do you want to know that for?"

"What were you doing?"

She took out a paper handkerchief and wiped her mouth.

"I was at home."

"Do you live alone?"

"No."

"With a girlfriend?"

"Yes."

"Was she also at home last Saturday evening?"

"No, she wasn't, as it happens. Why are you asking about that?"

"Do you remember what you gave your mother as a Christmas present fifteen years ago?"

"Eh?"

"A Christmas present," Münster repeated. "Nineteen eighty-two."

"How should I . . ."

"A carving knife," said Münster. "Is that right?"

He saw that her facial muscles were beginning to twitch here and there, and he realized there was probably not long to go before she started crying. *What the hell am I doing?* he thought. This job makes you a sadist.

"Why?" she mumbled. "I don't know what you mean. What are you getting at?"

"Just routine," said Münster. "Don't take it personally. Are you staying here overnight?"

She shook her head.

"I don't think so. I'll probably go back home tonight. . . . Unless Mom wants me to stay with her."

Why should she want that? Münster thought. Then he closed his notebook and reached his hand out over the table.

"Thank you, Fröken Leverkuhn," he said. "I'm sorry I had to torment you at a difficult time, but we would rather like to catch your father's murderer, as I'm sure you understand."

"Yes . . . of course."

She presented him with four cold fingers for half a second. Münster pushed back his chair and stood up.

"I think you'd better hurry before your meter runs out."

She glanced at the clock, stuffed the cigarettes and lighter into her handbag, and got to her feet.

"Thank you," she said. "I hope . . ."

He never learned what she hoped. Instead she tried to produce a smile, but when it refused to stick she turned on her heel and left him.

Ah well, Münster thought as he beckoned to the waitress. *One of those conversations.*

A condensed life in twenty minutes. Why was it that other people's lives could seem so clear-cut when my own almost always seemed to evade judgment and reflection?

He didn't know. One of those questions.

II

When Marie-Louise Leverkuhn had finished crying—a comparatively short outburst of emotion that lasted only a minute—Emmeline von Post removed her arm from her friend's shoulders and suggested a walk by the river. The weather was quite pleasant—the occasional shower was likely during the course of the day, but there were raincoats and Wellington boots available. That she could borrow.

Fru Leverkuhn blew her nose and declined the offer. Remained seated for a while at the kitchen table—like an injured and disheveled bird, it seemed to her hostess—and she explained that she needed a little more rest before she was ready to meet her children. Her daughter Ruth was expected about lunchtime, and it wasn't quite clear who would be expected to support whom.

Emmeline didn't quite understand the last bit, but kept a straight face even so and submitted to her newly widowed friend's wishes. Decided to go for a short walk herself instead—to the post office and the shopping center to buy a few necessities, now that there would be several mouths to feed.

And Marie-Louise could spend the time recovering as she thought best. While waiting for the children.

Emmeline set off as soon as the breakfast dishes had been washed, shortly before eleven, and when she returned with her grocery bags three quarters of an hour later, Marie-Louise had vanished.

The door to Mark's room was open, so it seemed that she had made no attempt to conceal the fact that she wasn't there. But there was no message, not in the room or anywhere else.

Well, Emmeline thought as she unpacked her bags and allocated the goods to the larder or the refrigerator as appropriate. *I expect she's just stepped out to buy a postage stamp or something of the sort. She'll be back soon, no doubt.*

And so she took a Swiss roll out of the freezer, switched on the coffee maker, and sat down at the kitchen table with a newspaper.

And waited.

She came down to the river next to the wooden cabin that served as the rowing club's house. A few young people were busy scraping the window frames. She hesitated for a moment before setting off westward along the unpaved bridle path through the deciduous woods. She felt almost immediately the raw, cold wind blowing off the dark water, and tied her shawl more tightly around her head. Wishing she had a wool hat instead, she dug her hands down into her coat pockets and clutched the package tighter under her arm.

She had been along this path before—two or three times in the summer together with Emmeline—and she began to picture what it was like farther on. Tried to remember if there was any one place that was better and more inaccessible than anywhere else, but couldn't decide for sure. She would have to make the best of it, this area along the bank of the river: waterlogged, covered in brushwood with hardly a building around—but of course it could never be 100 percent foolproof, she had realized and accepted that, seeing as there had been no opportunity to burn it, which would have been the best solution.

She had walked only a hundred yards or so when her bad knee started to act up—the typical prickling sensations and shooting

pains whenever she put her right foot down into the loose sand—
and it was clear that it would be risky to continue much farther.

But in all probability it wouldn't be necessary anyway. The
riverbank was covered in alders and brushwood, and the belt of
reeds extended a long way out into the water, more than 160 feet
or more in places. She could hardly have asked for anything better.
When she came to the first sidetrack leading inland, she paused
and looked around. No sign of anyone. She turned off along the
muddy path down to a jetty that ran in a sort of diamond shape
around a run-down boathouse. Walked carefully along the shaky,
slippery planks to where it changed direction like the apex of a
triangle, and leaned against the boathouse wall while she pressed
the air out of the package and tied the string tightly. Listened at-
tentively, but there was no sound save for the distant, mournful
cries of birds and the hum of traffic a long way off on the motorway. No sign of any people. No boats on the river. She took a
deep breath and hurled the package out into the reeds. Heard the
rattling noise as the brittle stalks snapped, and the dull plop when
it dropped into the water.

That's that, then, she thought. Looked around once more. Nothing. She was alone, and the deed was done.

She put her hands back into her pockets and started to retrace
her steps.

It took longer than she had expected. She had walked a long way,
and her knee was causing her serious pain now. She slowed down
and tried to avoid putting any weight on her heel, but it just felt
odd, and didn't help much in the loose sand. By the time she returned to the built-up area it had started raining quite hard again,
and she decided to allow herself a few minutes to rest. She found a
run-down and graffiti-covered bus shelter, sat down on the bench,
and tried to keep as warm as possible in the circumstances while
observing the few people who had ventured out of doors on this
rainy morning. Three or four grim-faced dog owners. A jogger in

a red tracksuit listening to his music player, and a down-and-out old man searching for empty bottles in the rubbish bins, dragging a shopping cart behind him. . . . A few steamed-up cars drove past, but no bus. But that didn't matter—she wouldn't know which one to catch anyway. After a while she was freezing cold, and although she knew full well that any hope of the rain easing off was mostly wishful thinking, she stood up and set off again. She noticed that she wasn't thinking straight: thoughts were buzzing inside her head like restless, nervous dreams; but before long everything was dominated by a desire to drink something hot. Or strong.

Or both.

When she finally returned to the neat little terraced house in Geldenerstraat it was ten minutes past one, and Emmeline von Post was being kept company at her kitchen table by Ruth Leverkuhn.

As soon as she saw her mother in the doorway, Ruth stood up. Cleared her throat, smoothed her skirt, and made a sort of half-hearted gesture with her hands.

Marie-Louise stood still and stared at her daughter with her arms hanging down by her sides.

Neither of them said a word. Five seconds passed. Emmeline scraped her coffee cup against the saucer and watched the rain her friend had brought in with her dripping onto the threshold and parts of the linoleum.

Do something, for God's sake, she thought. *Why does nobody say anything?*

12

"Well?" said Münster. "I hope you caught them in your trap?"

They had bagged one of the window booths at Adenaar's, and had made a start on the salad of the day.

"Yes, of course," said Ewa Moreno. "Kicking and screaming in a net of lies . . . No, I don't know. I spoke only to Wauters. Palinski was about to leave for the hospital for some sort of check. But I had the impression . . ."

She hesitated and stared out the window.

"What?" said Münster. "What sort of impression?"

"That they're hiding something. I asked Wauters straight out if they'd won some money, and I thought his reply seemed rehearsed. Raised eyebrows, broad gestures, the whole caboodle. I wouldn't be surprised if they've hit the jackpot."

"But you didn't press him?"

"I'm not in top form," said Moreno apologetically. "I told you that. I didn't want to mess things up. I thought it would be better to question them one at a time at the police station instead. A lamp shining into their faces and all that. But they both seemed to be genuinely at a loss regarding Bonger. Wauters claimed he'd been to the boat, looking for him, and Palinski said he intended to call him on the way home from the hospital."

Münster thought it over.

"So your guess is that they've won some money, but that it hasn't got anything to do with Bonger's disappearance?"

Moreno nodded.

"And hence nothing to do with Leverkuhn either," she said. "No, I reckon that would be too far an assumption. I think they are just scared of being suspected. Wauters at least is quite sharp, and he could well have realized the risk as soon as he heard what had happened to Leverkuhn. . . . There are lots of old crime novels in his bookcase."

"They might be reluctant to give the widow a quarter share as well," Münster pointed out. "Anyway, we'll give them a warm reception tomorrow morning. But let's face it, it's damned odd that Bonger should go up in smoke the same night that Leverkuhn is murdered, don't you think?"

"Of course," said Moreno. "Have we issued a wanted notice yet?"

Münster checked his watch.

"It went out an hour ago."

"Does he have any relatives?"

"A son in Africa. Nothing has been heard from him since 1985. And an elder sister with Alzheimer's, in Gemejnte Hospital. His wife died eight years ago—that was when he moved into the boat."

Moreno nodded and said nothing for a while.

"A strange crowd, this gang of old geezers," she said eventually.

"They had one another," said Münster. "Shall we have coffee?"

"Yes, let's," said Moreno.

In the end he couldn't hold back any longer.

"What about your private life?" he said. "How are things?"

Moreno contemplated the gray, misty view through the window once again, and Münster realized she was sizing him up. He passed the test, it seemed, when she took a deep breath and straightened her back.

"I moved out," she said.

"Away from Claus?"

He remembered his name in any case.

"Yes."

"Oh dear," said Münster, and waited.

"It's been a month now," she went on after a while. "I have a friend who's in Spain for six months, so I took the opportunity of subletting her place. . . . It took two days before I was convinced that I'd done the right thing, and that I'd wasted five years."

Münster tried to look on the bright side.

"Some people waste a whole life," he said.

"It's not that," said Moreno and sighed again. "It's not that at all. I'm prepared to put it behind me and start fresh. Experience is experience, after all."

"Without a doubt," said Münster. "What doesn't kill you makes you stronger. What *is* the matter, then?"

"Claus," she said, and the expression on her face was something he'd never seen before. "It's Claus that's the problem. I think . . . I don't think he's going to get over it."

Münster said nothing.

"For five years I've been under the impression that he was the strong half of the duo, and that it was me who didn't dare to let go—but now . . ."

She clenched her fists so tightly that her knuckles turned white.

". . . now he's so damned pitiful. I know it sounds cold and hard, but why can't he at least stop degrading himself in front of me?"

"He's begging and pleading, is he?" Münster asked.

"You can say that again."

"How often do you meet?"

Moreno sighed.

"Several times a week. And he calls me every day. He's taken sick leave as well. I loved him, but every time we talk, that love ebbs further and further away. . . . He says he's going to kill himself, and I'm almost starting to believe him. That's the worst part—that I believe him."

Münster rested his head on his hands, leaning closer to her. He suddenly realized that he wanted to touch her: just a gentle stroke over her cheek or along her arm, but he didn't dare. Come to think of it, he didn't recall having seen Claus Badher more than three or four times; he'd never spoken to him, but truthfully he didn't have an especially positive opinion of the young bank lawyer.

One of those pretty-boy financial yuppies, the type that changes his shirt three times a day and pours aftershave into his underpants.

But then again, perhaps there was just some kind of primitive and atavistic jealousy behind that judgment. He recalled that Reinhart once said it was perfectly normal to be jealous of every guy who went around with a woman who was more or less attractive. Healthy and natural. And you could be sure that anyone who didn't feel that way was definitely suffering from some nasty affliction or other. Constipation, for instance.

However, it wasn't always easy to scrutinize your own putative emotional life. Especially with regard to women.

Or so Intendent Münster thought, attempting to be honest in a melancholy sort of way.

"I understand," he said simply. "Is there anything I can do? You sound a bit depressed, if you'll pardon my saying so."

She pulled a face.

"I know," she said. "It's not that I hate the man, and I don't want him to lose control: I just want to be left in peace. It's so damned difficult when the whole of my environment seems to be shedding its skin like this. I haven't slept more than three hours a night for several weeks now."

Münster leaned back in his chair.

"The only things that can possibly help are time and coffee," he said. "Another cup?"

Moreno managed to produce a grimace that might have been intended to be a smile.

"You know," she said, "I sometimes get the feeling that men are nothing more than overgrown Boy Scouts in disguise—and not many are in disguise, at that."

"I've heard that before," said Münster. "But there is a female defect as well."

Moreno had raised her cup, but paused.

"Really? What?"

"The incomprehensible tendency to fall for overgrown Boy Scouts," Münster said. "Not to mention overgrown little boys whose voices are breaking, and rowdies, and swine in general. If you can explain to me why you can put up with being beaten and humiliated and raped and tortured by these macho gorillas year in and year out, then we can get around to discussing Boy Scout morals and disguises afterward!"

His anger struck without his having anticipated it, and he could see that Moreno had not been prepared for his attack.

"Oh dear," she said. "I suppose you have a point. Are there never any mature people at all?"

Münster sighed.

"A few, I suppose," he said. "It's not easy being human. Especially when you're tired and overworked all the time. . . . That's when you become inhuman."

"Yes, I suppose so," said Moreno.

Jung stared down into the water.

He was standing on Doggers Bridge about 150 feet from Bonger's houseboat, where he had just made his third fruitless visit. He'd had a third conversation with Fru Jümpers as well—more of an exchange of opinions really—but nothing had emerged that could bring the disappearance of the old boat owner any closer to a solution. Nothing at all. However, it was raining more heavily now: water was running down from his hair onto his face and the back of his neck, but it didn't bother him any longer. There was a limit beyond which it was impossible to get any wetter, and he had passed it some time ago. Moreover something was beginning to eat away inside his head.

Something quite complicated.

A theory.

Suppose, he thought as he watched a duck paddling away in an attempt to progress upstream without moving from the spot, suppose that Leverkuhn and Bonger fall out as they walk back home from Freddy's. . . . There were witnesses who testified that they had been arguing on the pavement outside the entrance door before they set off.

Suppose also that the argument becomes more heated, and Bonger goes all the way home with Leverkuhn. Eventually Leverkuhn goes to bed, but simmering with anger and fueled by alcohol, Bonger collects the carving knife and kills him.

Then Felix Bonger panics. He takes the knife with him, rushes out of the flat and away from Kolderweg (insofar as it's possible to rush when you're that age), hurries home along the dark streets and alleys to Bertrandgraacht, but by the time he reaches Doggers Bridge the realization and horror of what he's done gets to him. Regret and remorse. He stands on the bridge and stares at his blood-soaked weapon and the dark water.

Suppose, finally, Jung's fast-flowing stream of thought continued, *that he stands on this very spot.*

He paused and stared down at the canal. The duck finally gave in to another surge of current and turned around; a few seconds later it had disappeared into the shadows not far from Bonger's houseboat.

He stands right here beside the cold, wet railings! In the middle of the night. Would it be all that strange if he decided to take the consequences of what he had done?

Jung nodded to himself. It wasn't every day that he came up with a plausible theory.

And so—ergo!—there was without doubt a lot to suggest that they were both down there. In the mud at the bottom of the canal under this bridge.

Both the murder weapon and the murderer! Despite Heinemann's pessimistic calculations.

Jung leaned over the railings and tried to gaze down through the coal-black water. Then he shook his head.

You're out of your mind, he thought. *You're a dilettante. Leave thinking to those whom God blessed with the gift of a brain instead!*

He turned on his heel and walked off. Away from this murky canal and this murky speculation.

Mind you, he thought when he had come to slightly drier ground under the colonnade in Van Kolmerstraat, it wouldn't be totally out of place if he tried out his hypothesis on one of his colleagues. Rooth, for example. After all, it wasn't entirely impossible that it had happened exactly in this way. There were no logical red flags, and you never know. . . .

As said before.

Before Münster ended this lugubrious Monday, he ran through the witness testimonies with Krause. There was little useful information. Not much, but better than nothing, as Krause put it optimistically. A handful of people had seen Leverkuhn and Bonger outside Freddy's, and at least two of them were convinced that they had not left together. There had clearly been a degree of animosity between the two old friends, and it seemed as if Bonger had simply abandoned his friend and gone home on his own. So far, however, nobody had come forward to say they had seen either of the two men after they had left the restaurant—on their way to Kolderweg and Bertrandgraacht respectively.

They had also drawn a blank regarding Fru Leverkuhn's walk to and from Entwick Plejn a few hours later.

But then—as Krause also pointed out—it was still only Monday: the case was less than two days old, and the majority of people probably hadn't read about it yet.

So there was still hope.

For some obscure reason Münster had difficulty in sharing Krause's apple-cheeked can-do spirit, and when he went down to his car in the underground garage he noticed to his surprise that he felt old.

Old and tired.

It didn't help that Monday evening was when Synn attended her course in commercial French; nor the fact that his son, Bart, had borrowed a saxophone from a classmate and devoted every second of the evening to practicing. In the end Münster locked the instrument in the trunk of his car and explained that the ten-year-old was much too young for that sort of music.

Ten-year-olds should go to bed and keep quiet. It was half past ten.

For his own part he dropped off to sleep not long afterward, nagged by a bad conscience and without Synn by his side.

13

"I'm staying only until tonight," Mauritz Leverkuhn explained. "She doesn't want us hanging around, so why play the hypocrite?"

Yes, why indeed, Münster thought.

The man sitting opposite him on the visitor's chair was big and heavy, with a receding hairline and the same ruddy complexion as his sister. There was something superficial, disinterested, in his way of speaking and behaving—as if he weren't really with it—and Münster assumed that it had something to do with his profession.

Mauritz Leverkuhn worked as a salesman and distributor of paper cloths, serviettes, and candle rings to department stores and supermarkets.

"I'd just like some information," said Münster. "So far we don't have much to go on with regard to the murder of your father, so we need to follow up any leads we can manage to dig up."

"I understand," said Mauritz.

"When did you last see him?"

Mauritz thought for a few moments.

"A few months ago," he said. "I was here on an assignment, and I called in on them briefly. Drank coffee. Gave Mother a bottle of cherry liqueur—it was her birthday."

"So you didn't have much contact with your parents, generally speaking?"

Mauritz cleared his throat and adjusted his yellow-and-blue-striped tie.

"No," he said. "We didn't. . . . We don't have. None of us."

"Why?"

He shrugged.

"Is it necessary?"

Münster refrained from responding.

"Do you have any children?"

"No."

"So there aren't any grandchildren at all, then?"

Mauritz shook his head.

"Are you married?"

"No."

"Have you been?"

"No."

Münster waited a few seconds, but it was apparent that Mauritz had no intention of saying anything off his own bat.

"What's the relationship between you and your sisters?" he asked. "Do you see much of one another?"

"What has that got to do with it?"

He shifted his position on his chair and fingered the crease of his trousers.

"Nothing," said Münster. "It's difficult to say what is relevant at this stage. And what isn't."

We've got a real bundle of fun here, he thought—and it struck him that the same applied to the family as a whole. None of them were likely to be the life of any party: not the ones he'd been in contact with at least. Wood lice, as Reinhart used to call them.

But perhaps he was being unfair. He didn't feel all that much of a live wire himself, come to think of it.

"What about your eldest sister?" he asked. "She's unwell, if I'm not mistaken."

Mauritz suddenly looked hostile.

"You have no reason to drag her into this," he said. "Our family has nothing to do with what happened. Not me or my sisters. Or my mother."

"How can you be so sure?" said Münster.

"What?"

"How can you be so sure that none of them is involved? You don't have any contact with them."

"Shut your trap," said Mauritz.

Münster did as he was told. Then he pressed the intercom and asked Fröken Katz to serve them some coffee.

"Tell me what you were doing last Saturday night."

The coffee had induced a climate change for the better, but only marginally.

"I was at home," said Mauritz sullenly, after a couple of seconds' thought. "Watching the boxing match on TV."

Münster wrote that down as a matter of routine.

"What time was that?"

Mauritz shrugged.

"Between nine and twelve, roughly speaking. Surely you don't think that I drove here and murdered my father? Are you all right in the head?"

"I don't think anything," said Münster. "But I would like you to be a bit more cooperative."

"Oh yeah? And how do you think I'm going to be able to cooperate when I've got nothing to say?"

I don't know, Münster thought. *How many years is it since you last smiled at anything?*

"But what do you think?" he asked. "We have to try to find somebody who might have had a motive to kill your father. It's possible of course that it was an act of pure madness, but that's not certain. There might have been something behind it."

"What, for instance?" Mauritz wondered.

"That's something we hoped you might be able to tip us off about."

Mauritz snorted.

"Do you really think I'd shut up about something like that, even if I knew anything?"

Münster paused and checked the questions he had written down in advance.

"When did they move to Kolderweg?" he asked.

"Nineteen seventy-six. Why do you want to know that?"

Münster ignored the question.

"Why?"

"They sold the house. We youngsters had moved out."

Münster made a note of that.

"He got a new job as well. He'd been out of work for a while."

"What kind of a job?"

"Pixner Brewery. I'm sure you know about that already."

"Perhaps," said Münster. "And before that you lived down in Pampas, is that right?"

Mauritz nodded.

"Pampas, yes. Shoe boxes for the working class. Four rooms and a kitchen. Eighty square feet of lawn."

"Okay," said Münster. "And where did you move to when it became too cramped?"

"Aarlach. I started at the commercial college in 1975. This can't be important, surely?"

Münster pretended to check his notebook again. Mauritz had folded his arms over his chest and was gazing out the window at the rain-filled clouds. His aggressiveness seemed to have lapsed into genuine lethargy. As if he were sitting there reflecting the weather.

"Who do you think did it?" he asked speculatively.

Mauritz turned his head to look at Münster dismissively.

"How the hell should I know? I haven't had any real contact with my father for more than twenty years, and I've no idea who he used to knock around with. Can't we stop all this crap now so that I can get away from here?"

"All right," said Münster. "Just one more thing. Do you know if your father had any money? If he had any cash stashed away, for instance?"

Mauritz had already stood up.

"Garbage," he said. "He worked for half his life at Gahn's, and for the other half at the brewery. Those aren't the kind of places where you can scrape together a fortune. Good-bye, Intendent!"

He started to reach out over the desk with his hand, but changed his mind halfway through and put it in his pocket instead.

"Do you miss him?" Münster asked, but the only response he got was a vacant look. Nevertheless, Mauritz paused in the doorway.

"When I was a teenager I actually considered applying to police college," he said. "I'm glad I didn't."

"So are we," Münster muttered when the door had closed. "Very glad indeed."

When he was alone in the room, he went to the window and looked out over the town, as he often did. Over the streets, rooftops, and churches; over Wejmargraacht and Wollerims Park, where the gray mist enveloped the trees in a blanket of damp, obliterating outlines. *Like an amateurish watercolor painting,* he thought, *in which the colors have spread and mixed with one another and with the water.* The skyscrapers a little farther off, up on the ridge at Leimaar, could hardly be made out, and the thought struck him that if there was any town in the whole world where a murderer had a good chance of hiding away, it was here.

When he looked down he saw Mauritz Leverkuhn walking across the car park toward a white and fairly new Volvo. Some kind of company car, probably—with the trunk and backseat crammed full of serviettes and candle rings in every cheerful color imaginable. For the benefit of mankind and their endless striving after the greatest possible enjoyment.

I seem to be a bit disillusioned today, Münster thought, turning his back on the town.

. . .

Chief of Police Hiller was reminiscent of a randy frog.

At least that was Münster's immediate reaction when he came into the conference room where the run-through was set to take place, a few minutes late. The whole man seemed to be inflated, especially over his shirt collar; his eyes were bulging, his cheeks swollen, and his face was deep red.

"What the hell's the meaning of this?" he hissed, drops of spit glittering in the reflected light from the overhead projector, which was switched on, ready for use. "Explain what the hell this means!"

He was holding a newspaper in his hand, waving it at the cowering assembly—Intendent Heinemann; Inspectors Rooth, Jung, and Moreno; and in the far corner the promising young Constable Krause.

Münster sat down between Heinemann and Moreno without speaking.

"Well?" snorted Hiller, hurling the *Neuwe Blatt* onto the table so that Münster could see at last what the problem was.

The headline ran across all eight columns, and was followed by three exclamation marks:

POLICE ARE SEARCHING FOR REDHEADED DWARF!!!

and underneath, in less bold type:

IN CONNECTION WITH THE RETIREE MURDER

Heinemann put on his glasses.

"That's odd," he said. "I don't think I've been informed."

Hiller closed his eyes and clenched his fists. In an attempt to calm himself down, for his next comment came through clenched teeth.

"I want to know the meaning of this. And who is responsible."

Moreno glanced at the newspaper and cleared her throat.

"Red-haired dwarf?" she said. "It must be a joke."

"A joke?" snarled Hiller.

"I agree," said Rooth. "Surely none of you are looking for a dwarf?"

He looked inquiringly around the table, while Hiller chewed at his lower lip and tried to stand still.

"I'm not," said Heinemann.

Münster glanced at Jung. Realized that a disastrous burst of laughter was on the point of breaking out, and that he'd better intervene before it was too late.

"It's just a newspaper fuck-up," he said as slowly and pedagogically as he could. "Some bright spark has no doubt phoned the editorial office and spun them a yarn. And some other bright spark has swallowed the bait. Don't blame us!"

"Exactly," said Rooth.

Hiller's facial color went down to plum.

"What a fucking mess," he muttered. "Krause!"

Krause sat up straight.

"Yes?"

"Find out which prize idiot has written this drivel—I'll be damned if they're going to get away with it!"

"Yes, sir!" said Krause.

"Off you go, then!" the chief of police roared, and Krause slunk out. Hiller sat down at the end of the table and switched off the overhead projector.

"Moreover," he said, "we have too many people working on this case. Just a couple of you will be sufficient from now on. Münster!"

"Yes?" said Münster with a sigh.

"You and Moreno will sort out Leverkuhn from now on. Use Krause as well, but only if it's really necessary. Jung and Rooth will look after the rapes in Linzhuisen, and Heinemann—what were you working on last week?"

"That Dellinger business," said Heinemann.

"Continue with that," said Hiller. "I want reports from all of you by Friday."

He stood up and would have been out of the room in two seconds if he hadn't stumbled over Rooth's briefcase.

"Oops," said Rooth. "Sorry about that, but I think I need to have a quick word with Krause."

He picked up his briefcase and hurried off, while the chief of police brushed off his neatly creased knee and muttered something incomprehensible.

"Well, what do you think?" said Münster as he and Moreno sat down in the canteen. "A memorable performance?"

"There's no doubt about the entertainment value," said Moreno. "It must be the first time in a month that I almost burst out laughing. What an incredible idiot!"

"A Boy Scout, perhaps?" said Münster, and she actually smiled.

"Still, he says what he means," she said. "He doesn't try to fool anybody. Should we get down to work?"

"That's the idea. Have you any good ones?"

Moreno swirled her cup and analyzed the coffee grounds.

"No," she said. "No good ones."

"Nothing here either," said Münster. "So we'll have to make do with bad ones for the time being. We could bring Palinski in."

"Not a bad idea," said Moreno.

14

After two days out at Bossingen, Marie-Louise Leverkuhn returned to Kolderweg 17 on Tuesday afternoon.

The children had come, commiserated, and gone back home. Emmeline von Post had lamented and sympathized in every way possible, the heavens had wept more or less continuously. It was high time to return to reality and everyday life. It certainly was.

Marie-Lousie began by scrubbing the blood-soaked room. She was unable to get rid of the blood that had penetrated the floorboards and walls, despite her best efforts with strong scouring powder of various makes; nor was there much she could do about the stains on the woodwork of the bed—but then again, she didn't need the bed anymore. She dismantled it and dragged the whole caboodle out onto the landing for Arnold Van Eck to take care of. She then unrolled a large cowhair carpet that had been stored up in the attic for years and covered the floorboards. A couple of low-hanging tapestries took care of the wall.

After this hard labor she started going through her husband's wardrobe: it was a time-consuming and rather delicate undertaking. She didn't like doing it, but she had no choice. Some stuff ended up in the garbage, some in the laundry basket; but most of it was put into suitcases and plastic bags for taking to the charity shop in Windemeerstraat.

When this task was more or less finished, there was a ring at the door. It was Fru Van Eck, inviting her down for coffee and cake.

Marie-Louise hesitated at first. She had never been on particularly good terms with the caretaker's wife, but Fru Van Eck was insistent and in the end she heaved the plastic bag she had just finished filling into the wardrobe and accepted the invitation.

Life must go on, she thought, somewhat confused.

"Life must go on," said Fru Van Eck five minutes later as her husband sliced up the cake with raspberries and blackberries. "How are you feeling?"

"Not too bad," said Marie-Louise. "It takes time to get used to things."

"I can imagine that," said Fru Van Eck, eyeing Arnold for a few seconds with a thoughtful expression on her face.

"By the way, there was one thing," she said eventually. "Arnold, will you leave us alone for a minute or two, please? Go and buy a soccer pool coupon or something, but take that apron off!"

Arnold bowed obediently and left the ladies alone in the kitchen.

"There's one thing I didn't mention when the police were here," said Fru Van Eck when she heard the apartment door close.

Marie-Louise said nothing, merely stirred her cup of coffee, didn't look up.

"I thought perhaps we could discuss it and agree on what line we should take. Do help yourself to a slice of cake. Arnold baked it himself."

Marie-Louise shrugged and took a slice.

"Let's hear it, then," she said.

"Thanks a lot," said Rooth as he left Krause's office. "I'll make sure you get two tickets."

As he went through the door he found himself confronted by Joensuu and Kellerman, who were steering Adolf Bosch along the corridor. After a day-and-a-half-long search, they had eventually found him in a dodgy bar in the block just below the customs station. Rooth turned his nose up and squeezed past. There was a smell of old sweat and drunkenness surrounding the man: Krause immediately ushered him toward the PVC-covered sofa next to the door, and the constables used all their strength to force him to sit down on it.

"Ouch," said Bosch.

"Shut your trap," said Kellerman. "That was far from easy, believe you me."

"The bastard started peeing in the car," said Joensuu.

"Well done," said Krause. "You can go now."

Joensuu and Kellerman left and Krause closed the door. Bosch was already lying down on the short sofa, with his knees raised and his head on the armrest. Krause sat down at his desk and waited.

"I don't feel very well," said Bosch after half a minute.

"You never have," said Krause. "Stop with the act, you know what's what. If we want we can have you locked away for eighteen months. . . . Unless you tell me a thing or two about certain unpleasant characters. Sit up!"

Bosch was a narc. Or an informer, as he preferred to call himself. A good-for-nothing dropout in any case—but with just the right lack of backbone and civil courage required for the role. Krause observed him in disgust. He had always found it difficult to accept this form of cooperation. Bosch was constantly being admitted to various clinics and institutions for detox and rehab: nobody seriously thought he would live to be much older than the forty-five years he had managed to achieve, but despite everything, asking him to find out information often produced results. Much more often than one would have expected.

"When it comes to crooks, you can always rely on Adolf Bosch to stir up the shit," Van Veeteren used to say. "But never give him more than three days—he has no concept of time any longer than that."

The threat of being locked away and reprisals from the underworld made him sit up half-straight. His eyes looked shifty and he scratched away at his armpits.

"Are you listening?" said Krause.

"Any chance of a cig?"

Krause took a packet out of a drawer, where it was kept for this purpose, and handed it over.

"You can have what's left, but wait until you've left the building."

"Thanks," said Bosch, taking tight hold of the packet.

"It's in connection with a murder," said Krause. "That retiree in Kolderweg. Have you heard about it?"

Bosch nodded.

"But I have no idea who did it. I swear . . ."

"Spare us the innocent act," said Krause. "We think it was some junkie who had a bad trip. See what you can find out and report back to me the day after tomorrow."

"I'm a bit short of cash at the moment," said Bosch, looking worried.

"We'll see about that on Thursday."

"But I'm broke," said Bosch.

"Thursday," said Krause, pointing at the door.

"Thursday," muttered Bosch, and he left reluctantly.

Krause sighed and opened the window.

They stuck to the rule book with regard to Palinski. At first they considered drawing straws, but as Moreno was a woman Münster backed down and took the first round.

"Name?"

"Eh?" said Palinski. "You already know what it is."

"We're recording this conversation," explained Münster impatiently, pointing at the tape recorder. "Please state your name and date of birth."

"Is this an interrogation?"

"Yes. Name?"

"Palinski . . . Jan. Born 1924."

"Date?"

"April 10, but . . ."

"Here in Maardam?"

"Yes. But why are you treating me like this? Police car and everything. I've never been involved in anything all my life."

"You're involved in this now," said Münster. "Civil status?"

"Eh? . . . Bachelor, of course—or widower, depending on how you look at it. We were going to divorce twenty years ago, but she died before all the papers were signed and sealed. Run over by a truck in Palizerlaan. Shocking business."

"Current address?"

"Armastenplejn 42. But look here . . ."

"Do you realize the seriousness of the situation?" Münster interrupted him.

"Yes. Well, no."

"We suspect you are intentionally withholding important information."

"I would never do such a thing," said Palinski, clasping his hands. "Not from the police, at least."

From whom would you withhold important information, then? wondered Münster, and gave an impatient snort.

"Is it not the case," he went on, "that together with the other three gentlemen you have won quite a substantial amount of money, and that is what you were celebrating at Freddy's this past Saturday evening?"

"No."

Palinski looked down at the table.

"You're lying," said Münster. "Shall I tell you why you're lying?"

"No," said Palinski. "What do you mean? Huh . . ."

"Listen to me now," said Münster. "Last Saturday there were four of you. Now there are only two of you. Leverkuhn has been murdered, and Bonger has disappeared. There is a lot to suggest that he is no longer alive either. But you and Wauters are. There are only three possibilities."

"Eh?" said Palinski. "What do you mean by that?"

His head had begun shaking now, Münster noted, and he realized that what was about to happen was likely to be what Moreno foresaw. It was only a matter of time before he threw in the towel, but it seemed only fair to let his colleague look after the confession itself. More gentlemanly, if nothing else: that was why he hadn't wanted to draw straws.

"Three possibilities," he repeated slowly, holding up three fingers in front of Palinski's eyes. "Either you and Wauters have done them in together . . ."

"What the . . . ?" exclaimed Palinski, rising to his feet. "Come on, Intendent, you've gone far enough!"

"Sit down!" said Münster. "If you didn't do it together, it must have been Wauters on his own."

Palinski sat down and his jaws started moving but no words came.

"Unless of course you did it yourself!"

"You're out of your mind! I want to talk to a . . . Oh no, no, no! You're suggesting that I . . ."

Münster leaned forward over the table and his eyes drilled into his victim's.

"What conclusion would you draw yourself?" he asked. "Four elderly gentlemen win a large sum of money. Two of them decide to get rid of the other two in order to get a bigger slice of the cake. Or perhaps it's one of the four who intends wiping out the other three and getting the whole lot for himself. Doesn't it make you feel a little uncomfortable, Herr Palinski, knowing that two of your friends are dead? Don't you lie awake at night wondering when it will be your turn?"

Palinski had gone white in the face.

"You . . . you . . . you . . . ," he stammered, and Münster thought for a moment that he was going to flake out.

"How well do you know this Wauters, in fact?" asked Münster. "Isn't he the newest member of the gang?"

Palinski made no reply. He tried to swallow, but his protruding Adam's apple stopped halfway.

"Because if you are not afraid of Wauters, I have to conclude that you are the one behind it all, Herr Palinski!"

"I have never . . . ," protested Palinski. "I have never . . ."

But there was no continuation. Münster's reasoning had come home to him now, and it was obvious that his paradoxical predicament was dawning on him.

"We'll give you five minutes to think this over," said Münster, pushing his chair back. "If I were you I'd avoid any more evasive answers when we return."

He pressed the pause button. Stood up, left the room, and locked the door.

It took only a few minutes for Moreno to conclude the business. A certain degree of feminine concern in the questioning and a hint of compassion in her eyes were exactly what Jan Palinski's soul needed after Münster's bullying.

"For Christ's sake," said Palinski, "what the hell did he mean? Surely we wouldn't . . . I wouldn't . . ."

"Come clean," said Moreno. "You can't keep quiet about it any longer now. It will only do you more harm if you do, can't you see that?"

Palinski looked like a dog that has disobeyed its master.

"You think so?"

"Yes, certainly," said Moreno.

Palinski wrung his hands and sucked in his lips. Then he straightened his back and cleared his throat.

"It was Wauters," he said.

"Wauters?" said Moreno.

"Who said we should keep quiet about it."

Moreno nodded.

"He thought . . ."

Moreno waited.

"He thought that we would come under suspicion if it became public knowledge that we'd won."

"How much?" asked Moreno.

"Twenty thousand," said Palinski, looking shamefaced.

"How?"

"The lottery. Wauters had bought the ticket, it was his turn. We were going to get five thousand each. . . . But with Leverkuhn out of the picture it's almost seven."

"And minus Bonger, it's ten," said Moreno.

"Yes, by God," said Palinski. "But surely you don't believe it's as your colleague suggested? Surely you can see that we would never do anything like that?"

Moreno didn't reply. She leaned back in her chair and observed the nervous twitches in Palinski's face for a while.

"Just at the moment we don't think anything at all," she said. "But you are in no way cleared of suspicion, and we don't want you to leave Maardam."

"Good God," said Palinski. "It's not possible. What the hell is Wauters going to say?"

"You don't need to worry about that," said Moreno. "We'll take care of him. As far as you're concerned, you can go now—but we want you back here tomorrow morning so that you can sign the transcript of what you've said."

She switched off the tape recorder. Palinski stood up, his legs shaking.

"Am I a suspect?" he asked.

Moreno nodded.

"I apologize. . . . I really do apologize. If I'd had my way, we'd have told you this straight away, of course. But Wauters . . ."

"I understand," said Moreno. "We all make mistakes. Off you go now, this way."

Palinski slunk off through the door like a reprimanded and penitent schoolboy—but after a few seconds he reappeared.

"It's Wauters who has the lottery ticket," he said. "He hasn't cashed it in yet. Just so you know."

Then he apologized again and left.

Detective Inspector Moreno noticed that she was smiling.

15

Erich Reijsen was a well-groomed gentleman in his sixties with a wife and a terraced house in the same good condition as himself. Moreno had telephoned and made an appointment, and when she arrived the tea tray was already waiting in the living room, where a realistic electric fire was burning in the hearth.

She blinked in disbelief and sat down on the plush sofa.

"We don't eat anything sweet," said Herr Reijsen, gesturing toward the coarse rye bread and red pepper rings. "We started to live a healthy lifestyle as we grew older."

His weather-beaten face and neatly trimmed mustache bore witness to that—as did his wife's tight tracksuit and mop of blond hair kept in place by a red and gold headband.

"Help yourself," she said, demonstrating her successful facelift by opening her eyes wide. "My name's Blenda."

"Inspector Moreno," she said, fishing out her notebook from her briefcase. "I don't mean to be rude, but it's mainly Herr Reijsen I need to speak to."

"Of course," said Reijsen, and Blenda scampered off to some other part of the house. After only a few seconds Moreno could hear the characteristic whirring of an exercise bike at full speed.

"It's about Waldemar Leverkuhn," she said. "I take it you know what's happened?"

Reijsen nodded solemnly.

"We're trying to piece together a more well-rounded picture of him," said Moreno, as her host poured out some weak tea into yellow cups. "You were a colleague of his for . . . for how long?"

"Fifteen years," said Reijsen. "From the day he started work at Pixner until he retired. Nineteen ninety-one, I believe. I carried on working for five more years, and then the staff cuts began. I was offered early retirement and accepted it like a shot. I have to say that I haven't regretted it a single day."

Neither would I, Moreno thought in a quick flash of insight.

"What was he like?" she asked. "Can you tell me a little about Waldemar Leverkuhn?"

It took Erich Reijsen more than half an hour to exhaust the topic. It took about two minutes to realize that the visit was probably going to be fruitless. The portrait of Waldemar Leverkuhn as a reserved and grumpy person (but nevertheless upright and reliable) was one she already had, and her attentive host was unable to add any brushstrokes that changed it, or added anything new.

Nor did he have any dramatic revelations to make, no insightful comments or anything else that could be of the slightest relevance to the investigation.

In truth, she had difficulty at the moment in envisioning what a relevant piece of the puzzle might look like, so she dutifully noted most of what Herr Reijsen had to say. It sapped her strength, there was no denying it—both to write and to keep awake—and when she stood up after three slices of rye bread and as many cups of tea, her first instinct was to find her way to the bathroom and throw it all up. Both Herr Reijsen and the bread.

Her second instinct was to take a hammer and batter the exercise bike that had been emitting its reproachful whining for the whole of her visit, but she managed to restrain herself. After all, she did not have a hammer handy.

. . .

I'm an awful police officer, she thought shortly afterward, sitting at the wheel of her car again at last. *Certainly nothing for the force to be proud of. . . . It's a good thing we're not busy with something more serious than this case.*

She was not at all clear about what she meant by that last thought.

Something more serious? Was the death of Waldemar Leverkuhn not serious? She shook her head and bit her lower lip in the hope of waking up. It felt increasingly clear that all this accumulated tiredness was approaching a point beyond which it would be safer to switch to automatic pilot as far as work was concerned. Not rely on her own judgment. Not make any decisions. Not think.

Not until she had managed to get a few nights of decent sleep, in any case.

She started the car and set off for the town center. It was past five o'clock, and the town seemed to be comprised of approximately equal amounts of exhaust fumes, damp, and darkness—a mixture that corresponded pretty well with her own state. She stopped at Keymer Pleijn and did some shopping at Zimmermann's—yogurt, juice, and fifteen grapes; that was more than enough after the rye bread, she told herself—and when she parked outside her temporary refuge in Gerckstraat, she was convinced that there were only two things in the world that could put her back on her feet.

A long, hot bath and a large cognac.

Fortunately both these phenomena were within the realm of possibility, so she clambered out of the car. She broke with her usual practice and took the lift up to the fourth floor, and began to hum some pop song she must have heard on the car radio or in Zimmermann's.

When she opened the elevator door, the first thing she saw was Claus. He was sitting on the floor outside her flat, with a large bouquet of red roses in his lap.

He stared at her with blank, worn-out eyes.

"Ewa," he said.

The bread sitting in her stomach made its presence felt. *Hell,* she thought. *I don't have the strength for this.*

She slammed the lift door closed again and went back down. Half-ran over the paved area outside the entrance door and had just managed to sit down in her car again when he appeared in the lit-up doorway.

"Poor you," she mumbled as she rummaged for the ignition key. "I'm sorry, but I just don't have the strength."

Then she started the car and drove away to look for an acceptable hotel.

Münster was dreaming.

At first it was all perfectly innocent. Some sort of party with cheerful people in their best outfits, drinks in their hands and laughter in their faces. He recognized several of them—both colleagues and good friends, of both himself and Synn. Only the premises seemed to be unfamiliar: a confusion of various rooms, staircases, and corridors. And then, gradually, a hint of something unpleasant began to insinuate itself into the dream. Not to say frightening. . . . He went from one to another of these cubbyholes, each one smaller than the last, darker, occupied by increasingly unknown men and women up to more and more dodgy business. And all the time he kept bumping into people who wanted to speak to him, to drink a toast with him, but he felt unable to stay in any given place for more than a couple of minutes. . . . There was something beckoning to him, something he was looking for, but he didn't understand what it was until he was there.

He entered yet another room. It was dark, and at first he thought it was also empty—but then he heard a sound. Somebody whispered his name. He went farther in, and suddenly he felt a woman's hand on his chest. She huddled up to him, and he knew immediately that it was for her sake that he was here. Exclusively and only for her sake.

She was naked, and it was obvious that they were going to make love. She led him to a low, wide bed in front of a fire that had almost burned out, but the embers were still glowing. . . . Yes, it was obvious that they were going to make love, and he knew almost immediately that the woman was Ewa Moreno. Her mop of chestnut-brown hair, her eyes like halved almonds, her small, firm breasts that he had never seen before but nevertheless had always known that they would look exactly like this . . . and her skin reflecting the glowing embers—no, nothing could be clearer. In less than a second he was also naked, lying on the bed, and she was astride him, guiding him into her eager pussy, and he watched her gleaming body raising and lowering itself, and it was ineffably blissful. Then he noticed the door slowly opening without really registering it . . . until he saw his children, Bart and Marieke, standing there watching him only a few feet away, with their serious and somewhat sorrowful eyes.

He was woken up by his own cry. Synn stirred restlessly, and he could feel the cold sweat all over his skin like an armor plate of angst. He lay there motionless for a few seconds, then slid cautiously out of bed, tiptoed into the bathroom, and showered for ten minutes.

When he returned to the bedroom he saw that it was a quarter past four. He lifted the duvet and crept down to lie close to Synn's warm back. Close, very close.

Then he lay there, holding her tightly, without sleeping a wink all night.

Something is happening, he thought.

It mustn't happen.

16

Wednesday felt like a funeral in a foreign language. He almost crashed the car twice on the way to the police station, and for a while he seriously considered driving back home and going to bed instead. He had just flopped down at his desk, propping up his head with his hands, when Jung knocked on the door.

"Have you got a moment?"

Münster nodded.

"Two, if you need them."

Jung sat down.

"You look tired."

"What do you want?" asked Münster.

"Well," said Jung, squirming on the chair. "Nothing much really, just a thought that struck me."

"Really?"

"Well," said Jung. "I was thinking that the simplest solution to this Leverkuhn business would be that Bonger did it."

Münster yawned. "Go on."

Jung braced himself.

"Well, what if Bonger went home with Leverkuhn, or called around later, it doesn't really matter which . . . and killed him. I mean they had been arguing outside Freddy's, and if Bonger lost his temper, maybe he lost control of his senses."

"You think so?" said Münster.

"I don't know. But at least that would explain why he's disappeared, wouldn't it? At first I thought he had jumped into the canal when he sobered up and realized what he'd done, but of course he could simply be in hiding. He must know that he would be under suspicion. What do you think?"

Münster pondered for a moment.

"Okay," he said. "God knows, it's certainly a possibility. There's nothing to say that's not what happened in any case."

"Exactly," said Jung, looking pleased with himself. "I just wanted you to bear it in mind."

He stood up.

"Thank you," said Münster. "If Hiller agrees to let me have you for a few days, you could follow it up—check possible friends and acquaintances and so on. Regarding a hiding place, that is."

"I'd be glad to," said Jung. "Although he doesn't seem all that cooperative just now, Hiller. . . . Something to do with that dwarf. But let me know if he gives the okay."

When Jung left, Münster went to stand by the window. Pulled up the blind, rested his forehead against the cool glass, and gazed out at the completely unchanged town, which hardly seemed to have had the energy to get out of bed either.

Bonger? he thought. A dead simple solution. Why the hell not? Maybe he should do what Van Veeteren used to advise: Always do the simplest thing first. It's so damned easy to miss a checkmate in one move!

Then he looked at the clock and saw there was less than twenty minutes before his meeting with Marie-Louise Leverkuhn. He armed himself with coffee, pen, and notebook. Sat down at his desk again and tried to concentrate.

"To tell you the truth, we're having difficulty in coming to grips with this case, Fru Leverkuhn."

She made no reply.

"Nevertheless, we must work on the assumption that there is a motive behind the murder of your husband, that there is something in his background or general circumstances that has resulted in this terrible crime."

It was a heavy-handed opening, but he had decided to take that line. Marie-Louise didn't move a muscle.

"There is only one person who can know about such things, and that is, of course, you, Fru Leverkuhn. Have you had any thoughts about such matters in the last few days?"

"None at all."

She stared vacantly at him.

"You must have been thinking about what has happened?"

"I've been thinking about it, but nothing has come of it."

"Have you talked to many people you know?"

She shook her head.

"I don't know all that many people. My children. Emmeline. A few neighbors."

"But can you give me the names of your closest friends, apart from Emmeline von Post? That you and your husband used to socialize with."

She looked at the floor. *Aha,* Münster thought. *So that's how it is. That's where the problem lies.*

The most shameful thing in life, he'd read somewhere, was not having any friends. Being on your own. You can be as stupid as they come, a racist, a sadist, you can be obese and stink like a skunk, or be a practicing pedophile—but you have to have friends.

"We didn't socialize much," she said without looking up. "He had his friends, I had mine."

"No mutual friends?"

She shook her head.

"What about relatives?"

"Our children," she said again.

"You don't have any brothers or sisters?"

"No, not anymore."

"Whom did your husband use to meet, apart from the gentlemen at Freddy's?"

She thought for a moment.

"No one else, I think. Maybe Herr Engel now and then."

"Ruben Engel? In the same building?"

"Yes."

"And what about you?" Münster persisted. "You used to meet Fröken von Post a few times a month. Who else?"

"No one else," said Marie-Louise.

"Are you sure?" said Münster. "No former colleagues? You were working at that department store until a couple of years ago, isn't that right?"

"Fröken Svendsen," she said. "Regine Svendsen. We sometimes went out together, but she moved to Karpatz a few years ago. She found a new man, an old school friend who had also ended up on his own."

"Do you have her telephone number?"

"No."

Münster made a note and turned over a page.

"Tell me about your coming home last Saturday night."

"I've already done that several times."

"This will be the last time," Münster promised.

"Why?"

"You never know. Things sometimes come back to you that you overlooked shortly after the event. Especially if you were in shock."

She looked at him. Somewhat annoyed.

"I haven't overlooked anything."

"You came home at a few minutes past two, is that right?"

"Yes," said Fru Leverkuhn.

"And the entrance door was open?"

"Yes."

"The door to your apartment was unlocked, right?"

"I've already said so."

"Did you see anybody? In the street or on the staircase, or in the apartment?"

"No."

"You're sure?"

"Of course."

"So you went inside and discovered that something was wrong?"

"Yes."

"How?"

"What do you mean?"

"How did you know that something was wrong?"

She thought for a moment.

"There was a smell," she said.

"Of what?" Münster asked.

"Blood."

Münster pretended to be making notes while waiting for her to say more. But she didn't. He tried to recall the smell of blood, and established that it was distinctly possible that she could have detected it. If his memory served him right, he had read somewhere among all the information about her that, like her daughter, she had worked for a few years as a butcher. She presumably knew what she was talking about.

"You went into the room?"

"Yes."

"And switched the light on?"

"Yes."

"How did you react when you saw what had happened?"

She paused. Sat in silence again for a few seconds, then sat up straight and cleared her throat.

"I stood there and felt like throwing up," she said. "It sort of came in waves, but then it stopped. So I went back out to report it."

"You set off for Entwick Plejn?"

"Yes, I've told you already."

"Were there any other people about?"

She shook her head.

"I don't remember. I don't think so. It was raining."

"Did you go all the way to the police station?"

She thought that over again.

"No. There were no lights in the windows, I could see that from the other side of the square."

"And so you turned back?"

"Yes."

"And went the same way back home?"

"Yes."

Münster paused.

"Shall I tell you something odd, Fru Leverkuhn?" he said.

She didn't answer.

"You say you walked nearly one and a half miles through the town, and so far not a single witness has come forward to say they saw you. What do you say to that? I mean, the streets were not completely deserted."

No reply. Münster waited for half a minute.

"You're not lying are you, Fru Leverkuhn?"

She looked up and stared at him with mild contempt.

"Why on earth should I be telling lies?"

To save your own skin, Münster thought; but that was a dodgy thought, and he kept it to himself.

"Had he fallen out with any of those old friends?" he asked instead.

"Not as far as I know."

"With Herr Bonger, for instance?"

"I don't even know which is which."

"Have they never visited your apartment?"

"Never."

"But you knew that they had won some money, I take it?"

He had been leading up to that question for some time, but it was difficult to draw any conclusions from her reaction.

"Money?" was all she said.

"Twenty thousand," said Münster.

"Each?" she asked.

"Altogether," said Münster. "Five thousand each. But that's still quite a lot."

She shook her head slowly.

"He never mentioned that," she said.

Münster nodded.

"And you still haven't noticed anything missing from the apartment? Aside from the knife, that is."

"No."

"Nothing at all?"

"No. . . . Mind you, I haven't seen any trace of the five thousand guilders."

"They haven't collected the money yet," said Münster.

"That would explain it," said Fru Leverkuhn.

Münster sighed. He could feel weariness creeping up on him, and suddenly—in an instant—the pointlessness of it all took possession of him. He suddenly felt that he could see right through this old woman's vacant face, like looking through a pane of glass; and what he saw was a cul-de-sac, with himself standing there, staring at a brick wall. From less than two feet away. With his hands in his pockets and his shoulders slumped in despair. In some strange way he was able to look at his own back and the brick wall at the same time. Filthy bricks covered in faded graffiti, and a smell of eternal, acid rain. It was not a pleasant picture of the situation. Not pleasant at all. *I'd better retrace my steps,* he thought, and blinked a few times in order to come into contact with reality again.

"Thank you," he said. "I don't have any more questions for the moment, but I'd still like you to keep thinking, Fru Leverkuhn. Even the tiniest insignificant detail might help us get on the right track."

"I want you to leave me in peace."

"We want to find your husband's murderer, Fru Leverkuhn. And we shall find him."

For a moment he thought she looked deeply doubtful, and it was probably this look—together with the increasing feeling of graveliness behind his eyes—that made him raise his voice.

"We intend to find the murderer, Fru Leverkuhn, you can be absolutely certain of that!"

She looked at him in surprise. Then rose to her feet.

"Was there anything else?"

"Not right now," said Münster.

The rest of Wednesday passed by in more or less the same tone. Bonger's boat was as deserted as ever, testimony from people who had been out and about on Saturday night was conspicuous by its absence, and the only response from the so-called underworld came from an anonymous source, urging the police to stop rummaging around in the wrong pile of dirty laundry.

Tell us which pile of dirty laundry is the right one, then! Münster thought aggressively.

He purposely avoided contacting Inspector Moreno, and while he was struggling with an unusually unpalatable lunchtime pasta in the cafeteria, Krause informed him that Moreno had called earlier that morning and reported sick. At first Münster was relieved to hear that, but then he was filled with uncertainty that he dare not analyze too closely. The dream he had experienced the previous night was still hovering in the back of his mind—like an X-rated film he had watched by mistake—and he knew that it wasn't there purely by chance.

He spent the whole afternoon in his office, reading through all the reports and minutes connected with the case that had accumulated, without becoming much the wiser.

The case of Waldemar Leverkuhn?

That's the way it is, was how he summed it up in resignation as he left the police station at half past four. For reasons unknown, a perpetrator (a man? a woman?) had killed a harmless retiree—in the most bestial fashion imaginable. Four days had passed since the murder, and they were still nowhere near a solution.

Another elderly man had disappeared that same night, and the police knew just as much about that as well.

Nothing.

Yet again—he had lost count of how many times it had happened these last few days—some wise words from Van Veeteren came into his head.

Police work is like life, the chief inspector had announced over a Friday beer at Adenaar's a few years ago. *Ninety-five percent of it is wasted.*

Wasn't it about time they got around to that last five percent? Intendent Münster asked himself as he worked his way up through the labyrinth that formed the exit from the underground garage at the police station. Shouldn't the breakthrough be due any time now?

Or was it the case, it struck him as he emerged into Baderstraat, that those gloomy words of wisdom from Van Veeteren were a sort of nudge, encouraging him to call in at Krantze's antiquarian bookshop?

To pay a visit to the chief inspector?

It was a bold thought, of course—probably the only one that had struck him all day—and he decided to leave it in the back of his mind for the moment and see how it grew.

Then he put his foot down on the accelerator and began to long for Synn and the children.

II

17

"What did you say your name was?" asked Krause, furrowing his brow.

He jotted down the name and telephone number. Chewed at his pencil. There was something about this. . . .

"Address?"

He wrote that down as well and stared at it.

Surely it was . . . ?

No doubt about it. He asked, and had his suspicions confirmed. Could hear how excited his voice was becoming, and tried to cough it away. Said thank you for the call and promised that somebody would be there within half an hour. Replaced the receiver.

My God! he thought. *What the hell can this mean?*

He dialed Münster's number. Busy.

Moreno. No reply.

Van Eck? *Surely it can't be a coincidence,* he thought as he rose to his feet.

Münster beckoned him to come in as he continued talking on the telephone. Judging by the expression on his face, it must be Hiller at the other end of the line. Krause nodded to Moreno, who was sitting on one of the visitor chairs, leafing through a sheath of papers.

Rather listlessly, it seemed. She looked tired, Krause noted, and leaned back against the bookcase. Everyone was tired.

Münster managed to get rid of the chief of police and looked up.

"Well? What's the problem?"

"Umm," said Krause. "I just had a strange telephone call."

"Really?" said Münster.

"Really?" said Moreno.

"Arnold Van Eck. The caretaker in Kolderweg. He says his wife has disappeared."

"What?" said Moreno.

"What the hell?" said Münster.

Krause cleared his throat.

"That's what he claimed," he said. "Went up in smoke yesterday, it seems. I promised we'd be there pronto. Should I? . . . Or maybe . . . ?"

"No," said Münster. "Moreno and I will follow it up. That's . . ."

He failed to establish what it was. Collected his briefcase, scarf, and overcoat and hurried out the door. Moreno followed him, but paused for a moment in the doorway.

"Are you sure this isn't something Rooth has invented?" she said, looking searchingly at Krause. "He doesn't seem to be all that reliable at the moment."

Krause shrugged.

"Are you suggesting Rooth has kidnapped her, or something? You'd better go there and take a look and find out. If I remember correctly she's as big as a house. . . . It can't be all that easy to hide her away."

"Okay," said Moreno. "Stay here and we'll keep you informed."

"*I* don't make a habit of disappearing," said Krause.

Arnold Van Eck looked as if he'd sold the cream but lost the money. He must have been standing by the window, waiting for them, because he received them in the entrance hall, where they also met Fru Leverkuhn, who was carrying bags and suitcases full of her husband's clothes to a waiting taxi.

"They're going to the charity shop," she said. "I thought you lot would have been able to leave me alone for a day at least."

"It's not . . . It's . . . ," stammered Van Eck, shifting his feet nervously.

"It's not you we want to talk to today," Münster explained. "Herr Van Eck, perhaps we ought to go into your apartment."

The little caretaker nodded and led the way. His tiny frame looked more wretched than ever—it looked as if it could fall to pieces at any moment, so compelling were his tears and his despair. Münster wondered if he had slept a single wink that night.

"What happened?" he asked when they had sat down around the diminutive kitchen table covered by a blue-and-white-checked tablecloth, with a yellow artificial flower in a vase in the middle.

Van Eck flung out his arms in a gesture intended to express his impotence.

"She's gone."

"Gone?" said Moreno.

"Your wife?" asked Münster.

"Alas, yes," said Van Eck. "That's the way it is."

Alas, yes? Münster thought. *He's insane.* But then again he knew there were people who would never have been given the role of themselves if it had been a question of a film or a play rather than life itself. Arnold Van Eck was definitely one of them.

"Tell us about it," said Moreno.

Van Eck sniffed a few times and slid his thick spectacles farther up his shiny nose.

"It was yesterday," he said. "Yesterday evening . . . She disappeared sometime during the afternoon. Or evening."

He fell silent.

"How can you be sure that she hasn't just gone to visit somebody?" Moreno asked.

"I just know," said Van Eck. "It was Wednesday yesterday, and we always watch *Gangsters' Wives* on Wednesday. It's a television series."

"Yes, we know," said Moreno.

Gangsters? wondered Münster.

"She massages my legs as well," continued Van Eck. "Always on a Wednesday. It helps to prevent vascular spasms."

He demonstrated rather awkwardly how his wife would grasp and rub his thighs and calves. Münster couldn't believe his eyes, but he saw that Moreno was making notes without turning a hair, so he assumed for the time being at least that there was nothing to worry about. This was presumably how people behaved with each other in the autumn of their lives.

But how could Ewa Moreno know that?

"When did you see her last?" he asked.

"Five past five," said Van Eck without hesitation. "She went out to do some shopping, but she hadn't come back when I left to attend my course."

"What course is that?" Moreno asked.

"Porcelain painting. Six o'clock at Riitmeeterska, so it takes only a few minutes to get there. I left at about ten to."

"Porcelain painting?" said Münster.

"It's more interesting than you might think," Van Eck assured him, sitting up a bit straighter. "I'm only an amateur, I've been going for only four terms; but then the main idea isn't to produce masterpieces. Mind you, one day, perhaps. . . ."

For a brief second the caretaker's face lit up. Münster cleared his throat.

"What time did you get home?"

"Five past eight, as usual. Else wasn't home, and she hadn't returned by the time *Gangsters' Wives* started either. It begins at half past nine, and that was when I became really worried."

Moreno continued writing everything down. Münster recalled his dream from the other night and pinched himself discreetly on the arm to make sure that he really was sitting here in this yellow-and-pink-painted kitchen.

He didn't wake up, and he assumed that he hadn't been asleep.

"Where do you think she's gone?" asked Moreno.

Van Eck's cheek muscles twitched a couple of times, and once again he looked as if he were about to burst out crying.

"I don't know," he said. He produced a handkerchief from his trouser pocket and blew his nose. "It's beyond belief. She would never simply go away without saying where she was going. . . . She knows I'm not all that strong."

He folded his handkerchief meticulously, and blinked several times behind his thick lenses. *Love despite everything?* Münster thought. *There are so many kinds. . . .*

"A good friend, perhaps?" he said.

Van Eck made no reply. Put away his handkerchief.

"A good friend or relative who's suddenly fallen ill?" Moreno suggested.

Van Eck shook his head.

"She doesn't have many friends. She would have phoned—she's been missing for half a day now."

"And no message?" Moreno wondered.

"No."

"Has she ever gone away like this before?"

"Never."

"Have you called the hospitals? Something might have happened to her—a minor accident, it doesn't need to be anything serious."

"I've spoken to both Rumford and Gemejnte. They knew nothing—and in any case, she would have been in touch."

"Had you fallen out, perhaps? Quarreled?"

"We never quarrel."

"What was she wearing?" Münster asked.

Van Eck looked confused.

"Why do you want to know that?"

Münster sighed.

"Haven't you wondered about that?" he asked. "Have any of her jackets disappeared as well? Has she taken a suitcase with her? If you haven't checked that, perhaps you would be so kind as to do so now."

"Excuse me," said Van Eck as he hurried out into the hall. They could hear him rummaging around among coat hangers and shoes for a while, and then he came back.

"Yes," he said, "both her hat and coat are missing, and her handbag."

"So," said Moreno. "Could you please check if she's taken a bag with her—apart from her handbag, that is."

It took several minutes for Van Eck to investigate, but when he returned he was in no doubt.

"No bag," he said. "Both the suitcase and the shopping bag are in the wardrobe as usual. And she hasn't been down into the store-room in the basement. And what's more, I know she came back home after doing her shopping—she put things into the fridge and the pantry. Milk and potatoes and a few tins of stuff. And other odds and ends. Diegermann's caviar, for instance—we always buy that, the unsmoked variety. With dill."

"It's pretty good," said Münster.

"Have you mentioned this to any of the neighbors?" Moreno asked.

"No," said Van Eck, squirming in his chair.

"Any acquaintances?"

"No. I don't want this to come out, I mean, if it's nothing important. . . . I mean . . ."

He said nothing more. Münster and Moreno exchanged glances, and she was clearly on the same wavelength—she gestured with her head, then nodded. Münster cleared his throat.

"Well, Herr Van Eck," he said. "I think it would be best if you came to the police station with us. We can go through it all properly and write a report."

Van Eck took a deep breath.

"I agree," he said, and it was obvious that he was not in complete control of his voice. "Can I go to the bathroom first? My stomach's a bit upset, thanks to all this."

"Please do," said Moreno.

While they were waiting they took the opportunity of looking around the cramped two-bedroom apartment. It contained nothing that surprised them. A bedroom with an old-fashioned double bed with a teak headboard and net curtains in light blue and white. Living room with television set, glass-fronted display cupboard, and a drab three-piece sofa set in hard-wearing polyester. No books apart from a reference work in ten bright red volumes—but lots of magazines and a mass of landscape reproductions on the walls, and hand-painted porcelain vases on the bureau and tables. The kitchen where they had been sitting was barely big enough for three people: refrigerator, stove, and sink from the late fifties, by the looks of it, and the potted plants on the window ledges seemed to have grown and multiplied of their own accord. The artificial flower on the table looked much more natural. All the floors were covered in carpets of different styles, colors, and qualities, and the only thing that Münster could possibly interpret as an expression of personal taste was a stuffed giraffe's head over the hat shelf in the hall—but that was probably because he had never seen a detached giraffe's head before.

Moreno shrugged, with a sigh of resignation, and they went back to the kitchen.

"What about the neighbors?" she said. "Should I stay here and listen to whatever they have to say? I suppose it would be helpful if we could establish when she was last seen."

Münster nodded.

"Yes, good thinking," he said. "Should I send Krause or somebody to help?"

"In an hour," said Moreno. "Then at least I won't need to walk back to the station."

She checked her watch. Van Eck's stomach was taking its time.

"What do you think?" she said. "I must say I haven't a clue. Why on earth should this woman disappear?"

"Beats me," said Münster. "It must mean something, of course, and I have the feeling we need to take it seriously. Even if it all seems like a farce."

He leaned back in his chair and looked out the window. The melancholy weather was persisting. Heavy clouds were rolling in from the sea, and the pane was dappled, even though it wasn't actually raining.

Gloom, Münster thought. *Who wouldn't want to vanish in weather like this?*

There was the sound of the toilet flushing. Van Eck came out.

"I've finished," he said, as if he were a three-year-old at a potty-training camp.

"Okay, then let's go," said Münster. "Inspector Moreno will stay behind and investigate a few things."

Van Eck's lower lip started trembling, and Moreno tapped him cautiously on the shoulder.

"This will sort itself out, don't worry," she said. "There's bound to be a perfectly natural explanation."

Presumably, Münster thought. *So much seems to be natural nowadays.*

18

Inspector Moreno checked out of Hotel Bender at about four o'clock on Thursday afternoon. The nose-ringed receptionist tried to make her pay for a second night, since she had occupied the room after twelve noon, but she refused. For the first time in ages (or maybe the first time ever? she asked herself) she chose to use her work status for her personal gain.

As it was only a matter of 140 guilders, perhaps she could be excused.

"I'm a detective inspector," she explained. "We needed the room in order to keep an eye on a certain transaction taking place in this hotel. That mission is now completed. Unless you want your name mentioned in less than flattering circumstances, I suggest you charge me for one night and no more."

The young man, as thin as a rake, thought for a couple of seconds.

"I understand," he said then. "Let's say just the one night."

There was no Claus sitting outside her door when she got home, but she phoned him as soon as she had downed half a glass of wine.

She explained, without beating around the bush or becoming emotional, that she had a demand to make. An ultimatum, if he liked. If there was going to be any possibility of repairing the relationship they used to have—and even as she spoke those words she realized that by doing so she was giving him false hope—she demanded two weeks without being disturbed.

No telephone calls, no greetings. No damned roses.

Two whole weeks. Fourteen days from today. Did he agree?

He did, he announced after what seemed rather too long a silence. But only if he really could count on their meeting and discussing things properly once that time had run out.

And that neither of them would initiate anything else during those two weeks.

Initiate? Moreno thought. *Anything else?*

She agreed to the discussion, and avoided the other demand by making no comment and hanging up.

Then she drank the remaining wine. *So there,* she thought. *I've delayed his execution by two weeks. Cowardly. But it feels good.*

She curled up in a corner of the sofa with another glass of wine and the notes she had made at Kolderweg. Adjusted the cushions and switched on the reading lamp: the light it produced was so restricted that it almost felt like sitting inside a one-man tent, a tiny bright cone in the darkness where she could hide herself away, cut off from all the surroundings that she would rather forget. Men, darkness, and so on.

At last, she thought. *Time to concentrate on the case, and pay no attention to herself or the world around her.*

Especially herself.

She had written down the tenants in Kolderweg 17 on the first page of her notebook. From the top down:

3. Ruben Engel	Leonore Mathisen
2. Waldemar Leverkuhn/	Tobose Menakdise/
Marie-Louise Leverkuhn	Filippa de Booning
1. Arnold Van Eck/Else Van Eck	Empty apartment

The facts were first and foremost that Waldemar Leverkuhn was dead. She crossed his name out and continued.

Marie-Louise Leverkuhn? What was there to say about the widow?

Not a lot. She had returned from the charity shop shortly after noon. Moreno had a short conversation with her, but in view of what the poor woman had already been through in terms of traumatic experiences and vigorous interviews, she restricted herself to what was absolutely necessary. Fru Leverkuhn said she had drunk coffee with Else Van Eck in the latter's apartment on Tuesday afternoon, had then bumped into her on the stairs the following morning (when she was on her way to the police station to talk to Intendent Münster), but apart from that she had neither seen nor heard anything of the caretaker's wife, she claimed.

Moreno wrote a check mark after Marie-Louise Leverkuhn. And a question mark after Else Van Eck.

Herr Van Eck had returned from the police station at about half past one in a rather pathetic state, and Moreno checked him as well.

That left the acrobatic lovers Menakdise and de Booning on the second floor, and Herr Engel and Fröken Mathisen on the third. Viewed dispassionately these four were not yet involved in the case. Neutral observers (question mark again) and possible witnesses.

She had started with the young couple.

Or, rather, with Filippa de Booning, as Tobose Menakdise was studying medicine and had lectures all day. However, Fröken de Booning promised to ask him when he came home if he had seen or heard anything in connection with the caretaker's wife that could throw some light on her disappearance. She herself had nothing to contribute. She had been at home most of Wednesday—studying for an upcoming exam on cultural anthropology—but she hadn't seen any sign of Fru Van Eck at all.

"Thank goodness," she added, then bit her tongue. "Sorry, but she always pays us special attention. I take it you know why?"

Moreno smiled and nodded. She felt a sudden ache in her inner thigh as she momentarily envisioned the redheaded and pale-skinned Filippa in her sexual wrestling match with Tobose, who—if the framed photograph in the hall was to be believed—was blacker than the blackest black.

You two are still alive, she thought. *Congratulations.*

Ruben Engel had had just as little to contribute—even less if you took the aching inner thigh into consideration. He had felt out of sorts and spent the whole of Wednesday in bed, he explained. Not just the evening. Moreno looked around and drew the provisional conclusion that it might have been due to his taking the wrong medication. If you didn't feel too well in the morning, it presumably didn't help if you then proceeded to swig glass after glass of claret, beer, and mulled wine for the rest of the day. Engel also seemed to be very upset about what was going on elsewhere in the building, she noted, and she had difficulty in ignoring his moaning and groaning about law and order and moral decadence. But there were obvious elements of the dirty old man in his outpourings: there was little doubt that he did his best to drag out her visit for as long as possible. She declined his offer of coffee, mulled wine, and gin, and eventually managed to extricate herself by half-promising to keep him informed about how the case was developing. In person.

What an unpleasant old fart, she thought when she finally succeeded in leaving his flat.

But then again, she told herself, it can't be all that much fun being old, lonely, and smelly.

No fun at all.

The only possible gleam of light came from Fröken Mathisen, who Moreno thought seemed reminiscent in appearance of a cream puff pastry. Big, spongy, and rather delicious. What Mathisen had to say was perhaps nothing to write home about, but what she was quite clear about was that she had gone out at about seven o'clock on Wednesday evening, a few minutes past, if she remembered correctly, and that she was pretty sure she had heard noises coming from the caretaker's apartment as she walked past the door. She couldn't be more precise about what sort of sounds they were, apart from being sure that it seemed as if somebody was busy doing something in the hall—that somebody being Fru Van Eck, seeing as her husband was over at Riitmeerska, painting decorations onto porcelain ornaments.

Moreno read through her notes on this conversation, and checked it off together with the remaining names—de Booning, Engel, and Mathisen.

There was not much more to add. Krause had come to relieve her at about noon and spent the afternoon interrogating the neighbors. Not too complicated considering Fru Van Eck had been a well-known figure in the neighborhood.

Sure enough, she had been to three of the shops in Kolderplejn, had left the last of them at about a quarter to six, and had been seen by at least two witnesses walking back home. So it wasn't difficult to make a timetable for what seemed to be the crucial part of Wednesday evening:

> c. 6:00 Fru Van Eck arrives home
> c. 7:00 Fru Van Eck is still at home (in the hall)
> c. 8:00 Fru Van Eck has disappeared

It could possibly be added that none of Krause's many witnesses had seen the caretaker's substantial wife after six p.m.

Moreno contemplated her summary. *Brilliant detective work!* she concluded, and closed her notebook.

Münster and Jung took it in turns with Arnold Van Eck.

Bearing in mind developments at Kolderweg, Hiller had agreed to release both Rooth and Jung and transfer them to the Leverkuhn case, as long as Münster needed them. The serial rapist in Linzhuisen had been lying low for more than two months, and that investigation had come to a standstill.

Despite persistent efforts, mainly by Jung—there was something about Arnold Van Eck's character that made Münster reluctant to interrogate him and even made him angry (perhaps it was that image of the run-over kitten spooking him again)—they did not succeed in extracting much information beyond what had emerged during the conversation at the kitchen table. Their picture of the somewhat peculiar and childless marriage became a little clearer, but on the whole no progress was made regarding the actual disappearance of the wife. No matter how hard Jung tried to penetrate the relationship and the shared lives of the couple, Van Eck was unable to produce even a hint of an explanation as to why his wife would have left him voluntarily.

If she had done so thirty or forty years ago, it would of course have been the most natural thing in the world—even Van Eck himself could see that. But now—why leave him now?

And so, both Münster and Jung concluded, she had not done so. There must be some other explanation. And a pretty powerful one at that: Fru Van Eck was not the sort of woman you could knock over with a feather duster, as Jung put it before leaving.

When he was alone in his office Münster listened to the whole tape again, and if he were to be honest he thought it sounded, at least in part, more like a therapeutic conversation than an interrogation.

But be that as it may, the fact remained: Else Van Eck, five feet eleven inches tall, weight 207 pounds, sixty-five years old, had disappeared. Probably wearing a bluish gray coat, well-fitting brown ENOC shoes (size 11), various other items, and a black felt hat. She had left her home sometime between seven and eight p.m. (the precise time had been established with the aid of Constable Krause, who had informed them of Fröken Mathisen's observations) on Wednesday evening.

The Wanted notice was sent out as early as two o'clock, but by five o'clock, when Münster was preparing to go home, there had still been no response from that great detective, the general public.

But perhaps it would have been overly optimistic to expect oth-

erwise. Perhaps they had a better chance of receiving a tip following the feeler Krause had sent out into the underworld regarding
Leverkuhn, but they had so far drawn a blank there as well. The
informant Adolf Bosch had turned up shortly after three, delivered his report, and been paid his two hundred guilders, albeit in
reverse order: Bosch wasn't born yesterday, and the result of his
dodgy researches had been aptly summed up by his own words:
"Not a thing, Constable Krause, not a fucking thing!"

Before going home for the night Münster allowed himself half an
hour's introspection in his office. He locked the door. Switched off
the light. Wheeled his desk chair over to the window and put his
feet up onto the window ledge.

Leaned back and contemplated the view. It was beautiful in
a way, he couldn't deny that. Beautiful and threatening. The sky
hovered over the town like a slowly but inexorably darkening lead
dome. The vain attempts to illuminate things from the buzzing
streets below seemed merely to emphasize the indomitable nature
of the darkness rather than to offer it any resistance.

A bit like his own work. The chief inspector used to talk about
that—the fact that it's not until we start fighting evil that we begin
to realize how all-embracing it is. Only when we light a candle in
the darkness do we see how vast it is.

He shook his head in an attempt to rid himself of these questionable thoughts. They were not productive—all they did was
provide unnecessary nourishment to feelings of weariness and impotence, which of course had their best growing conditions at this
falling, sinking time of year.

Despite Jung's and his own talk of wet, bare tree trunks and all
the rest of it. Inner landscapes?

Anyway, the case! he thought and closed his eyes. *The case of
Waldemar Leverkuhn.*

Or was it the case of Bonger? Or Else Van Eck?

How sure was he that they were interconnected, these three

strands? There was an old rule of thumb that said that if the dead bodies of two movie projectionists were discovered, it was by no means certain that the murders were connected. But if a third one was found—well, you could reasonably assume that all the movie projectionists in the world should be given special protection.

And now here we are with three retirees. One murdered and two disappeared. Did that mean that all the retirees in the world should be given special protection?

One would hope not, Münster thought. Because it was not difficult to restrict the links quite radically. Leverkuhn and Bonger had been good friends. Leverkuhn and Fru Van Eck lived in the same block of flats. But on the other hand, Bonger and Fru Van Eck had no known connections at all, so if there was in fact some kind of common denominator, it must be Leverkuhn.

And Leverkuhn was the only one of them who was definitely dead. Very dead.

Münster sighed and wished he were a smoker. If he had been, he would have lit up at this point; as it was, he had to make do with clasping his hands behind the back of his neck and leaning still farther back on his chair.

What about the disappearances? he thought. There were differences between them. Big differences. As far as Bonger was concerned, he could have gone up in smoke at any time during the night of the murder—or even later. No one had seen any trace of him after he had left Freddy's, but no one missed him until well into Sunday. At a guess he had never arrived back at his houseboat at all, but that was only a hypothesis. There were masses of alternatives and variations.

It was different in the case of Else Van Eck. Here the margins were reduced to an hour between seven and eight on Wednesday evening, and bearing in mind her size and general profile, that was not a very large space to pass through. Witnesses should—no, *must,* surely—turn up, Münster thought. We shall have to carry out yet another door-to-door operation tomorrow!

Then he just sat there for a while with his eyes closed, and imagined the three puzzle pieces dancing around in a deep and increasingly dark space—like that logo of some film company until the letters clung to one another and formed its name, or at least its abbreviation. He couldn't remember the name of the film company, and the puzzle pieces Leverkuhn, Bonger, and Van Eck never clung to one another. They simply continued whirling around and around in the same unfathomable and never-ending loops, receding farther and farther away, it seemed, deeper and deeper into blacker space.

He made a big effort and opened his eyes. Noted that it was past five o'clock and decided to go home.

I'd bet my life, he thought as he wormed his way into his jacket, *I'd bet my life that if all the detective officers in the world got an hour's extra sleep per night, five hours per day would be saved. Due to the fact that our brains would have the strength to think more clearly.*

Surely it must be better to cut back on wasted time rather than on sleep? Surely sleep can never be wasted?

What's all this buzzing around in my head? he thought. *Am I growing old? And I haven't made love for two weeks either.*

19

"I can't shake this feeling," said Rooth.

"What feeling?" said Jung.

"That I'm sort of lost as far as this investigation is concerned. I can't get the hang of what the hell is going on. I think I ought to be working on a different case."

Jung eyed him with a cool smile.

"Such as? I don't have the feeling that we've covered ourselves with glory as far as that jerk in Linzhuisen is concerned either. . . . Perhaps you ought to pack it in altogether?"

Rooth sighed self-critically. Rummaged around in his pockets for something to pop into his mouth, but found only a lump of ancient chewing gum wrapped up in an old movie ticket. There was a knock on the door and Krause came in with an envelope.

"Pictures of Else Van Eck," he announced.

"Okay," said Jung, accepting them. "Can you tell Joensuu and Kellerman to come to my office—and whoever else it was . . ."

"Klempje and Proszek."

"Right," said Rooth. "Let's go for broke."

Krause left. Jung took the photographs out of the envelope and examined them. Passed one over to Rooth, who stood up and started scratching his head demonstratively.

"What's the matter with you?" said Jung.

"It's remarkable," said Rooth.

"What is?"

"That so much can disappear without a trace. Everything disappears eventually, I mean, but even so?"

"Hmm," said Jung. "You have a theory, is that what you're trying to say?"

"Well," said Rooth. "Theory and theory . . . I don't really dare to make any further comment about this business. No, keep your own counsel, that's best."

"For Christ's sake," said Jung. "What the hell are you talking about? Even if they've succeeded in bugging this office, there isn't a newspaper in the whole of Europe that could print anything you say. Do you get what I'm saying?"

"All right," said Rooth. "It has to do with her bulk."

"Bulk?"

"Bulk, yes. I simply can't believe that a gigantic woman like Else Van Eck could simply disappear like this."

"Like this? What do you mean?"

Rooth sat down again.

"Don't you get it?"

"No."

"And they made you an inspector?"

Jung gathered together the pictures and put them back in the envelope.

"High and mighty unshaven cop speaks with forked tongue," he said.

"I think she's still in the building," said Rooth.

"Eh?"

"That Van Eck woman. She's still in Kolderweg 17."

"What do you mean?"

Rooth sighed again.

"Just that it's hardly credible that she could have left the building without anyone seeing her. So she must still be there."

"Where?" asked Jung.

Rooth shrugged.

"I have no idea. In the attic, or down in the cellar."

"You're assuming she's dead?"

"That's possible," said Rooth. "She might have been butchered and embalmed. Or tied up and muzzled. Who cares? The point is that we ought to do a thorough search of the building instead of wandering around the neighborhood."

Jung said nothing for a while.

"You have a point," he said. "Why don't you go to Münster and talk it over with him?"

"That's exactly what I intend to do," said Rooth, standing up again. "I just wanted to give you some insight into how a bigger brain works first."

"Thank you," said Jung. "It's been both interesting and instructive."

Two minutes later the four constables turned up. Jung inspected the quartet while thinking over the priorities.

"I think we can manage with two of you for the time being," he said. "Klampe and Proszek. Joensuu and Kellerman can wait down in the duty officer's room for the time being. We've received some new . . . indications."

Constables Klempje and Proszek spent six hours on Friday showing enlarged photographs of Else Van Eck to a total of 362 persons in and around Kolderweg. A large proportion of those people recognized the woman in the photograph immediately, but a comparatively small number had seen her later than six p.m. on Wednesday.

None at all, to be precise.

"Why the hell don't they just put a Wanted notice in the newspapers instead of making us work our socks off?" Proszek wondered when they finally managed to find a sufficiently sheltered corner in the Café Bendix in Kolderplejn. "This is making me look impotent."

"You always have been," said Klempje. "There'll be one tomorrow."

"One what?"

"A Wanted notice."

"For God's sake," said Proszek. "In that case what's the point of our dicking around like this?"

Klempe shrugged.

"Perhaps they're in a hurry?"

"Kiss my ass," said Proszek. "And cheers. Where the hell are Joensuu and Kellerman, by the way? Lounging about and lording it over at some stakeout again, no doubt."

Neither Joensuu nor Kellerman would have regarded what they were doing on Friday as lording it, assuming they had an opportunity to comment, which they didn't. They spent five hours and forty-five minutes searching Kolderweg 17 from attic to boiler room. They were assisted by two German shepherds with two red-haired handlers and, for at least half the search, Detective Inspector Rooth in his capacity as leader of the operation.

The property was built at the end of the 1890s: there was an abundance of remarkable passages, corridors, and abandoned cupboards, and nobody still alive had ever seen a plan of the building. That is if you could believe the owner, a certain Herr Tibor, who turned up in a Bentley with a large collection of keys at lunchtime. But when Rooth himself called off the operation two hours later, it could be stated with confidence that no woman of Else Van Eck's dimensions—in no circumstances (and no other woman come to that!)—could have been hidden away in any of the building's nooks or crannies.

Dead or alive.

Several of the tenants were feeling distinctly upset, however. Joensuu's protestations that it was just a routine investigation lost credibility as first the attic spaces were emptied, then bathtubs were turned upside down and the bottoms of sofas were cut open.

"Hooligans!" snarled Herr Engel when the German shepherd investigated the collection of bottles under his bed. "Where's that woman who came to see me the other day? At least she displayed a modicum of tact and good sense."

What did I say! thought Inspector Rooth when it was all over. *I'm going to keep this case at arm's length.*

"Well, how did it go with your theory?" Jung asked when Rooth returned to the police station.

"Great," said Rooth. "I have another theory now. About how it happened."

"You don't say," said Jung, looking up from the piles of papers.

"Fröken Mathisen ground her down in the mincing machine and let Mussolini gobble her up."

"I thought Mussolini was a vegetarian?" said Jung.

"Wrong," said Rooth. "It was Hitler who was a vegetarian."

"If you say so," said Jung.

The run-through with Chief of Police Hiller on Friday afternoon was not a very memorable event. Two dwarf acacias had died during the week, despite having received all the care, nourishment, and love of which a human being is capable.

The chief of police wasn't mourning, although he did have black bags under his eyes.

Things were not much better on the human level. Münster recounted the situation with the assistance of Moreno and Jung (who had spent most of the day locating and interviewing various relatives and acquaintances of Else and Arnold Van Eck—and made about as much progress as a string quartet in a school for the deaf), and after an extremely uninspiring hour it was decided to keep more or less all the officers currently on the case, to send out a lengthy press communiqué, and to leave all doors wide open for the mass media and any member of the public who might be able to provide relevant information.

Help, thought Münster when he had finally returned to his office. *That's what we need. We don't know a damned thing, and what's required now is help.*

TV, newspapers, anything at all. The general public, that great detective.

Tips, that's what they needed.

And yet, it was still only a three-piece puzzle.

Leverkuhn. Bonger. Else Van Eck.

When he tried to think about how it felt, the only conclusion he could draw was that it was not especially uplifting.

20

"You do realize it's Saturday, don't you?" said Synn.

"I called him yesterday," said Münster. "The only time he had available was a couple of hours this morning. Do you think he's found himself a woman?"

Synn raised an eyebrow.

"You're not suggesting that he would give her preference over work, are you? He must be unique in the world of men if he does, I must say."

Münster tried to respond but found that there was some kind of spiritual eructation in the way, and no words came out.

"Synn, for goodness sake . . . ," he managed to utter in the end, but she had already turned her back on him.

He drank his coffee and left the kitchen. As he stood in the hall tying his shoelaces, he could hear her messing around with the children upstairs.

She loves me even so, he thought hopefully. *When all is said and done, she still does.*

"I'll be home by one at the latest!" he shouted up the stairs. "I'll do some shopping on the way back."

"Buy me something!"

Marieke came sliding down the stairs.

"Buy me something! I want something! Wrapped up in paper!"

He lifted her up. Gave her a hug, buried his nose in her newly washed hair, and decided he would buy no less than three presents. Something for Marieke, something for Bartje, something for Synn.

A hundred roses for Synn.

I must put a stop to the deterioration in our relationship, he thought. *I really must.*

But if roses would be the right thing to fill the cracks—well, that was something he would have to think long and hard about.

He put Marieke down and hurried out into the rain.

"You're looking well, Chief Inspector," said Münster.

Van Veeteren sucked the froth off his beer.

"Kindly refrain from using those words, Münster," he said. "I've known you long enough; we don't need to use titles."

"Thank you," said Münster. "But in any case, you're looking well. That's what I was trying to convey."

Van Veeteren took a deep swig and smacked his lips with pleasure.

"Yes," he said. "I've had a word with the good Lord, and we've agreed on seven good years after the wandering through the darkness. And I'll be damned if that isn't what I deserve—when I'm sixty-five. He can do whatever He likes with me."

"Really?" said Münster. "I must say I've started feeling a bit older and Reinhart is on leave of absence, so things get a bit difficult at times."

"Don't they have a new chief inspector up their sleeves?"

Münster shook his head.

"I think they're waiting for two things. To see if you come back . . ."

"I'm not coming back," said Van Veeteren.

". . . and if you don't, I reckon Heinemann has to retire first. Nobody can see him in that role, and he's next in line."

"But Hiller became chief of police," Van Veeteren reminded him.

He picked up his pack of tobacco, placed a little cigarette machine on the table, and started rolling.

"I've given up toothpicks," he explained. "I was becoming addicted. And this rolling almost makes it a craft. . . . Anyway, what the hell is it you want? We don't need to sit around all day being as polite as a couple of Chinamen."

Münster took a swig of his beer and looked out over the rainy square, where people were rushing from one stall to another. He wondered vaguely how many times he'd sat here at Adenaar's with the chief inspector. Listening to his bad-tempered expositions and gloomy observations . . . and noting the absolutely clear and incorruptible spirit that was always present under the surface. *No, it was not difficult to understand why he had jumped off the bandwagon,* Münster thought. *He'd been on it for thirty-five years, after all.*

And it was not surprising that the good Lord had granted him seven good years. Münster would have done the same.

"Well?" Van Veeteren asked again.

"Yes, there was something I wanted to ask you about."

"Leverkuhn?"

Münster nodded. "How could the chief . . . how did you know that?"

Van Veeteren lit his cigarette and inhaled as if he had just invented the first cigarette.

"Five a day," he said. "This is number one. What did you say?"

"You knew that I wanted to talk to you about Leverkuhn. How?"

"I guessed," said Van Veeteren modestly. "It's not the first time. And I still read the newspapers."

Münster nodded, somewhat embarrassed. It was true. On two previous occasions since Van Veeteren had left the stage, Münster had plucked up courage and discussed ongoing investigations with him. The first time, nearly a year ago, he had been reluctant to get him involved again, but he had soon realized that the old bloodhound instinct had not died out altogether. And that the chief inspector even derived a certain grim satisfaction from being consulted in this fashion.

But the fact that he would never admit as much for even a second was another matter, of course.

"I understand," said Münster. "Thank you for being willing to help. And to listen. Anyway, of course it's about Leverkuhn, no point in denying it."

Van Veeteren emptied his glass.

"I've read about it, as I said. It seems a bit special. If you buy me another beer it would no doubt improve my sense of hearing."

There was a slight twitch in the muscles of one cheek. Münster drained his own glass and went to the bar.

Two beers and forty-five minutes later, they had finished. Van Veeteren leaned back in his chair and nodded thoughtfully.

"No, this certainly doesn't seem to be a straightforward case," he said. "Things seem to be pulling in different directions. The threads seem to be unwinding instead of coming together."

"Exactly," said Münster. "Leverkuhn, Bonger, and Fru Van Eck. I've been thinking about it, and there seems to be just enough that links them together to suggest that their fates were connected—but yet not enough to suggest a motive."

"That could well be, yes," said Van Veeteren mysteriously. "But I think you should be careful not to take that jigsaw puzzle analogy too far. It can be so damned annoying to have a piece too many."

"Eh?" said Münster. "What do you mean by that?"

Van Veeteren didn't answer. Sat up in his chair and began playing with his cigarette machine instead. Münster looked out the window again. *Another of those meaningless comments,* he thought, and felt a little pang of irritation that was as familiar to him as a favorite jacket.

A piece too many? No, he decided that it was just an example of the chief inspector's weakness for smoke screens and mystification, nothing more. But what was the point of that in a situation like this?

"What about the wife?" said Van Veeteren. "What do you make of her?"

Münster thought for a moment.

"Introverted," he said eventually. "She seems to have a lot buttoned up inside her that she's reluctant to let come out. Although I don't really know—there's no such thing as normal reactions when you come home and find your husband murdered like that. Why do you ask?"

Van Veeteren ignored that question as well. Sat squeezing his newly rolled cigarette and seemed to be lost in thought.

"Anyway," said Münster. "I just wanted to talk it through. Thank you for listening."

Van Veeteren lit the cigarette and blew smoke over a begonia that was probably just as dead as the chief of police's acacias.

"Tuesday afternoon," he said. "Give me a few days to think things over, and then maybe we can have a game of badminton. I need to get some exercise. But don't expect too much—regarding your case, that is," he added, tapping his brow with his knuckles. "I'm a bit more focused on beauty and pleasure nowadays."

"Tuesday, then," said Münster, writing it down in his notebook. "Yes, I'd heard rumors about that—a new woman, is that right?"

Van Veeteren put the cigarette machine into his jacket pocket and looked inscrutable.

The presents added up to nearly 500 guilders, topped by a red dress for Synn costing 295. *What the hell,* Münster thought. *You only live once.*

What had she said the other day?

What if we die soon?

He shuddered and got into his car. However you looked at it, life was no more than the total of all these days, and at some point, of course, you start being more interested in the days that have passed rather than the ones yet to come.

But there are moments in life—let's hope so in any case—when you have an opportunity to devote yourself to the here and now.

Such as a Saturday and Sunday in November like this.

Damn, Intendent Münster thought. *I wish to God I had one of those cop's brains that you can switch on and off in accordance with working hours.*

If there is such a thing, of course. He remembered an old conversation with the chief inspector—presumably at Adenaar's as usual—about the concept of intuition.

The brain functions best when you leave it in peace, Van Veeteren had argued. Keep tucked away the questions and information you have and think about something else. If there's an answer, it will come tumbling out sooner or later.

Like hell it will! Münster thought pessimistically. *I suppose there are brains and then there are brains. . . .*

Whatever, after the conversation with the chief inspector and the shopping at the height of the Saturday rush hour, there was no doubt that he felt switched off—so he could let his brain work away undisturbed in the background and see if anything came tumbling out.

He looked at his watch. Ten past one. It was a Saturday in November, it was raining, and he had nothing to do except devote himself to his family.

21

During the night between Friday and Saturday Inspector Moreno slept for more than twelve hours, and when she woke up at about half past ten on the Saturday morning, it took some time before she realized where she was.

And that she was alone.

That the five years with Claus Badher were at an end, and that from now on she had only herself to worry about. It felt strange. Not least the fact that a month had passed since she left him, but it was only now that she realized that her fate was in her own hands.

As if to check whether those hands were strong enough to carry it, she took them out from under the warm bedcovers and examined them for a while. Didn't think that they looked up to much—but that's the way it is with women's hands. Underdeveloped and a bit childlike. There was an enormous difference between them and the large, sinewy equipment with which men were blessed. Usable and nice to look at. Now that she came to think about it, she couldn't recall ever having seen an attractive woman's hand. They were like chickens' wings, it struck her—dysfunctional and pathetic. Perhaps there was food for thought in this striking difference—the extent to which it typified something basic when it came to the difference between men and women?

An expression of essential differences? Their hands?

And never the twain shall meet, she thought: but then she saw in her mind's eye a black man's hand on a white woman's breast, and it occurred to her that the twain can in fact meet.

By the time she entered the shower she had realized that the hand and the breast in the image she had conjured up were not in any way Claus's and hers, but Tobose Menakdise's and Filippa de Booning's, and she was suddenly back in the middle of the investigation.

You talk about what fills the mind, she seemed to remember somebody saying. But so what? The more thoughts she devoted to the Leverkuhn case and the fewer to Claus, the better.

And the healthier it would be for her mistreated spiritual life.

There was always the hope that there might be other alternatives with which to rack her brain. In that spirit she set out after breakfast on a long walk along Willemsgraacht, toward the Lauern lakes and Lohr. Strolled through the light rain and thought about all sorts of things, but mostly about her parents—and her brother in Rome, whom she hadn't seen for more than two years. Her parents in Groenstadt didn't live far away, but that contact wasn't everything it might have been either. It was easy to form opinions about the Leverkuhns' family relationships, but to be honest, her own were not much better.

And then there was her sister, Maud. She had no idea where Maud was—in Hamburg maybe—or what state she was in.

Perhaps the anthropologists were right, she thought, *that when the northern European nuclear family had exhausted its role as an economic and social factor, it had also lost its emotional significance.*

Emotions were no more than superstructure and empty show. Men and women met, had children, then wandered off in different directions. Heading for wherever it was they were going before they happened to meet, for their various goals. Yes, perhaps that was how you ought to look at it. In any case, there were plenty of examples of this in the animal world, and a human being is basically an animal, after all.

This last point made her realize that she was also a female, and that this week she was in the middle of her monthly cycle and was going to find it difficult to do without a man. In the long run, at least. *What a pity,* she thought, *what a pity that a human being should be so badly constructed that there was such a disconnect between brain, heart, and sex sometimes. Usually.*

Always?

The café at Czerpinski's Mill was open, and she decided to indulge herself in a cup of tea before returning home. But she would have to be quick about it: it was already a quarter to three, and in no circumstance did she want to be strolling around in the dark.

She had barely entered the premises before noticing that sitting at one of the tables in the circular room were Benjamin Wauters and Jan Palinski—they didn't recognize her, or at least showed no sign of having done so, but she realized that it was a sign.

A sign that there was no point in trying to keep her work at a distance anymore.

She hung on for a bit longer. On Saturday evening she called both her brother and her parents, watched a French film from the sixties on television, and hand-washed two sweaters. But when Sunday morning announced itself with a high, clear blue sky, she knew that it was all in vain. It was simply too urgent. The case. Her work. A few hours of private investigation without any great expectations. It was in the nature of things, and there was no point in pretending otherwise.

There is something deep inside me, she thought, *that makes me do this. A drive, an urge that I never acknowledge, that actually steers my life. Or at least my professional life. I like poking my nose into things! I enjoy putting other people under a magnifying glass. Their motivation and their actions.*

Besides, I'm in the middle of the month. I'd better look after the sublimation myself.

She smiled at that last thought as she stood waiting for the bus to Kolderweg. Working instead of making love? How totally absurd! If Claus could follow her thoughts for five minutes he would probably never dare to meet her again.

But perhaps that's the situation in all relationships?

With all women and their men with their beautiful hands?

The bus was approaching.

The door was opened by a woman she had never seen before, and for a moment Moreno suspected the possibility of a breakthrough. But then the woman introduced herself as Helena Winther, the younger sister of Arnold Van Eck, and that hope was lost.

"I arrived yesterday," she explained. "I thought I needed to—he's not very strong."

She was a slim woman in her mid-fifties, with the same anemic appearance as her brother, but with a handshake that suggested a certain strength of character.

"You don't live here in Maardam, then?"

"No, in Aarlach. My husband has a business there."

She led the way into the living room, where Van Eck was sitting hunched in front of the television. He looked as if he had stopped crying only a short while ago.

"Good morning," said Moreno. "How are you feeling?"

"Awful," said Van Eck with a cough. "There's such a void."

Moreno nodded.

"I can imagine," she said. "I thought I'd just call in and see if anything had occurred to you. These things usually come out of the blue, as I said before."

"It's a mystery!" Van Eck exclaimed. "A complete mystery!"

I wonder if he thinks the same way as he talks, Moreno thought. Whatever, he must surely be a special case even in that male sector she had been thinking about?

"Do you remember if your wife acted in an unusual way during the days before she disappeared?" she asked. "Said or did something she didn't usually say or do?"

Van Eck sighed from the very depths of his martyred soul.

"No," he said. "Nothing like that. I've been lying awake at night, thinking and thinking, but everything is a complete mystery. It's like a nightmare even though I'm awake."

"And you don't remember noticing anything unusual when you came back home after your course last Wednesday? That first impression you had the moment you crossed the threshold, if you follow me."

Van Eck shook his head.

"Do you think your wife had any male friends you didn't know about?"

"Eh?"

For a second Van Eck looked cross-eyed behind the thick lenses of his spectacles, and Moreno realized that the question—like any possible answer to it—was way beyond his imagination.

She also realized that she wasn't going to get anything more out of him, but before moving on to the people who lived upstairs she had a few words with his sister in the kitchen.

"Do you have much contact with your brother and your sister-in-law?" she asked.

Helena Winther shrugged.

"Not a lot," she said. "There's the age difference, of course, but we do meet now and then. My husband and Arnold are very different, though."

"And Else?"

Winther looked out the window and hesitated before answering.

"She's a bit unusual," she said. "But you'll have gathered that. They are not the most normal couple in the world, but in a way they make a real pair. You've seen what he's like without her."

"Is he taking any sedatives?"

She shook her head.

"He never takes medicine. He's never even taken an aspirin for as long as he's lived."

"Why not?"

Winther said nothing, just looked at Moreno with her eyebrows slightly raised, and for a few seconds it was as if the whole masculine mystique was weighed up and fathomed out between those four female eyes.

And found to be unfathomable. Moreno noticed that she was smiling inwardly.

"You have no idea about what might have happened?"

"None at all. As he says, it's a complete mystery. She's not the type who disappears. On the contrary, if you know what I mean."

With a slight nod Moreno indicated that she did. Then she shook hands with both her and her brother, and promised to do her utmost to throw light on these sad circumstances.

Ruben Engel wasn't exactly smelling of violets today either, but he seemed to be sober and there was a half-finished crossword lying on the kitchen table.

"For the little gray cells," he explained, standing up and pointing a dirty index finger at his forehead. "Welcome—and that's a greeting I don't extend to all police officers."

Moreno took the compliment with a practiced smile.

"There are just a few things I've been thinking about," she said. "If you have time, that is."

"Of course."

Engel hitched up his trousers, which had a tendency to fall, and indicated the vacant chair. She sat down and waited for a couple of seconds.

"What is the link between Leverkuhn and Fru Van Eck?"

"Eh?" said Engel, sitting down.

Moreno leaned forward over the table and braced herself.

"Listen," she said. "What I mean is that there must be some sort of crucial link between these two events in the same building, some vital little factor that explains why it's these two people who have been . . . been moved out of the way. It could be anything at all, but it's almost impossible for an outsider to catch on. You have been living close to both of them for twenty years, Herr Engel, so you ought to be just the person to come up with something. Can you recall anything at all where both Waldemar Leverkuhn and Else Van Eck had their fingers in the same pie, so to speak?"

"Are you suggesting they were having an affair?"

Moreno choked back a sigh.

"Not at all. It doesn't need to be anything as big as that, but it's hard to be more precise when you don't really know what you are looking for."

"Yes," said Engel, "it is."

He clamped his jaws together with a loud click, and she gathered that just now he was thinking of her in terms of a cop rather than a woman.

"Are you worried at all that something might happen to you, Herr Engel?"

Memories of his masculinity naturally got in the way of his giving her an honest answer to that question. He cleared his throat, straightened his back until it creaked, but she could see nevertheless that fear was coursing through his whole body.

Lay there ominously like dark water under one-night-old ice.

"I'm not especially frightened, young lady," he claimed, trying to keep his gaze steady. "One learns to get by in the world we live in."

"Are there any neighbors you feel slightly less confident about?" she insisted. "When you bump into them on the stairs, for instance?"

"The neighbors? No, no, of course not!"

He burst out coughing, and as the attack slowly ebbed away Moreno sat there motionless, weighing up his final comment.

Was it really as clear a dismissal of any such thought as he tried to make it sound? Or?

Two hours later, as she slid down into a bubble bath smelling of eucalyptus, she still had not made up her mind about that.

. . .

Inspector Ewa Moreno also slept soundly on Sunday night without waking up at all, and as she sat in the trolley in the cold light of dawn the next morning, on her way to the police station, she realized that she had finally caught up with herself. The lack of sleep that had been building up had now been satisfied, and for the first time in weeks she felt eager to start work.

Ready to get to grips with whatever lay in store for her.

But she could hardly have been prepared for what Intendent Münster had to tell her when she entered his office.

"Anything new?" she asked.

"You can say that again," said Münster, looking up from the pile of papers he was leafing through. "She confessed."

"What?" said Moreno.

"Fru Leverkuhn. She rang at a quarter past seven this morning and confessed that she had murdered her husband."

Moreno sat down on a chair.

"Well, I'll be damned!" she said. "So it was her after all?"

"That's what she claims," said Münster.

III

22

The police spent three days with her, and then she was left more or less alone. From the second week onward her visitors were restricted to a handful of people.

Her lawyer, Bachmann, came in almost every day—in the beginning, at least. She had met him in connection with the first interrogation at the police station, and he hadn't made a particularly good impression on her. A well-dressed, overweight man of about fifty with thick, wavy hair that he probably dyed. A large signet ring and strong, white teeth. He suggested from the very start that they should follow the manslaughter line, and she went along with it without really thinking about it.

She didn't like the man, but reckoned that the more she let him have his own way, the less time she would need to spend discussing matters with him. In the middle of the month, he stayed away several times for a few days on end; but in December, as the date of the trial approached, there was a lot to run through again. She didn't really understand why, but never asked.

Get it over with quickly, she thought: and that was the only request she put to him. Don't let it become one of those long-drawn-out affairs with special pleading and the cross-examination of witnesses and all the rest that she had seen on television.

Bachmann put his hand on his heart, assuring her that he would do his best. Although there were several things that were unclear, and one simply can't get away with anything in court.

Every time he pointed this out he gave her a quick smile, but she never responded with one of her own.

The chaplain was named Kolding, and was about her age. A low-key preacher who always brought with him a flask of tea and a tin of cookies, and generally sat on the chair in her cell for half an hour or so, without saying very much. On his first visit he explained that he didn't want to harass her, but it was his intention to call in every two or three days. In case there was something she would like to take up with him.

There never was, but she had nothing against his sitting there. He was tall and thin, slightly stooping in view of his age, and he reminded her of the vicar who conducted her confirmation classes. She once asked him if they were relatives, but of course they were not.

However, he had worked for a while in the Maalwort parish in Pampas. This emerged from one of their sparse conversations, but as she had been to church only once or twice during all the years they had lived only a stone's throw away, there was not much to say about this circumstance either.

Nevertheless, he would sit there in the corner several afternoons a week. And made himself available, as he had promised. Perhaps he was simply tired, and needed to rest for a while, she sometimes thought.

At least he did not annoy her.

Other people who took the trouble to come and visit her were her two children and the assiduous Emmeline von Post.

Before the trial began, when she counted up the visits, she concluded that Mauritz had been three times, and Ruth and Emmeline twice each. On her birthday, the second of December, Mauritz and Ruth turned up together with a chocolate cake and three white lilies—which for some reason she found so absurd that she had difficulty not bursting into laughter.

Otherwise she made a big effort—during all these visits and greetings—to behave politely and courteously; but the circumstances sometimes meant that the atmosphere inside her pale yellow cell felt tense and strained. Especially with Mauritz, there were a few occasions when heated words were exchanged about trivialities—but then, she hadn't expected anything else.

On the whole, however, her time in prison—the six weeks of waiting before the trial began—was a period of rest and recovery, and when she went to bed the evening before the proceedings started, she inevitably felt a bit worried about what lay in store, but also calm and quite confident that her inner strength would carry her through these difficult times as well.

As it had done thus far.

The trial began on a Tuesday afternoon, and her lawyer had promised her that it would be all over by Friday evening. Assuming no complications arose, that is, and there was hardly any reason to expect that they would.

The first few hours in the courtroom were characterized by ceremonial posturing and a slow pace that made her wonder. She had been placed behind an oblong wooden table with bottles of mineral water, paper mugs, and a notepad. On her right was her lawyer, smelling of his usual aftershave; on her left was a youngish woman dressed in blue, whose role was unclear to Marie-Louise Leverkuhn. But she didn't ask about it.

This was not one of the bigger courtrooms, as far as she knew. The space for members of the public and journalists was limited to about twenty chairs behind a bar at the far end of the rectangular room. Just now, on this first afternoon, the audience was restricted to six people: two balding journalists and four women reassuringly well into retirement age. It was a relief to find that there were so few, but she suspected there would be more people sitting on the high-backed chairs later in the performance. Once it was properly under way.

Sitting opposite her, enthroned on a dais barely four inches high, was Judge Hart, behind a broad table covered in a green cloth hanging down to the floor on all sides—so that one didn't need to look at his feet. Or up skirts, she fancied, if the judge happened to be a woman. But she didn't know. In any case, her own administrator of justice was a man of generous proportions in his sixties. He reminded her very much of a French actor whose name she couldn't remember, no matter how hard she tried. Ended in -eaux, she seemed to recall.

To the right of the judge were two other officers of justice—young and immaculately groomed men wearing glasses and impeccable suits—and to the left was the jury.

In the early stages everything was aimed at the six members of this jury: four men and two women, and as far as she could make out it was all intended to establish the irreproachable and impartial nature of their characters when it came to the trial that was about to start.

When they had all been approved, Judge Hart declared that the proceedings could begin and handed over to the prosecutor, Fru Grootner, a woman in late middle age wearing a beige suit and with a mouth so wide that it sometimes seemed to continue for some distance outside the face itself. She stood in front of her table on the other side of the center aisle, leaning back with her ample bosom as a counterbalance, and pleaded her cause for more than forty-five minutes. As far as Marie-Louise Leverkuhn could understand it was based on the premise that in the early hours of October 26 she had stabbed to death Waldemar Leverkuhn with premeditation and in full control of her senses, so that the only crime she could possibly be accused of was first-degree murder. And hence this was the count that she would have to answer for.

Does she really believe what she's saying? Leverkuhn wondered to herself. But it was hard to judge what was hiding behind the

torrent of words and the streamlined spectacles that, on closer ex-
amination, proved to have precisely the Cupid's bow form that was
missing from her lips.

When the prosecutor had finished, it was the defense's turn.
Bachmann stood up with all the dignity he could muster, stroked
his right hand several times over his mahogany-brown hair, and
then announced that the defense would contest the charge and
instead plead guilty to manslaughter.

He elaborated on this forcefully and verbosely for almost as
long as the broad-mouthed prosecutor had spouted forth, and
Marie-Louise felt frequently as if her eyelids were closing.

Perhaps she hadn't slept as well as she'd thought last night?

Perhaps she was too old for this kind of thing. Would everything be over and done with more quickly if she were to plead
guilty to murder?

When proceedings were suspended for the day shortly after four
o'clock, she hadn't needed to utter a single word. Nor answer a single question. Bachmann had already explained that this was how
things would go on the first day, but even so she felt somewhat
confused as she was led out by the lady in blue who had remained
at her side all the time.

It's like being at the dentist's or in the hospital, she thought with a
mixture of relief and disappointment. *One is without doubt the leading character, but doesn't have a single word to say about it.*

That was presumably the norm in courts of law as well.

23

"A longer racket," said Van Veeteren, feeling his back. "That's what's needed, dammit. I don't understand why they don't invent something of the sort."

"Why?" said Münster.

"So that you don't need to bend so far down for stop balls, of course. My back isn't what it used to be. Never has been."

Münster considered these words of wisdom and switched on the shower. He had won all three sets as usual, but the chief inspector—former chief inspector—had offered stiff competition. The scores were 15–9, 15–11, 15–6, which suggested that Van Veeteren was in better shape now than he had been before leaving the police station.

Surely he can't have much further to go before passing the sixty mark? Münster thought, trying to brush aside the possibility that the fairly even outcome of the match might have something to do with his own state at the moment.

"Adenaar's now?" wondered Van Veeteren as they came up to the foyer. "I gather you have something else on your chest?"

Münster coughed a little self-consciously.

"If you have time, Chief Inspector."

"Stop using those words, will you?" grunted Van Veeteren.

"I'm sorry," said Münster. "It takes time to get used to it."

"I know that only too well," said Van Veeteren, holding the door open.

"I suppose it's Leverkuhn that's worrying you, is it?"

Münster looked out in the direction of the square and took a deep breath.

"Yes," he admitted. "The trial started this afternoon. I just can't get it out of my head."

Van Veeteren took out his unwieldy cigarette machine and started filling it with tobacco.

"Those are the worst kind," he said. "The ones that won't allow you to sleep at night."

"Exactly," said Münster. "I dream about this cursed case. I can't make head or tail of it, whether I'm awake or asleep. Despite the fact that I've been through it hundreds of times, both with Jung and Moreno. It doesn't help."

"Reinhart?" Van Veeteren asked.

"On leave of absence," said Münster with a sigh. "Playing with his daughter."

"Ah, yes, of course," said Van Veeteren, pressing down the lid of the machine so that a rolled cigarette fell onto the table. With a contented expression on his face he placed the cigarette between his lips and lit it. Münster watched his activities in silence.

"Do you think she's innocent?" asked Van Veeteren after his first drag. "What's the problem?"

Münster shrugged.

"I don't know," he admitted. "I suppose it must have been her, but that's not the end of the case. We have Fru Van Eck and that damned Bonger as well. Nobody's seen any trace of either of them since they vanished, and that was more than a month ago now."

"And Fru Leverkuhn has nothing to do with them?"

"Not a thing. If you can believe what she says, that is. We pressed her pretty hard once she confessed, but she didn't give an inch. She owns up to stabbing her husband in a fit of anger, but she's as innocent as a newborn babe as far as the others are concerned, she claims."

"Why did she kill her husband?"

"Why indeed?" said Münster glumly. "She just says it was the last straw."

"Hmm," said Van Veeteren. "What kind of a straw could that have been, was she more precise about it? If we assume that the camel's back was full."

"That he'd won some money, but didn't intend to give her a penny. She says she came home and found him lying in bed bragging about all the things he was going to buy, and after a while she'd had enough."

Van Veeteren drew on his cigarette and thought for a moment.

"I suppose it could happen like that," he said. "Is she the type?"

Münster scratched his head.

"I don't know," he said. "If we assume that she's been leading that camel all her life—or throughout their marriage at any rate—well, I suppose it could be true; but it's hard for an outsider to judge. That's her story—that she's been having to put up with this and that for what seemed to be forever, and she simply couldn't take it anymore. Something snapped inside her, she says, and so she did it."

Van Veeteren leaned back and stared up at the ceiling.

"Theories?" he said eventually. "Do you have any? What do you think? About this lady Van Eck, for instance?"

Münster suddenly looked almost unhappy.

"I haven't a damn clue," he said. "Not the slightest. As I said before, I find it difficult to believe that these three cases aren't connected in some way. It seems unlikely that Bonger, Leverkuhn, and Fru Van Eck would all kick the bucket at the same time purely by chance."

"You don't know that Bonger and Van Eck are dead," Van Veeteren pointed out. "Or have I missed something?"

Münster sighed.

"You're right," he said. "But it doesn't exactly make things any easier if they've simply gone missing."

Van Veeteren said nothing for a few seconds.

"Maybe not," he said eventually. "What have you done about it? From the point of view of the investigation, I mean. Presumably you haven't just wandered around thinking about this?"

"Not a lot," Münster admitted. "Since the prosecutor charged Fru Leverkuhn, we've only been going through the routine motions as far as Bonger and Fru Van Eck are concerned."

"Who's in charge of the investigation?" asked Van Veeteren.

"I am," said Münster, taking another swig of beer. "But once Fru Leverkuhn is sentenced Hiller is probably going to shelve the other cases. That will be next week. There are a few other things to keep us occupied."

"Really?" said Van Veeteren.

He drained his glass and signaled for another. While waiting for it to be served, he sat in silence with his chin resting on his knuckles as he gazed out the window at the traffic and the pigeons in Karlsplats. When the beer arrived he sucked off the froth first, then emptied it in one enormous swig.

"Very good!" he announced. "All that exercise makes you thirsty. Why exactly did you want to speak to me?"

Münster looked embarrassed. *He never learns,* Van Veeteren thought. *But then, perhaps it's not a bad thing to have a few red cheeks in the police force. It makes things seem nice and peaceful.*

"Well?"

Münster cleared his throat.

"All that stuff about intuition. I thought I'd ask the chief . . . ask you to do me a favor, to be frank."

"I'm all ears," said Van Veeteren.

Münster squirmed on his chair.

"The trial," he said. "It would be good to get an idea of whether she really is as guilty and as innocent as she says. Fru Leverkuhn, that is. If somebody with an eye for such things could go and take a look at her. Whether she's found guilty or not."

"Which she will be?" said Van Veeteren.

"I think so," said Münster.

Van Veeteren frowned and contemplated his cigarette machine.

"All right," he said. "I'll go there and take a look at her, then."

"Excellent," said Münster. "Many thanks. Room four. But it'll be all over by Friday, if I'm not mistaken."

"I'll go tomorrow," said Van Veeteren. "The eagle's eye never sleeps."

Huh, big chief is never wrong, Münster thought. But he said nothing.

24

"Tell me about when you came home in the early hours of October twenty-sixth!"

Prosecutor Grootner pushed up her spectacles and waited. Marie-Louise Leverkuhn took a sip of water from the glass on the table in front of her. Cleared her throat and straightened her back.

"I got home at about two o'clock," she said. "There had been a power cut on the railway line to Bossingen and Löhr. We were standing still for an hour. I'd been to visit a friend."

She looked up at the public gallery, as if she were looking for a face. The prosecutor made no attempt to hurry her, and after a while she continued of her own accord.

"My husband woke up as I came through the door into the bedroom and started making abusive remarks."

"Abusive remarks?" wondered the prosecutor.

"Because I'd woken him up. He claimed I'd done it on purpose. Then he went on and on."

"How did he go on?"

"He said he'd won some money, and that he was going to spend it so that he didn't have to see me so often."

"Did he usually say things like that?"

"It happened. When he'd been drinking."

"Was he drunk that evening?"

"Yes."

"How drunk?"

"He was pretty far gone. Slurring when he spoke."

Short pause. The prosecutor nodded thoughtfully several times.

"Please continue, Fru Leverkuhn."

"Well, I went out into the kitchen and saw the knife lying on the cutting board. I'd used it when I'd been cutting up some ham that afternoon."

"What did you think when you saw the knife?"

"Nothing. I just picked it up to wash it and put it back in the drawer."

"Is that what you did?"

"I beg your pardon?"

"Did you wash the knife?"

"No."

"Tell us what you did instead."

Leverkuhn brushed aside an annoying strand of hair and seemed to be hesitating about what to say next. The prosecutor eyed her without moving a muscle.

"I was standing with the knife in my hand. And then my husband shouted something."

"What?"

"I'd rather not say. It was a very rude insult."

"What did you do?"

"I felt that I just couldn't go on like this any longer. I don't think I really understood what I was doing. I went into the bedroom, and then I stabbed him in the stomach."

"Did he try to defend himself?"

"He didn't have time."

"And then?"

"I just carried on stabbing. It felt . . ."

"Yes?"

"It felt as if it wasn't me holding the knife. As if it was somebody else. It was very odd."

Prosecutor Grootner paused again, then went for a little walk.

When she returned to her starting point, a few feet in front of the table, she first coughed into her hand, then turned her head so that she seemed to be speaking to a point somewhere diagonally above where the accused was sitting. As if she were talking to somebody else.

"I find it a bit difficult to believe this," she said. "You have been married to your husband for more than forty years. You have shared the same home and bed and endured the same hardships during a long life, but now you suddenly lose your head without any real reason. You said you were used to, um, exchanges of opinion like that, didn't you?"

"I don't know," said Leverkuhn, looking down at the table. "It's just that this was something extra. . . ."

"This wasn't something you'd considered doing earlier?"

"No."

"You'd never even given it a thought?"

"No."

"Not earlier that evening, for instance?"

"No."

"Are you suggesting that you didn't know what you were doing when you murdered your husband?"

"Objection!" shouted Bachmann. "It has not been established that she murdered her husband."

"Allowed," muttered the judge without moving his mouth. The prosecutor shrugged, and her heavy bosom bobbed up and down.

"Did you know what you were doing when you stabbed your husband?" she said.

"Yes, of course."

A faint murmur ran through the gallery, and Judge Hart called for silence by raising his gaze half an inch.

"What did you intend to do by stabbing him?"

"To kill him, of course. To shut him up."

The prosecutor nodded again, several times, and looked pleased.

"Then what did you do?"

"I rinsed the knife under the tap in the kitchen. Then I wrapped it up in a newspaper and went out."

"Why?"

Leverkuhn hesitated.

"I don't know. I suppose I wanted to make it look as if somebody else had done it."

"Where did you go?"

"Toward Entwick Plejn. I threw the knife and the newspaper into a rubbish bin."

"Where?"

"I can't remember. Maybe in Entwickstraat, but I'm not sure. I was a bit confused."

"And then?"

"Then I went back home and phoned the police. I pretended that I'd found my husband dead, but that wasn't the case. . . ."

"Didn't you get a lot of blood on you when you killed your husband?"

"Only a bit. I washed it off at the same time as I rinsed the knife."

The prosecutor seemed to be thinking for a few seconds. Then she slowly turned her back on the accused. Pushed up her spectacles again and let her gaze wander over the members of the jury.

"Thank you, Fru Leverkuhn," she said, in a voice lowered by half an octave. "I don't think we need to doubt that you acted with great presence of mind and purposefulness at the time. And I no longer think there is a single one of us who doubts that you murdered your husband with premeditation. Thank you, no more questions."

Bachmann had stood up, but didn't bother to protest. He had bags under his eyes, she noticed. Looked tired and somewhat resigned. She had the impression that his fee depended in some way on whether he won or lost the case, but she wasn't sure. It wasn't easy to know the ways of this strange world.

Not easy at all.

. . .

Nor did she know how common it was for the judge himself to ask questions, but when Bachmann had finished his rather pointless interrogation—all the time she found it difficult to understand what he was after and what he wanted her to say, and when he sat down he looked even more dispirited—the great man cleared his throat emphatically and announced that certain things needed clarifying.

But first he asked if she would like a little rest before he started questioning her.

No, she said that was not necessary.

"Certain things need clarifying," Judge Hart said again, clasping his hairy hands on the Bible in front of him. A murmur ran through the public gallery and Prosecutor Grootner suddenly began scribbling away on her notepad. Bachmann stroked his hair and looked like a morose question mark.

"What made you confess?"

He looked down on her from his slightly raised position with a skeptical frown between his bushy eyebrows.

"My conscience," she said.

"Your conscience?"

"Yes."

"And what made your conscience stir after more than a week?"

Marie-Louise Leverkuhn was certainly ten years older than Judge Hart, but nevertheless there was suddenly an element of teacher-schoolgirl in the situation. A teenager caught smoking in the bathroom and now summoned to the headmaster for a telling-off.

"I don't know," she said after a short pause for thought. "I thought about it for a few days and then decided it was wrong to carry on lying."

"What made you lie in the first place?"

"Fear," she said without hesitation. "Of the consequences . . . court and prison and so on."

"Do you regret what you did?"

She examined her hands for a while.

"Yes," she said. "Of course I regret it. It's terrible, killing another human being. You have to take your punishment."

Judge Hart leaned back.

"Why didn't you throw the knife into a canal instead of a dustbin?"

"I didn't think."

"Have you been asked that question before?"

"Yes."

"But why bother to get rid of the knife in the first place? Wouldn't it have been sufficient to rinse the blood off it and put it back in its place in the kitchen?"

Leverkuhn frowned briefly before answering.

"I don't remember what I was thinking," she said, "but I supposed people would realize that was the knife I'd used if they found it. I wasn't thinking clearly."

The judge nodded and looked mildly reproachful.

"I'm sure you weren't," he said. "But don't you think it rather odd that you immediately told the police that the knife was missing?"

She did not answer. Judge Hart pulled a hair out of his nostril and examined it for a moment before flicking it over his shoulder and continuing.

"Did you meet Fru Van Eck at all during the days before she disappeared?"

Bachmann started gesturing, but seemed to realize that it wasn't appropriate to protest when it was the judge himself asking the questions. He moved his chair noisily and leaned back nonchalantly instead. Looked up at the ceiling. As if what was happening had nothing to do with him.

"I had coffee with her and her husband one afternoon. They invited me."

"That was on Tuesday, wasn't it?"

She thought about it.

"Yes, it must have been."

"And then she disappeared on the Wednesday?"

"As far as I know, yes. Why are you asking about that?"

The judge made a vague gesture with his hands, as if to say that they might just as well chat about these events, seeing as they were all gathered together here.

"Just one more little question," he said eventually. "It doesn't happen to be the case that you needed this time—these seven days or however long it was—for some special purpose?"

"I don't understand what you mean," said Leverkuhn.

Judge Hart took out a large red handkerchief and blew his nose.

"I think you do," he muttered. "But you may leave the dock now."

Marie-Louise Leverkuhn thanked him and did as she had been told.

Judge Hart, Van Veeteren thought as he came out into the street and opened up his umbrella. *What a terrific police officer the old distorter of the law would have made!*

25

Moreno knocked and entered. Münster looked up from the reports he was reading.

"Have a seat," he said. "How did it go?"

She flopped down onto the chair without even unbuttoning her brown suede jacket. She shook her head a few times, and he realized that she was on the verge of tears.

"Not well," she said.

Münster put his pen in his breast pocket and slid the pile of files to one side. He waited for the continuation, but there wasn't one.

"I see," he said in the end. "Feel free to tell me about it."

Ewa Moreno dug her hands into her pockets and took a deep breath. Münster noted that he did the opposite—held his breath.

"I explained to him that it was all over now. Definitely over and done with. He's off to the USA for a course tomorrow morning. He said that if I don't change my mind, he won't be coming back. So that's where we're at."

She fell silent and looked past his shoulder, out the window. Münster swallowed, and for a fleeting moment acknowledged that if he had been in Claus Bladher's shoes he would probably have done the same.

"You mean . . . ?" he said.

"Yes," said Moreno. "That's what he meant. I know it. He's intending to take his own life."

Five seconds passed.

"It's not that serious. A lot of people say things like that."

"Maybe," said Moreno. "And a lot of people do it. God, I some-times wish I could just disappear into a black hole. Everything feels so damned hopeless. I've tried to persuade him to at least talk to somebody. . . . To seek some kind of help. To do anything at all that leaves me out of it—but you men are just the way you are."

"The macho mystery?" said Münster.

"Yes. We've already talked about that."

She shrugged apologetically.

"Do you have somebody to talk to yourself?" Münster asked.

A slight blush colored her face.

"Oh sure," she said. "An old detective intendent I happen to know, among others. No, enough of this. Isn't there any work I can immerse myself in?"

"A whole ocean," said Münster. "Plus some stagnant backwater called the Leverkuhn case. Could that be something for you?"

"You're not going to shelve it?"

"I can't," said Münster. "I've tried, but I dream about it at night."

Moreno nodded and took her hands out of her pockets.

"Okay," she said. "What do you want me to do?"

"I've been thinking about that daughter I spoke to," said Mün-ster. "Could that be something worth following up?"

"Odd," said Rooth.

"What is?" said Jung.

"Can't you see?"

"No, I'm blind."

Rooth snorted.

"Look at the other houseboats. That one . . . and that one!"

He pointed. Jung looked and stamped his feet in an attempt to create a bit of heat.

"I'm freezing," he said. "Tell me what you're onto, or I'll throw you into the canal."

"Spoken like a true gentleman," said Rooth. "It's not moored next to the quay, you idiot. Why the hell is he anchored three feet out into the water?"

Jung registered that this really was the case. Bonger's canal boat—which he was now gaping at for the seventh or eighth time—was not moored with its rail next to the stone quayside. Instead it was held in place by four ropes as thick as your arm and a couple of fenders made out of rough wooden logs with car tires fixed to the end, wedged between the hull of the boat and the quay eighteen inches above the waterline. The narrow gangplank, which he had crossed a month ago, ran for about five feet over open water very nearly to the bows of the boat. Come to think of it, he had to admit it was a bit odd.

"All right," said Jung. "But what's the significance?"

"How the hell should I know?" said Rooth. "But it's an unusual setup. Anyway, should we call in on the old witch?"

Jung bit his lip.

"Maybe we should have brought her something."

"Brought her something? What the hell are you saying?"

"She's a bit of an eccentric, I've explained that already. We'd be more likely to get somewhere with her if we presented her with a drop of something tasty."

Rooth shuddered.

"Curse this wind," he said. "Okay, there's a liquor store on the corner over there. Hop over and buy a half bottle of gin, and I'll wait here for you."

Ten minutes later they were ensconced in the galley with Fru Jümpers. Just as Jung had predicted, the gin was much appreciated—especially as it was the coldest day so far this winter, and the lady of the boat had a visitor.

The visitor's name was Barga—Jung couldn't make out whether this was her first name or her surname—a robust woman of an uncertain age. Probably somewhere between forty and seventy. Despite the fact that it was relatively warm on board, both ladies were wearing rubber boots, thick woolen sweaters, and long scarves wrapped around their heads and necks. Without much in the way of ceremony, four tin mugs appeared on the table and were promptly filled with two fingers of gin and coffee. Then a sugar cube, and a toast was proposed.

"Aah!" exclaimed Barga. "God is not as dead as they say."

"But He's on His last legs," said Fru Jümpers. "Believe you me!"

"Hmm," said Jung. "On that note, did you happen to see Herr Bonger lately? That's why we've called on you, of course."

"Bonger?" said Barga, unwinding her headscarf slightly. "No, that's a goddamn mystery. Makes you wonder what the police do in this town."

"These gentlemen are from the police," said the hostess, with a wry smile.

"Well, I'll be damned," said Barga. "Still, I suppose somebody has to do it, as the ass-licker said."

"Exactly," said Rooth. "So you also knew Herr Bonger?"

"You can bet your ass I did, Officer," said Barga. "Better than anybody else, I reckon. . . ." She glanced at her friend. "With the possible exception of this old cow."

"Do you also live on the canal?" Jung asked.

"No fear," said Barga. "On the contrary. . . . Up under the roof beams in Kleinstraat, that's where I have my abode. But I do descend down here now and then."

"Descend down here, kiss my ass!" snorted Fru Jümpers, unscrewing the top of the bottle again. "Can I offer anybody a drop more?"

"Just a little one," said Jung.

"A fairly big one," said Rooth.

Fru Jümpers poured out the gin and Barga laughed so expansively that the fillings in her teeth glittered.

"A fairly big one!" she repeated in delight. "Are you really a police officer, my dear?"

"I wasn't good enough to do anything else," said Rooth. "But this Bonger character—if you knew him so well, perhaps you have some idea of where he might be?"

A few seconds passed while the large woman's facial expression

turned serious. She peered between swollen eyelids at Fru Jümpers, who was meticulously blending the coffee and gin. Then she
cleared her throat.

"Either he's been murdered," she said.

She lifted her mug. Three seconds passed.

"Or?" said Jung.

"Or he's done a runner."

"Don't talk crap," said Fru Jümpers.

"Why would he do a runner?" asked Rooth.

"Business," said Barga secretively. "He had no choice."

Jung stared skeptically at her and Rooth shook his head.

"What kind of business?"

"Debts," said Barga, tapping the table three times with her fist.
"He owed a lot of money. They were after him; I spoke to him just
a few days before he disappeared. He's gone underground, that's
all there is to it. You don't play around with the characters in that
branch."

"What branch?" wondered Rooth.

"It could have something to do with his sister as well," said
Barga, gazing down into her mug as if her friend had got the proportions wrong.

"I didn't know he had a sister," said Jung. "Where does she live?"

"Nobody knows," interjected Fru Jümpers. "She also vanished
in mysterious circumstances. . . . When would it be now? Fifteen
years ago? About that. Lost her mind and turned up later in Lim-
burg, or so they say."

"What branch were you talking about?" Rooth insisted.

"I'm not saying, so I haven't said anything," said Barga, fishing
out a crumpled cigarette. "It's not good to give your tongue its
head."

"For Christ's sake," Jung said with a sigh.

"Cheers!" said Fru Jümpers. "Pay no attention to her. She always rambles on like that when she doesn't know what she's talking about. She's been senile for the last thirty years."

"Bah," said Barga, lighting a cigarette. "Bonger had problems, there's no doubt about that. My tip is that he's in Hamburg or maybe South America, and that he'll make damn well sure he doesn't come back here."

There was silence for a few seconds while the mugs were emptied. Then Rooth thought it was time to change tack.

"Why is his boat moored as it is?" he asked. "It seems a bit odd."

Fru Jümpers belched. "It's been moored like that for twenty years. The former owner did it—he was a Muslim of some kind or other and wanted open water on all sides of his boat, said it was good for his karma or something."

Jung suspected she had mixed up the religions, but let it pass. He glanced at Rooth, who was looking increasingly tormented. *Best to leave it at that,* he thought.

"Anyway, we'd better be making a move," he said, draining the last drops from his mug.

"You may be right," said Rooth. "Thank you very much. It's been most interesting."

"Bye-bye," said Barga, waving her cigarette around. "Make sure you clean up some of the riffraff so that it's safe for a respectable lady to walk home."

"Huh, kiss my ass," said Fru Jümpers.

"What the hell did we come here for?" wondered Rooth when they were back on the frosty quay.

Jung shrugged.

"Beats me. Münster just wanted us to check up on the situation. He seems to have trouble in letting this case go."

Rooth nodded glumly.

"He certainly does," he said. "As far as I'm concerned I'd like to forget all about this visit. I've come across fairer maidens in my time."

"I should hope so," said Jung. "But what do you think about that Barga?"

Rooth shuddered.

"Away with the fairies," he said. "Nothing of what she said made sense. First it was a mystery, then she knew all about it. . . . But if Bonger really did owe money, surely this was an ideal situation for him to pay it back, now that they'd won the lottery."

"Exactly what I was thinking," said Jung.

"I doubt it," said Rooth. "Can we move on now?"

"By all means," said Jung.

Moreno drove up to Wernice. She doubted if she would be well received by Ruth Leverkuhn, and while she sat waiting for the bascule bridge over the Maar to go up and down, she also wondered about the point of the visit. Always assuming there was one. Ruth Leverkuhn had sounded off-putting on the telephone, finding it hard to understand why the police needed to stick their noses further into this personal tragedy than they had done already.

Her father had been murdered in his bed.

Her mother had confessed to doing it.

Wasn't that enough?

Was it really necessary to pester the survivors, and didn't the police have more important things to do?

Moreno had to admit she could understand Leverkuhn's point of view.

The visit didn't turn out to be especially successful.

Ruth Leverkuhn received her in a loose-fitting wine-red tracksuit with the text PUP FOR THE CUP in flaking yellow letters over her chest. She had a wet towel wound around her head, dripping water on her bosom and shoulders, and on her feet were wrinkled, thick skiing socks. On the whole she was not a pretty sight.

"Migraine," she explained. "I'm in the middle of an attack. Can we keep this as short as possible?"

"I realize this must be very traumatic for you," Moreno began, "but there are a few things we'd like to shed some light on."

"Really?" said Leverkuhn. "What exactly?"

She led the way into a living room with low, soft sofas, Oriental fans, and a mass of brightly colored fluffy cushions. The apartment was on the fifth floor, and the picture window gave a splendid view over the flat landscape with scattered clumps of bare deciduous trees, church towers, and arrow-straight canals. The sky was covered in rain clouds, and mist was starting to roll in from the sea like a shroud. Moreno stood for a few moments taking in the scenery before sinking down among the fluff.

"What a lovely view you have!" she said. "It must be very pleasant to sit here, watching dusk fall."

But Leverkuhn was not particularly interested in beauty today. She muttered something and sat down opposite Moreno on the other side of the low cane table.

"What do you want to know?" she asked after a few seconds of silence.

Moreno took a deep breath.

"Were you surprised?" she said.

"What?" said Leverkuhn.

"When you heard she had confessed. Did you get another shock, or had you suspected that it was your mother who was guilty?"

Leverkuhn adjusted the wet towel over her forehead.

"I don't see the point of this," she said. "The fact is that my mother has killed my father. Isn't that enough? Why do you want details? Why do you want to drag us even further through the mud? Can't you understand how it feels?"

Her voice sounded unsteady. Moreno guessed that it was to do with the migraine medicine, and began wondering once again why she was sitting there. Using her job as cover for her own therapy was not especially attractive, now that she came to think about it.

"So you weren't surprised when your mother confessed?" she said.

No reply.

"And then we have the other two strange occurrences," Moreno continued. "Herr Bonger and Fru Van Eck. Did you know them?"

Leverkuhn shook her head.

"But you have met them?"

"I suppose I must have seen the Van Ecks once or twice. But I've no idea who Bonger is."

"One of your father's friends," said Moreno.

"Did he have any friends?"

It slipped out before she could stop it. Moreno could see clearly that she wanted to bite her tongue off.

"What do you mean by that?"

Leverkuhn shrugged.

"Nothing."

"Was your father a solitary person?"

No reply.

"You don't know much about his habits in recent years, then? Friends and such?"

"No."

"Do you know if they socialized with the Van Ecks occasionally? Your father and mother, that is? Either of them?"

"I have no idea."

"How often did you visit your parents?"

"Hardly ever. You know that already. We don't have a good relationship."

"So you didn't like your father?"

But now Ruth Leverkuhn had had enough.

"I . . . I'm not going to answer any more questions," she said. "You have no right to come poking around into my private life. Don't you think we've suffered enough from all this?"

"Yes," said Moreno. "Of course I do. But no matter how awful it might seem, we have to try to find our way to the truth. That's our job."

That sounded a bit pompous—find our way to the truth!—and she wondered where that formulation could have come from. A few moments passed before Leverkuhn answered.

"The truth?" she said, slowly and thoughtfully, turning her head and apparently directing her attention at the sky and the landscape. "You don't know what you're talking about. Why should anybody go digging after something which is ugly and repulsive? If the truth were a beautiful pearl, then yes, I could understand why anyone should want to go hunting after it; but as it is . . . well, why not let it lie hidden, if somebody is managing to hide it so well?"

Those were momentous words coming from such a sloppy woman, Moreno thought, and as she drove back home she wondered what they could mean.

The ugly snout of the truth?

Was it merely a general reflection about a family with bad internal relationships, and the feeling of hopelessness after the final catastrophe? Or was it something more than that?

Something more tangible and concrete?

As dusk was falling and she drove into Maardam over the Fourth of November Bridge and along Zwille, she still hadn't found an answer to these questions.

Apart from an irritating feeling that she was absolutely sure about.

There was more to this story than had come to light. A lot more. And therefore good reason to continue with these efforts to penetrate the darkness.

Even if the pearls were black and cracked.

26

The trial of Marie-Louise Leverkuhn dragged on over three long afternoons in the presence of dwindling audiences in the public gallery. The only person who seemed to have any doubts about her guilt—going by the grim expressions on his face—was Judge Hart, who occasionally intervened with questions that neither the prosecutor nor defense counsel seemed to have bothered with.

Nor had she, come to that.

Otherwise, it seemed that the line of truth was going to be drawn somewhere in the gray area between murder and manslaughter. In accordance with a series of points difficult to pin down, such as *reasonable doubt, temporary state of unsound mind, degree of legal competency, time for reflection in prevailing circumstances*—and so on.

She found these questions pointless. Instead of listening while they were being argued about, she often sat observing members of the jury. These unimpeachable men and women holding her fate in their hands—or imagining that they did so, at least. For some reason it was one of the two women who captured her interest. A dark-haired woman aged sixty-something—not much younger than she was. Slim and wiry, but with a certain stature that was noticeable mainly in the way she held her head: she hardly ever looked at the person who happened to be speaking—usually the prosecutor or the tiresome Bachmann—but seemed to be concentrating on something else. Something inside herself.

Or more elevated. *I could entrust myself to a woman like that,* thought Marie-Louise Leverkuhn.

The prosecution had called three witnesses in all, the defense one. She was never quite sure precisely what role the prosecutor's henchmen were supposed to be playing: if she understood it rightly, they comprised a doctor, a pathologist, and some kind of police officer. Their evidence merely confirmed what was claimed to be known already, and perhaps that was the point: Judge Hart asked a few questions that could have opened up new avenues of thought, but nobody seemed to be particularly interested. Nothing was really at stake, and the ventilation in the rather chilly room left a lot to be desired—best to get it all over with as painlessly as possible, everybody seemed to be agreed on that. Nevertheless, interrogation of the witnesses for the prosecution took almost two hours.

Emmeline von Post, the defense's so-called character witness, took up considerably less time (probably about a quarter of an hour; she didn't check). All in all it was a rather painful episode. But nothing else could reasonably have been expected. Bachmann hadn't told her that he intended to put Emmeline on the stand—if he had, she would have prevented him. No doubt about that.

After Emmeline von Post had come to the stand, confirmed who she was, and sworn the oath, barely half a minute passed before she burst out crying. Judge Hart adjourned proceedings while a female usher hurried up to administer a carafe of water, some tissues, and a dose of humane sympathy.

Bachmann then managed to continue for a few minutes before she collapsed in tears again. Another pause ensued, with snuffling and more tissues, and when the poor woman finally seemed to be more or less composed, Bachmann took his courage in both hands and asked her the crucial question without beating around the bush.

"You have known the accused almost all your life, Fru von Post.

Given your familiarity with her character, do you consider it credible that she would murder her husband with premeditation in the way that the prosecution has tried to suggest?"

Emmeline von Post (who naturally had no idea of what the prosecution had tried to suggest, as she had not had the right to be present in court until it was her turn) sobbed several times. Then she replied in a comparatively steady voice: "She would never hurt a fly. I can swear to that."

Bachmann had no more questions.

Nor did Prosecutor Grootner.

Not even Judge Hart.

The final pleas were made on Friday, a performance confusingly similar to the opening session on Tuesday. When it was over Hart declared the proceedings closed. Sentence would be passed the following Thursday: until then Marie-Louise Leverkuhn would be remanded as had been the case since her arrest thirty-nine days ago—in cell number 12 in the women's section of the jail in the Maardam police station.

As she sat in the car taking her back to her cell she felt more relieved than anything else. To the best of her knowledge nothing had gone wrong during the trial (apart from the Emmeline von Post farce, but that had nothing to do with the main business), and all that remained now was a few days of waiting.

No more decisions. No questions. No lies.

It rained almost all weekend. Somewhere below her little window was a corrugated iron roof, on which the variations in the rain were just as clear as the notes from a musical instrument. She liked it: lying stretched out on the bed with the green blanket pulled up to her chin and the window slightly open. . . . Yes, there was something deeply soothing about it. Something inside her was finally able to rest.

Something had come home after a long, long journey.

It was remarkable.

The chaplain came to see her as usual. A short visit on both Saturday and Sunday. He sat there in his corner half asleep, as if keeping watch at a deathbed. She liked the idea of that as well.

Bachmann had threatened to put in an appearance and talk her through the situation, but she realized that it was no more than an empty promise typical of his profession. He had looked very depressed during the final days of the trial, and she had not encouraged him to come to visit her. And so he didn't.

Ruth phoned on Friday evening and Mauritz did the same early on Saturday morning, but it was Sunday afternoon before Ruth's large body flopped down on the chair.

"Mom," she said after the initial silence.

"Yes, what do you want?" said Marie-Louise Leverkuhn.

That was a question her daughter was unable to answer, and not much more was said. After twenty minutes she vented a deep sigh and left her mother to her own devices.

It felt almost like a sort of victory when the door was locked behind her, Marie-Louise thought. It was strange that she should think that, of course; but that's the way it was.

Things had turned out the way they had, and that's the way it was. Only a few minutes after Ruth had left, she fell asleep and had a dream.

She was on a train. It was racing through flat, monotonous countryside, at such high speed that it was almost impossible to make out anything that flashed past the dirty, scratched window.

Even so, she knew that what was out there was life. Her own life. Flashing past at high speed. She was sitting with her back to the engine, and it soon became clear that she was getting younger the farther they traveled. The same applied to her fellow passengers. The young woman sitting opposite her was suddenly no more than a little girl, and the elderly man in the corner with the shaking hands and bewildered eyes was soon transformed into a smart, blue-eyed young man in uniform.

A journey backward through life. On and on it went until everyone was only a small child, and when someone in the carriage became so small that he or she looked like a newborn baby, the train stopped at a station. A few people in long, white coats with stethoscopes around their necks came on board and picked up the pink little lumps from the dirty seats. Made them all belch and cry a little, collected the blue ticket that they were each holding in their tiny hands, and left the train with the little creatures over their shoulders.

When it was her turn—it was an unusually big and fat doctor with wings on his back who lifted her up—it turned out that she didn't have a ticket.

"Haven't you got a ticket?" asked the man sternly—she could now see that he was an angel. "In that case you can't be born."

"Thank you, oh, thank you!" She smiled up into his florid face. "If I can't be born, I suppose that means I don't need to live?"

"Ho ho," said the angel cryptically and put her back down on the seat.

And so she continued the train journey into eternity, through the night of the unborn.

And she was happy. When she woke up she had butterflies in her stomach.

I don't need to live.

Mauritz also came on Sunday. At about half past six, just after the warden had been in to collect the dinner tray.

He had spent five hours in the car driving there and seemed stressed and irritated. Although perhaps it was just his customary insecurity that lay behind it. He rang for coffee, said that he wanted some, but when it was actually standing on the shaky plastic table, he never touched it.

He also had difficulty in finding anything to say, just as Ruth had done. All they talked about were things like prison routines and the situation on the candle-ring front in the run-up to Christmas. Mainly red and green this year, it seemed. She wished he would leave, and after half an hour said as much.

He had assumed there would be this kind of difficulty, and so he had written a letter. He stood up and produced it from an inside pocket in his ugly blazer with the firm's emblem on the breast pocket. He handed it over without a word, then rang the bell and was let out.

It was only one and a half pages long. She read it three times. Then she tore it up into tiny pieces and flushed it down the toilet in the scruffy little booth in the corner of the cell.

It took a while. The pieces kept floating back up to the surface, and as she stood there pressing the flush button over and over again, she made up her mind what to do next.

She called the warden again, asked for pencil and paper, and shortly afterward sat down at the little table to search for the right words.

The only surprise she felt at her decision was how easy it had been to make. Half an hour later she drank tea and ate a couple of sandwiches with an eager appetite, as if life were still something relevant to her.

27

Moreno had gotten in touch with Krystyna Gravenstein via the secretary at Doggers grammar school, where she had worked until she retired three years ago.

Gravenstein welcomed her into the little two-bedroom apartment in Palitzerstraat, at the top of the building with a view over the river and Megsje Bois. Moreno wondered if everybody had such splendid views from their homes nowadays when she entered the apartment, and recalled Ruth Leverkuhn's picture window. It seemed to be the case, at least for home owners on the distaff side. Fröken Gravenstein was a slim little woman with a mass of chalk-white hair and owl eyes behind thick spectacles. Tweed suit and crocheted shawl over her shoulders. She moved a pile of books from a tubular steel armchair and urged the inspector to sit down, sat down herself on a revolving chair in front of a desk, and spun around. Of the two rooms, one served as a bedroom and the other a study. Moreno guessed that nothing else was required. The desk, with a view of rooftops and the open sky, was covered in papers, books, dictionaries, and a computer. Bookshelves covered the walls from floor to ceiling and were chockablock with books.

"I've started to do a bit of translating since I finished at the school," Gravenstein explained, with a faint suggestion of a smile. "You have to find something to do. Italian and French. It helps to make the pension go a bit further as well."

Moreno nodded in agreement.

"Literature, I assume?" she asked.

"Yes," said Gravenstein. "Mostly poetry, but I've done the occasional novel as well."

"So you used to teach at Doggers, right? Romance languages?"

"For thirty-seven years . . . Thirty-seven . . ."

She shrugged and looked somewhat apologetic. Moreno gathered that she didn't exactly long to be back in front of classes again. And that it was time to come to the point.

"You were a colleague of Else Van Eck's, I understand," she began. "That's why I want to talk to you. Are you aware of what has happened?"

"She's vanished," said Gravenstein, adjusting her spectacles.

"Exactly," said Moreno. "She's been missing for nearly seven weeks now, and we still don't have a clue where she is. There are good reasons for suspecting she is no longer with us. Were you close to her as a colleague?"

Her hostess shook her head and looked worried.

"No," she said. "Certainly not. Nobody was—I'm sorry to have to say that, but it's the way it was. We never met in our free time—apart from the odd occasion when the French Society had something interesting in its program."

"How long did you work together?"

Gravenstein worked it out.

"Nearly twenty years," she said. "Else Van Eck is a . . . a remarkable woman. Or was."

"In what way?" wondered Moreno.

Fröken Gravenstein adjusted her shawl while she thought that over.

"Unsociable," she said in the end. "She had no desire to associate with or even to talk to the rest of us teachers. She wasn't unpleasant, but she didn't bother with other people. She was self-sufficient, if you know what I mean."

"What was she like as a teacher?"

Gravenstein gave a hint of a smile.

"Excellent," she said. "That might sound unlikely, but it's a fact. Once the pupils had gotten used to her, they liked her. Maybe young people find it easier to get on with weirdos—I think so. And she loved French. She never taught any other subject, and—well, she was a walking dictionary. And grammar book as well. Obviously she would never have been able to stay on as a member of the staff if she hadn't had those qualities. Not in view of the way she was."

Moreno thought for a moment.

"And why was she the way she was?"

"I haven't the slightest idea. I never got to know her, and know nothing about her private life."

"What about her professional life?" Moreno asked. "Do you know why she became a French teacher?"

Gravenstein hesitated.

"There is a story," she said.

"A story?" Moreno said.

Fröken Gravenstein bit her lip and contemplated her hands. Seemed to be discussing something with herself.

"One of those myths," she said. "The kind that circulate among pupils about almost every teacher. Sometimes there's a grain of truth in them, sometimes there isn't. But you can't put too much faith in them."

"And what was the mythology surrounding Else Van Eck?" Moreno asked.

"A love story."

Moreno nodded encouragingly.

"Young and unhappy love," explained Gravenstein. "A Frenchman. They were engaged and were going to get married, but then he left her for somebody else."

Moreno said nothing, waited for a while.

"Not especially imaginative," she said eventually.

"There's more to come," said Fröken Gravenstein. "According

to legend, she started reading French for his sake, and she continued doing so. His name was said to be Albert, and after a while he regretted what he'd done. Tried to win her back. But Else refused to forgive him. When it finally got through to him what he'd done, he hurled himself in front of a train and died. Gare du Nord. Hmm . . ."

"Hmm," Moreno agreed. "And when was this supposed to have happened?"

Gravenstein threw her arms out wide.

"I don't know. When she was young, of course. Shortly after the war, I assume."

Moreno sighed. Krystyna Gravenstein suddenly smiled broadly.

"Everybody must have a story," she said. "For those who don't, we need to invent one."

She glanced up at the rows of books as she said that, and Moreno realized that it was a quotation. And that the words had a certain relevance to Gravenstein's life as well.

What's my story? Moreno thought in the elevator on the way down. *Claus? My police work? Or do I have to invent one?*

She shuddered when she realized that there were less than seven days to go to Christmas, and she had no idea how she was going to spend the holiday.

I might as well volunteer to work over all the time, she thought. *If I could make things easier for a colleague, why not?*

Then she thought for a while about Albert.

A Frenchman who had taken his own life fifty years ago or more? For the sake of Else Van Eck. Would it be possible to track him down?

And could it have anything at all to do with this case that Intendent Münster insisted on persevering with and poking about in?

No, nothing at all, she decided. Could anything possibly be more far-fetched? Nevertheless, she decided to report the matter.

To tell the story. The myth. If anything, it would be nice to sit and talk about it for a while with Münster. Surely she could grant herself that much?

Anyway, Krystyna Gravenstein seemed to have sorted out quite a pleasant way of spending her old age, Moreno thought. Sitting up under the roof beams among lots of books high above the town, and doing nothing but reading and writing. . . . Not a bad existence.

But before you get that far, of course, you had to find your way through life. She sighed and started walking back to the police station.

Münster checked his watch. Then counted the Christmas presents in the backseat.

Twelve in an hour and a half. Not bad. That gave him plenty of time for his visit to Pampas, and he gathered that the widowed Fru de Grooit didn't like being rushed. Peace and quiet, and there's a time for everything—that's what it had sounded like on the telephone.

He parked in the street outside the low, drab, brown house. Sat there for a minute, composing himself and wondering what exactly it was that prevented him from letting go of this business.

In his infinite wisdom Chief of Police Hiller had declared that in the name of all that's holy there was no rational reason for wasting any more resources on this case. Waldemar Leverkuhn had been murdered. His wife had confessed to doing it, and on Thursday she would be found guilty of either murder or manslaughter. He didn't give a crap which. A certain Felix Bonger had gone missing and a certain Else Van Eck had gone missing.

"So what?" Hiller had asked, and Münster knew that he was right. The average number of people who went missing in their district was fifteen to eighteen per year, and the fact that two of them happened to disappear at about the same time as the Leverkuhn business was pure coincidence.

Naturally the police continued to look for the two missing persons—just as they did for all the others who had gone up in smoke—but it wasn't a job for highly paid (overpaid!) detectives.

Waste of fucking time. Full stop. Exit Hiller.

It's a damned nuisance, having to work on the sly, Münster thought as he got out of the car.

But if you are an uncompromising seeker of the truth, you must grin and bear it.

"Really, I couldn't believe my eyes when I read about it in the paper," said Fru de Grooit. "Take a cookie. They used to live over there, and we called on one another almost every day."

She pointed out the cluttered window at the house on the other side of the hedge.

"Over there," she repeated. "Between 1952 and 1976. We moved in when the house was new in 1948, and since my husband died I've often thought I ought to move out, but I've never gotten around to it. Don't be afraid to dunk if you want to. It's terrible. We're normal people here in Pampas. Honest working people, not murderers. I talk too much, do interrupt me if you need to. My husband always used to say you have to interrupt me in order to shut me up."

"Did you know the Leverkuhns well?" Münster asked.

"Well . . . no, not really," said Fru de Grooit, blinking a little nervously. "We always had more to do with the Van Klusters and the Bolmeks on the other side and opposite, not so much with the Leverkuhns, no. . . . It wasn't that . . ."

She fell silent and looked thoughtful.

"Wasn't what?" Münster asked.

"It wasn't that they weren't good neighbors and good people, but they tended to keep their distance. They were like that, especially him."

"Waldemar Leverkuhn?"

"Herr Leverkuhn, yes. A reserved man, not easy to talk to;

but an honest worker, nobody could possibly suggest anything else. . . . It's awful. Do you think she really murdered him in that terrible way? I don't know what to think anymore. How was the coffee?"

"Good," said Münster.

It looked for a moment as if Fru de Grooit was going to start crying. Münster coughed to distract her while he thought of something to say, but he couldn't think of anything that might console her.

"Did you know Fru Leverkuhn a little better, then?" was the best he could do. "Better than him, that is. Woman to woman."

But Fru de Grooit shook her head.

"No," she said. "She wasn't the type to get chummy with, and if you ever needed to borrow some sugar or flour, it was natural to go to one of the other neighbors—the Van Klusters or Bolmeks. On the other side and opposite. Has she really killed him?"

"It looks like it," said Münster. "What were the children like?"

Fru de Grooit fiddled with her coffee cup and didn't reply immediately.

"They were also reserved," she said after a while. "They didn't have any real friends, none of them. Mauritz was exactly the same age as our Bertrand, we had him late, but they never became good friends. We tried ten, twenty times, but he always preferred to be at home on his own, playing with his electric train set, Mauritz did—and don't think that Bertrand was allowed to join in. There was something . . . something mean, something off-putting about the boy. I think he had a rough time at school as well. And with girls—no, it wasn't exactly a home with open doors, certainly not."

"Have you had any contact with them in recent years?" Münster asked. "Since they left here?"

"None at all," said Fru de Grooit. "They moved out and disappeared. From one day to the next. The children had already flown the nest, of course, so it was easier for them with an apartment— they were never very interested in the garden. They didn't even leave an address. We heard later that things had gone badly for Irene. . . ."

"Really?" said Münster, pretending to be surprised.

"Nerves," said Fru de Grooit. "She just couldn't cope, that's all there was to it. Some people just can't cope, that's the way it's always been. They put her in a home, I don't know if she's come out again. They were introverted as well, the sisters—you never saw them with boys. Always kept themselves to themselves. No, it wasn't a happy family, if you can put it like that. But one knows so little about it."

She fell silent again, sighed, and stirred her coffee. Münster wondered what he had hoped to get out of this conversation, but realized that it was just a matter of blind chance. Yet again.

Maybe something will crop up, maybe not.

That's not a bad motto for police work overall, he thought. *A vain and arbitrary search for a needle in a haystack, that's exactly what it always seemed to be like.*

Or, as Reinhart preferred to put it: a cop is a blind tortoise looking for a snowball in the desert.

There were plenty of appropriate images.

"I remember one incident," said Fru de Grooit after a few moments of silence. "That Mauritz didn't have an easy time at school, as I said. He was in the same class as our Bertrand, and on one occasion he'd been beaten up by some older boys. I don't know how serious it was, or what lay behind it, but in any case, he didn't dare go back to school. . . . And he didn't dare stay at home either, scared of what his parents would say or do—Fru Leverkuhn was out of work when it happened. So he would pretend to go off to school in the morning, but instead of being in school he was hiding away in the shed at the back of their house all day. He can't have been more than about eleven or twelve at the time: his sisters knew about it and looked after him. . . . One of them was also without a job and so was at home all day and she used to smuggle sandwiches out to him. He sat there day after day, for about two weeks at least. . . ."

"Didn't the school ask about where he was?" Münster asked.

She shrugged. Brushed some imaginary crumbs off the tablecloth.

"Eventually, yes. I think he got a good beating from his dad then. For being such a coward."

"Not a very good way of making him any braver," said Münster.

"No," said Fru de Grooit. "But that's the way he was, Waldemar."

"How was he?" asked Münster.

"Hard, sort of."

"You didn't like him, I gather?"

Fru de Grooit looked a little embarrassed.

"I don't really know," she said. "It was a long time ago. We didn't have a lot to do with them, and you have to leave people in peace if that's what they want. It takes all sorts. . . . Everybody is happy in his own way."

"You're absolutely right," said Münster.

He went for a walk among the little detached houses in Pampas when he left Fru de Grooit. He was pretty fed up with the little houses, but the weather was pleasant enough for walking.

This Pampas was a rather special part of town, it couldn't be denied. And he hadn't been here for ages. The low-lying, almost swampy area next to the river had not been built on until shortly after the war, when all at once these rows of tiny houses sprang up, all of them with only three or four rooms, on plots barely large enough to accommodate them. A local council project to provide owner-occupied houses for hardworking laborers and junior office workers, if he understood it correctly. A sort of clumsy attempt to boost the lower classes in the direction of equality, and all of them—more than six hundred houses—were still standing in more or less unchanged condition after nearly fifty years. Repaired and modernized and extended here and there, but nevertheless remarkably intact.

Postwar optimism, Münster thought. *A monument to an age.*

And to a generation that was disappearing into the grave.

Like Fru de Grooit and the Leverkuhns.

I'll never get any further with this damned case, he thought as he settled behind the wheel of his car. *It's going to stand as still as Pampas. Nothing more is going to happen.*

But that is where Intendent Münster was wrong.

In spades.

28

If Vera Kretschke's boyfriend hadn't given her the boot the previous evening—on December 20—she would presumably have slept a bit better.

If she had slept a bit better, she would obviously have been able to run all the way around her jogging route without any problems. She usually did.

If she had managed to run all the way, she certainly wouldn't have stopped after one and a half miles and started walking instead of running.

And if she hadn't started walking as slowly as she did, well, she would never have noticed that yellow bit of plastic sticking up from the undergrowth in among the trees a few feet from the path.

Probably not, in any case.

And then . . . then that awful image would not be filling her head like a lump of hot goo, preventing her from having much in the way of rational thoughts.

That's what she was thinking as she lay in bed that same evening in her old, secure, childhood room, waiting for Reuben to ring despite everything—if not to apologize and take back what he'd said, then at least so that she could tell him what had happened while she was out jogging that morning.

Jogging and walking.

. . .

What an ugly sight, she thought, and stopped. *Why couldn't people dispose of things in the right place instead of out here in the forest?*

Weyler's Woods was not a large nature park, but it was popular and well looked after. There were recycling bins and garbage bins alongside all the paths for walkers and joggers that crisscrossed the forest in all directions, and she didn't usually need to stop and pick up rubbish that had been dumped like this.

Occasionally a popsicle stick or an empty cigarette packet, perhaps, but not a big plastic carrier bag.

Vera Kretschke was the chairman of her school's environmental society—had been for the last three semesters—and she felt a certain responsibility.

She stepped out resolutely into the undergrowth. Shook the raindrops off the young birch sapling before ducking down underneath it and pulling out the plastic grocery bag. Most of it had been hidden under leaves and twigs, and she had to pull quite hard to get it loose.

Dirty bastards, she thought. *Filthy pigs.*

Then she looked inside the bag.

It contained a head. A woman's head.

She started vomiting without being able to stop. It came spurting out of her, just as it had done that time a few years ago when she'd eaten something dodgy at the Indian restaurant in the center of town.

Some of it came into the bag as well. Which naturally didn't make matters any better.

And Reuben didn't phone, so there was another sleepless night in store for poor Vera Kretschke.

"Fucking hell!" roared Inspector Fuller. "This sort of thing simply shouldn't happen."

Warder Schmidt shook his large head and looked unhappy.

"But it has happened. . . ."

"How the hell did she do it?" said Fuller.

Schmidt sighed.

"Ripped up the blanket to make a rope, I think. And then used that little bit of pipe high up in the corner—we've talked about that before."

"I take it you've cut her down?"

"No . . ." Schmidt shuffled and squirmed uneasily. "No, we thought you might like to take a look at her first."

"Holy shit," muttered Fuller, getting to his feet.

"We found her only a couple of minutes ago," said Schmidt apologetically. "Wacker is there now, but she's dead, there's no doubt about that. And there's a letter on the table as well."

But Inspector Fuller had already elbowed his way past and was charging down the corridor toward cell number 12.

Damn, thought Schmidt. *And it's my birthday today.*

When Fuller had established that Fru Leverkuhn really was in the state that had been reported, he arranged for a dozen photographs to be taken and had her cut down. Then he sent for a doctor, took a couple of tablets to calm his upset stomach, and phoned Intendent Münster.

Münster took the elevator down and eyed the dead woman on the bed in her cell for ten seconds. Asked Fuller how the hell something like this could happen, then took the elevator back up to his office.

He read the letter twice, rang Moreno, and explained the situation.

"Quite unambiguous," said Moreno after reading Marie-Louise Leverkuhn's final message to the world.

"Yes, very clear," said Münster. "She's done her husband in, and now it was her turn. She was a woman of action, nobody can take that from her."

He stood up and looked out at the rain.

"But it's a bugger that she's committed suicide in her cell," he muttered. "They'll have to revise their procedures. Hiller looked like a plum about to explode when he heard about it."

"I can imagine," said Moreno. "But she did it well. Did you see the rope she made? Plaited four strands thick, it must have taken her several hours. A man would never have been able to do it."

Münster said nothing. A few seconds of silence passed.

"Why did she do it?" asked Moreno. "I mean, I can understand that she didn't particularly fancy spending the last years of her life in prison, but . . . was that all?"

"What else could it be?" said Münster. "I guess that's a good enough reason. If there's anything to wonder about, it's why she waited until now. It's not exactly straightforward to commit suicide in a prison cell. Even if you are skilled, and the routines are bad. Or what do you think? Why now?"

Moreno shrugged.

"I don't know. But there doesn't seem to be much point in speculating now. We've got the key, after all."

Münster sighed and turned around.

"What a pointless life," he said.

"Marie-Louise Leverkuhn's?"

"Yes. Can you see any point in it? She murdered her husband, then killed herself. One of her children is in a psychiatric hospital, and the other two are not exactly the life of any party. No grandchildren. Well, you tell me if there's some point that I've missed."

Moreno glanced at the letter again. Folded it up and put it back in the envelope.

"No," she said. "But that's the way it is. It's not likely to be a story with a happy ending if we're involved in it."

"I suppose so," said Münster. "But there ought to be limits nevertheless. . . . The occasional diamond among all the shit. What are you doing for Christmas?"

Moreno pulled a face.

"The main thing is that I don't have to see Claus," she said. "He's due back tomorrow. At first I intended working over the holidays, but then I bumped into an old friend who had just been dumped. We're taking six bottles of wine with us to her house by the sea."

Münster smiled. Didn't dare ask about details of the Claus situation. Or what state she was in now. There were certain things that had nothing to do with him, and the less he asked, the better. It was safer that way.

"Good for you," he said. "Make sure you don't swim out too far."

"I promise," she said.

"I'm working tomorrow," said Münster as he shuffled the cards for Marieke. "Then I'm off for six days."

"About time," said Synn. "I don't want this autumn back again. We need to find a strategy to overcome this, we really do."

"A strategy?" said Münster.

"Star-tea-gee," said Marieke. "Jack of clubs."

"I'm serious," said Synn. "It's better to throttle the depression before it makes a mess of everything. We have to make time to live. Remember that my mother went to the wall at the age of forty-five. She lived to be seventy, but she didn't smile once during the last twenty-five years."

"I know," said Münster. "But you're only thirty-eight. And you look like twenty-two."

"Seven of hearts," said Marieke. "Your turn! How old are you, Daddy?"

"A hundred and three," said Münster. "But I feel older. All right, I agree with you. We need to do something."

For a second he tried to compare his life with that of the Leverkuhn family: tried to see where they stood in relation to one another—but the thought was so absurd that it collapsed immediately.

"We'll start the day after tomorrow," he said. "Was there any mail today?"

"Only bills and this," said Synn, handing him a white envelope. He opened it and took out a sheet of paper folded twice.

It was a brief message. Only three words. Dated two days ago.

It's not her.
V.V.

"Queen of spades," said Marieke. "Your turn!"
"Oh hell . . . ," said Intendent Münster.

29

Judgment in the Marie-Louise Leverkuhn case was announced the morning of Monday, December 22, in the Maardam courthouse.

Unanimously, the jury had found Fru Leverkuhn guilty of the first-degree murder of her husband, Waldemar Severin Leverkuhn, in accordance with paragraphs forty-three and forty-four of the penal code. She was sentenced to six years in prison, the shortest time allowed by the law: Judge Hart announced in all seriousness that this reflected the fact that the guilty person was already dead and hence was not expected to serve the sentence.

He then explained that an appeal against the verdict could be lodged in accordance with usual procedures within ninety days, slammed his enormous gavel down on the desk, and declared the case closed.

Pathologist Meusse dried his hands on his coat and looked up.

"Yes, what is it?"

Rooth cleared his throat.

"It's about a skull. . . ."

"That skull," added Jung.

Meusse glared at them over the edge of his misted-up glasses and beckoned them to follow him. He led the way through a series of chilly rooms before finally coming to a stop in front of a large refrigerator.

"It's in here," he said, opening the door. "Unless I'm mistaken."

He took out a white plastic sack and lifted up a decapitated woman's head by her hair. It was swollen and discolored, with blotches and pustules of every hue from ocher to deep lilac. The eyes were closed, but a few centimeters of dark brown tongue were sticking out of the mouth. The nose looked like a lump of excrement. Jung could feel his stomach turning over and hoped he wouldn't be forced to leave the room.

"Holy shit!" said Rooth.

"Yes, it's not going to win a beauty contest," said Meusse. "She could have been lying there for a couple of months, I think. The plastic bag was high quality, otherwise more might have been nibbled away."

Rooth swallowed and averted his gaze. For want of anything else he found himself looking at Jung, who was standing about a foot away. Jung felt another spasm in his stomach and closed his eyes.

"Do you recognize her?" asked Rooth, his voice shaking.

Jung opened his eyes and nodded vaguely.

"I think so," he said. "Can you say anything about the cause of death?"

Meusse put the head back into the bag.

"Not yet," he said. "She took a few hefty blows with something heavy on the crown of her head, but God only knows if that's what killed her. But she must have blacked out in any case, it's one hell of a contusion. You reckon you know who she is?"

"We think so," said Rooth. "Two months, is that what you said?"

"Plus or minus a few weeks," said Meusse. "You'll get more accurate data the day after tomorrow."

"That will be Christmas Eve," said Rooth.

"You don't say?" said Meusse.

"How was she decapitated?" asked Jung.

Meusse stroked over his own bald head a few times as if to check that it was still in place.

"A knife," he said. "A butcher's cleaver, I think. Not the instruments I would have chosen myself for that kind of operation, but it clearly worked okay."

"Clearly," said Rooth.

"How old?" asked Jung.

Meusse snorted.

"If you know who it is, you ought to know how old she is," he muttered, and started walking back to his office.

"Just double-checking," Rooth explained. "Our lady was close to seventy. Does that fit?"

"Not too bad," said Meusse. "This head seems to be between sixty-five and seventy-five, according to my preliminary calculations. But I didn't receive her until yesterday afternoon, so I don't want to be more precise than that yet."

Jung nodded. He had never heard Meusse being prepared to give an exact estimation, but on the other hand, he had never heard of Meusse ever guessing wrong. If Meusse said that the head they had just been gaping at belonged to a woman of about seventy who had been beaten to death with a blunt instrument hitting the crown of her head about two months ago, there were doubtless good reasons for believing that this was in fact the case.

And that the woman in question was Else Van Eck, and no one else.

"Hmm," said Rooth when they emerged from the Forensic Medicine Department and turned up their collars to keep out the driving drizzle. "That was a turn-up for the bloody books. Changes things quite a bit, I suspect."

"Maybe we ought to give Münster a ring," said Jung.

"No doubt we should," said Rooth. "But I'm thinking we ought to get a bite to eat first; this is going to cause masses of work and trouble, I can feel it coming."

"I'm sure you're right," said Jung. "It's in the air."

IV

30

He woke up and didn't know who he was.

It took a second, or half of one, but it had been there. The moment of complete blankness in which no past existed. No memories. No defeats.

No falseness, no inadequacies.

Not even a name.

Half a second. Merely a drop in a large ocean of humanity. Then it came back.

"Hmmm . . . ," mumbled the woman by his side. Turned over and buried her head more deeply in the pillow. Pressed herself closer to him.

Ah well, he thought. *It could be worse.* He looked at the clock. Half past seven. He remembered the date as well. The first of January! Good Lord, they hadn't gone to bed until after two; and as they were in bed, then . . .

He smiled.

Noticed that he was smiling. There was an unusual twitching in his cheek muscles, but by Jove, it was a smile. Half past seven after two or three hours' sleep! On the first day of the year.

He adjusted the pillows and observed her. Ulrike Fremdli. With chestnut-brown hair and one breast peeping out through a gap in the covers. A large and mature woman's breast with a nipple that had served two children, and on a New Year's morning like this it certainly seemed to be delivering a message of peace and goodwill. Of friendship and brotherhood and love between all people on earth, among all these drops in this ocean . . .

Good Lord, Van Veeteren thought. *I'm losing the plot. Life is a symphony.*

He stayed in bed and scarcely dared to breathe. As if the slightest movement would be enough to break this fragile moment.

I want to die at a moment like this, he thought.

Then a dream took possession of him again.

Remarkable. It was as if it had been sitting around the corner, waiting as the morning spun its treacherous web of illusory happiness: waiting to stab him as soon as he had lowered his guard. Wasn't that just typical? Absolutely typical.

It was a peculiar dream.

A dark and gloomy old castle. With arches and staircases and large, dimly lit halls. Empty and cold, with restless flickering shadows flitting along rough stone walls. Night, evidently; and threatening voices in the distance, and adjacent rooms . . . and the piercing sound of iron against iron, as if knives were being sharpened; and he's scurrying along through all this, from room to room, hunting for something, unclear what.

He comes to a cell: very small, next to one wall a diminutive altar with a Madonna relief, carved out of the dark stone of the wall, next to another wall a man asleep on a wooden bed. A thick horsehair blanket is pulled up over his shoulders and head, but even so he knows that it's Erich.

His son Erich.

His wayward and accident-prone Erich. He hesitates, and as he stands there in the narrow doorway, not knowing what to do or what is expected of him, he hears the piercing sound of the knives getting louder, then suddenly, suddenly, he sees one of those daggers hovering in the room. Hanging in midair above the man sleeping on the bench. A big, heavy dagger, lit up by jagged beams, glistening, rotating slowly until the tip of its razor-sharp blade is pointing straight down at the man. At Erich, his son.

He hesitates again. Then moves carefully forward and takes

away the blanket from the sleeping man's head. And it's not Erich lying there. It's Münster.

Intendent Münster lying asleep on his side, at peace with his hands under his head, totally unaware, and Van Veeteren doesn't understand what is happening. He puts the blanket back where it was, just as carefully, hears voices and heavy footsteps approaching, and before he has time to leave the room and reach safety, he wakes up.

"It was like Macbeth. The funny thing is that I was so sure it was Erich lying there, but it turned out to be Münster."

Ulrike Fremdli yawned and rested her head on her hands. Eyed him over the kitchen table with a look that was almost cross-eyed with exhaustion. *Charmingly cross-eyed,* he thought.

"You're a remarkable person," she said.

"Hogwash," said Van Veeteren.

"Not at all," said Ulrike, stroking her hair away from her face. "Curiouser and curiouser. The first time you turn up in my life it's because you are trying to find out who murdered my husband. Then you wait for more than a year before getting in touch again, and now you sit here on the morning of New Year's Day and want me to interpret your dreams. Thank you for last night, by the way. It wasn't too bad."

"Thank *you*," said Van Veeteren, and realized that he was smiling again. It was beginning to be a habit. "Anyway, women are better at dreams," he said. "Some women, at any rate."

"I think so," said Ulrike. "I agree with you in general, but you have a gift that makes you just as intuitive as I am. I'd always imagined that an old detective inspector would be much more resolute, but perhaps that's just a prejudice?"

"Hmm, yes," said Van Veeteren. "We know so little."

"Really?"

He cut a slice of cheese and chewed it thoughtfully. Ulrike stuck out her naked foot under the table and stroked his calf with it.

"Hmm," said Van Veeteren again. "Only a tiny bit of all there is to know. And if we don't have a keen ear, it's a damned minuscule bit."

"Go on," said Ulrike.

"Well," said Van Veeteren. "This is one of my private hobbies, of course, but since you seem to be too tired to contradict me, maybe I can expand a bit on it. . . ."

She stretched out the other foot as well.

"Quite a humble little theory in fact," he said. "It ought to suit a clever woman like you. A woman with humble feet . . . no, carry on, please do. Anyway, let's assume that there is an infinite number of connections and correspondences and patterns in the world, and that the cleverest of us might be able—to dare!—to comprehend . . . let's say a hundredth part of them. The dumbest of us might comprehend a thousandth, or a ten-thousandth. Let's not go into how much I can grasp. Most of it comes to us in ways different from what the so-called Western way of thinking is prepared to accept. The deductive terror. Despite the fact that this in no way contradicts it. Or threatens it. Quite the reverse, actually, for it must surely be easier to comprehend things than to comprehend how we comprehend them. Our knowledge of the world must always be greater than our knowledge of knowledge. . . . Well, er, something like that."

Ulrike thought for a moment.

"It sounds plausible," she said. "But I'm not properly awake."

"There are so many patterns," Van Veeteren continued. "We get so much information that we generally just let it flash over our heads. A thousand pounds of stimuli every second. We don't have time to work on them. This is all obvious, but all I really understand is obvious, I have to admit."

"Dreams?" said Ulrike.

"For example. But good God! A dagger hovering over Intendent Münster! You're not going to tell me that that's a coincidence? He's in danger, even a child can understand that."

"You thought it was Erich," Ulrike pointed out.

Van Veeteren sighed.

"Erich has been in the danger zone for as long as I can remember," he said. "That wouldn't be anything new."

"How old is he?"

Van Veeteren had to think that over.

"Twenty-six," he said. "It's about time I should stop worrying about him."

Ulrike shook her head.

"Why should you do that?" she asked. "Once your child, always your child. Even if they're a hundred years old."

Van Veeteren observed her for a while in silence. Felt the warm soles of her feet against his legs. *Good God,* he thought. *This woman . . .*

It was only the fourth or fifth time they had spent a whole night together, and now, just as on all the previous occasions, he was forced to ask himself why it didn't happen more often. As far as he could tell he didn't seem to be causing her all that much suffering, so why be so damned cautious? Be as unabashed as a hermit. Not as doubtful as a donkey. As far as he was concerned . . . well, as far as he was concerned he wasn't suffering in the least.

He looked out the window at a New Year's Day that seemed very uncertain. It had been raining during the night, and the sky and the earth seemed to be conjoined by a blue-gray light that certainly didn't intend to keep darkness at bay for many hours. It struck him that there were grounds for thinking the sun had been extinguished at some point in November—he couldn't recall seeing it since then.

"Lovely weather," he said. "Shall we go back to bed for a while?"

"Good idea," said Ulrike Fremdli.

When they next woke up it was two o'clock.

"When are your children due?" he asked in horror.

"This evening," she said. "They're not dangerous."

"My solicitude concerns them and nothing else," said Van

Veeteren, sitting up. "I don't want to give them a shock, first thing in the new year."

Ulrike pulled him back down onto the bed.

"You're staying," she said. "They're grown up now and have flown the nest, both of them. And they've seen a thing or two."

Van Veeteren pondered.

"Why do we have weekdays when we can have Sundays exclusively?" he asked slyly.

Ulrike furrowed her brow, then sat astride him.

"Don't think I'm in a hurry," she said. "But one Sunday every other month is on the thin side."

Van Veeteren stretched out his hands and let her heavy breasts rest on them.

"You may be right," he said. "All right, I'll stay then. I'll soon be sixty, so maybe it's time to tie up a few loose ends."

"The year is starting off well," said Ulrike.

"It could have started worse," said Van Veeteren.

But later, as he lay in bed waiting for her to finish in the bathroom, his thoughts reverted to last night's dream.

Erich? he thought. *Münster? Intendent Münster?*

Is this a dagger I see before me?

Incomprehensible.

At least for somebody who generally comprehends only a tiny part that is obvious.

31

"Happy New Year," said Chief of Police Hiller, adjusting his tie. "Good to see you back, Reinhart. We all hope that your leave of absence did you good."

"Thank you, everybody," said Reinhart. "Yes, it was relatively bearable. But I don't understand why I'm being given this case. There seem to be enough people working on it already. Don't tell me you've got stuck?"

"Hmm," said Hiller. "I think we'll leave it to Intendent Münster to fill you in on that score."

Münster took out his notebook and looked around the table. Reinhart was right, that couldn't be denied. There suddenly seemed to be a lot of officers on the case. Himself. Rooth and Heinemann. Jung and Moreno. And now Reinhart. Not counting Hiller, of course.

"I suggest we go through what has happened since that find out in Weyler's Woods," said Münster. "It wouldn't hurt for us all to get an overview, while Reinhart gets up to speed."

Hiller nodded approvingly and made clicking noises with the new Ballograf pen he'd been given as a Christmas present.

"Right, it was the twenty-first of December when a young girl, Vera Kretschke, found a head hidden in a plastic bag. It was pretty clear from early on that it belonged to Else Van Eck, who had been missing since the end of October. Her husband, Arnold Van Eck, identified her right away: it was a bit too much for him, and he's been in the hospital out at Majorna ever since. . . ."

"Poor bastard," said Reinhart.

"Apparently he hasn't spoken for a week," said Moreno.

"During the eleven days that have passed since, we've discovered three more bags, but she's still not complete. Her left leg and part of her torso are still missing—her pelvis, to be more precise. Two more bags, presumably. Twelve officers are still searching, but it's not an easy task, of course, even if we assume that everything was dumped in Weyler's Woods. Nothing has been buried so far: the murderer just covered the bags up as best he could, with leaves and twigs and such."

"He didn't have a shovel," said Rooth. "Careless type."

"Quite possibly," said Münster. "In any case, according to Meusse she's been dead for up to two months, so there's nothing to suggest that she wasn't murdered the same night she disappeared . . . the twenty-ninth or soon after. The butchery isn't too badly done—I'm quoting Meusse—and could well have been performed by someone with a certain amount of professional skill, although the tools used were of poor quality. An ordinary, fairly blunt carving knife or something similar. Plus a cleaver, in all likelihood. The actual cause of death seems to have been several powerful blows to the head with a heavy instrument. The parietal bone was smashed, and bits of bone penetrated the brain; but the killer probably also severed the carotid artery before he started cutting her up. As for the plastic bags, they are widely available and can be bought by the roll in seven out of ten grocer's shops or supermarkets. The only thing that might be worth noting is that they were yellow. You can buy dark green ones of the same type, a color that would've been preferable if you didn't want them to be easily found."

"He probably didn't have any others at home," said Rooth.

"It might be as simple as that," Münster agreed. "All the body parts found so far have been naked. No clothes, no other details that could have left clues. Fingerprints are out of the question, of course, given the length of time that's passed."

He paused and looked around the table again.

"It won't help us much even if we do find the missing parts," said Jung.

"No," said Rooth. "Presumably not. But it's no fun sitting with a puzzle with two pieces missing."

"It's not exactly a fun puzzle, no matter what," said Moreno.

"It seems not," said Reinhart. "What do you have in the way of suspicions?"

There was silence for a few seconds, broken only by the clicking of the chief of police's new pen.

"Let's consider what we know first," said Münster, "and then we can start speculating. We've spoken to a lot of people, mainly neighbors in the same building—there aren't many relatives and friends—and overall, it has to be said that we haven't found very much. Fru Van Eck disappeared on the evening of Wednesday, the twenty-ninth of October, while her husband was attending a course at the Riitmeeterska school. She was last seen shortly after six o'clock that evening—one of the neighbors thinks she heard her in her apartment at around seven—but she wasn't there when Arnold Van Eck got home at eight o'clock. Nobody has been able to tell us any more than that."

"Could it be one of them?" wondered Reinhart. "The neighbors, I mean. And is it certain that she was the one in the flat at seven o'clock?"

"It could have been one of the other people in the building," said Münster. "Hypothetically, at least. I think it's best to discuss that later, when we start looking at links with the other case— Waldemar Leverkuhn. But as for the person who was heard inside the flat, it could have been anybody at all."

"The murderer, for instance?" said Reinhart.

"For instance," said Münster.

"What's with these Leverkuhns?" wondered Reinhart.

Münster sighed and turned over a page.

"I don't really know, to be honest," he said. "On the surface it all seems crystal clear. . . ."

"Some surfaces can be both crystal clear and paper thin," said Reinhart. "I've been following it to some extent in the newspapers, but we all know how they report things."

"Start from the beginning," said the chief of police.

"Start from the twenty-fifth of October," said Münster. "That's when it all begins. Fru Leverkuhn comes home and finds her husband stabbed to death in his bed. We launch an investigation, and after ten days she calls us and confesses to having done it herself. In an attack of anger. We spend a week interrogating her thoroughly, and before long both we and the prosecutor think we have enough evidence. Anyway, things then follow the usual path, the trial begins in the middle of December, and it's over after three or four days. Nothing remarkable. The prosecutor presses for murder, the defense for manslaughter. While waiting for the verdict, on Sunday the twenty-first, she hangs herself in her cell. . . . She plaits a rope from strips of blanket and manages to hook it onto a jutting piece of pipe in a corner of her cell. Obviously, a lot has been said about how that could happen, so perhaps we don't need to go into it here. She's left a suicide note as well, in which she wrote that she had decided to take her own life in view of the circumstances."

"The circumstances?" said Reinhart. "What circumstances?"

"That she had killed her husband, and had nothing to look forward to apart from several years behind bars," said Moreno.

"It's not exactly difficult to understand her motive," said Münster. "But what is difficult to explain is why she waited so long. Why she allowed herself to be arrested and charged, and then put on a show in court before putting an end to it all."

"Didn't she write anything about that in the letter?" wondered Reinhart.

Münster shook his head.

"No. It was just a few lines, and of course you can't expect logical reasoning. She must have been pretty exhausted mentally, and a decision like that must've taken a lot of thought."

"You'd think so," said Rooth.

Heinemann cleared his throat and put his glasses on the table.

"I've spoken to a woman by the name of Regine Svendsen," he began pensively. "A former colleague of Fru Leverkuhn's. We spoke about precisely these psychological aspects. She seems to have known Leverkuhn well—until a few years ago, at least. It's risky to jump to conclusions in cases like this, and she was careful to stress that . . ."

"What did she say?" said Rooth. "If we cut the crap."

"Well," said Heinemann. "You could say Fru Leverkuhn was a very strong woman. Quite capable of doing all kinds of things. There was a sort of incorruptibility about her, according to Fru Svendsen. Or something to that effect."

"Really?" said Münster. "Well, clearly she has displayed an ability to take action, there's no denying that."

"Have you found any diaries?" Heinemann asked.

"Diaries?" said Münster.

"Yes," said Heinemann. "I spoke to this woman only yesterday—she'd been away, so I haven't been able to report on it until now. Anyway, she claims that Marie-Louise Leverkuhn kept a diary all her life, and if that's the case and we could manage to take a look at it—or them—well, maybe we could get some insight into things. . . ."

There was a moment's silence, then Hiller cleared his throat.

"Yes, indeed," he said. "I suggest you go look for these diaries—it shouldn't be too difficult, surely?"

Münster looked at Moreno.

"We've . . . we've searched Leverkuhn's flat," said Moreno. "But we weren't looking for diaries."

"According to Fru Svendsen there should be eight to ten," said Heinemann. "She's seen them, but never read them, of course. Ordinary notebooks with black oilcloth covers. Each one covering three or four years. Just short notes, presumably."

"That would cover no more than thirty years," said Reinhart. "I thought she was older than that?"

Heinemann shrugged.

"Don't ask me," he said. "But I thought it was worth mentioning."

Münster made a note and thought about it, but hadn't reached a conclusion before the chief of police once again took command.

"Get over there and start looking!" he said. "Search the whole damned apartment and dig them out. The place is still under guard, I take it? That wouldn't be unusual?"

"Not unusual at all," said Münster with a sigh. "Obviously. I don't think she had a notebook with her while she was under arrest in any case—but she might have stopped keeping a diary in her old age. How long has it been since this Regine Svendsen was last in touch with her?"

"About five years," said Heinemann. "They worked together at Lippmann's."

Reinhart had been filling his pipe for several minutes, under Hiller's stern gaze. Now he put it in his mouth, leaned back in his chair and clasped his hands behind his head.

"The link, what about that link?" he said. "And wasn't there somebody else who came to a bad end?"

Münster sighed again.

"Absolutely right," he said. "We have a Felix Bonger who's disappeared as well. One of Leverkuhn's friends. He hasn't been seen since the night Leverkuhn was killed."

Chief of Police Hiller had had enough. He stopped observing Reinhart's tobacco activities and tapped demonstratively on the table with his Ballograf.

"Now listen here," he said. "You have to make up your minds whether these cases are linked or not—I thought we'd already done that. Is there anything—anything at all!—to suggest that Leverkuhn's and Fru Van Eck's deaths are connected in any way?"

"Well," said Münster, "I have to say it's unusual for two people living in the same building to be murdered within only a few days of each other, and—"

"I regard the Leverkuhn case as finished and done with!" interrupted Hiller. "At least as long as nothing completely new comes to light. What we have to do now is to find out who murdered Else Van Eck. Mind you, if it was Fru Leverkuhn who did her in as well, that would suit me perfectly well."

"A neat solution," said Reinhart. "The chief of police ought to have become a police officer."

Hiller was irritated for a moment, but then he continued with undiminished authority: "As for this Bonger character, he's disappeared, so we'll pursue the same procedures as we would for any other similar case—routine missing-persons procedures, that is." He glanced at his watch. "I have a meeting in five minutes."

"We should take a smoke break," said Reinhart. "We're about due for one."

"Does anybody else wish to say anything?" asked Münster diplomatically.

"Personally, I could do with a cup of coffee," said Rooth.

"You look tired," said Moreno, closing the door.

"That's probably because I am tired," said Münster. "I was supposed to be off for a week over the holidays: it ended up being only two and a half days."

"Not much fun when you have a family, I suppose."

Münster pulled a face.

"Yes, having a family is great. It's all this work that isn't so great. It makes you lose heart."

Moreno sat down opposite him and waited for him to continue.

"How are things with you?" Münster asked instead.

"Odd," said Moreno after a short pause.

"Odd?"

She laughed.

"Yes, odd. But okay, basically. Does a heartless intendent have the strength to listen? It'll only take half a minute."

Münster nodded.

"Well, Claus came home from New York, despite everything,"

Moreno said while trying to scrape a little coffee stain off her pale yellow sweater with a fingernail. "It struck me straightaway that he had changed somehow. . . . I think I said this, didn't I? I couldn't put my finger on it, but it finally came out yesterday. He's found somebody else."

"What?" said Münster. "What the hell . . . ?"

"Yes. A month ago he was ready to take his own life for my sake, but now he has a flourishing new relationship. He met her at a restaurant in Greenwich Village, they flew home on the same plane, and they've evidently found each other. Her name's Brigitte, and she's a script girl with a television company. Huh, men . . ."

"Enough of that," said Münster. "Don't tar everybody with the same brush, for Christ's sake! I refuse to associate myself with this kind of . . . of juvenile behavior."

Moreno smiled. Stopped scraping and contemplated the stain, which was still there.

"Okay," she said. "I know. In any case, I think it's brilliant, even if it is a bit odd, as I said. Shall we drop the battle of the sexes?"

"By all means," said Münster. "I've had more than my fair share of that as well."

Moreno looked vaguely sympathetic, but said nothing. Münster took a drink out of the can of soda water on his desk and tried not to belch, but belched even so. In that polite way, which brought tears to his eyes.

"The Leverkuhn case," he said, taking a deep breath. "Are you with me on it?"

"Yes, I'm with you."

"Act three. Or is it act four? Anyway, the division of labor is clear, in broad outline at least. Rooth and Jung will lead the search for the diaries at the Leverkuhns' place. Reinhart and Heinemann will take care of Van Eck. You and I have a bit more freedom. I'll ignore what Hiller said about what's resolved and what isn't. I'm going to have another go at Leverkuhn's children. All three, I think."

"Even the daughter who's locked away?" asked Moreno.

"Even her," said Münster.

"Do you think it was Marie-Louise Leverkuhn who disposed of Else Van Eck as well?"

Münster made no reply at first. Leafed somewhat listlessly through the pile of paper on his desk. Drank the rest of the soda water and threw the empty can into the wastepaper basket.

"I don't know," he said. "She flatly denied it, and why should she bother to do that when she had already admitted to killing her husband? And she took her own life, too. Why would she want to kill Van Eck? What motive could she have had?"

"Don't ask me," said Moreno. "But you think they're connected?"

"Yes," said Münster. "I think so. I don't know how, but damn it, I'm going to find out."

He could hear the trace of weariness in his last sentence, and he could see that Moreno heard it as well. She looked at him for a moment, her brow furrowed as she searched for something consoling to say. But she found nothing.

I wish she would just walk around the desk and give me a hug, Münster thought, closing his eyes. *Or we could get undressed and go to bed.*

But nothing like that happened either.

32

"Hello?"

"Hello. My name's Jung, Maardam police. Am I talking to Emmeline von Post?"

"Yes, that's me. Good morning."

"I have just one question, so maybe we can sort it out on the telephone?"

"Good Lord, what's it about?"

"Marie-Louise Leverkuhn. We're winding up the case, and we want to sort out all the final details."

"I understand," said Emmeline.

Oh no you don't, thought Jung. *But you're not supposed to either.*

"Did Fru Leverkuhn keep a diary?" he asked.

There were a few seconds of astonished silence before Emmeline answered.

"Yes, of course. She used to keep a diary. But why on earth do you want to know about that?"

"Routine," said Jung routinely.

"I see. . . . Oh, it's all so awful."

"Absolutely awful," said Jung. "Had she been doing it long? Keeping a diary?"

"I think so," said Emmeline. "Yes, she was keeping one when we were at commercial college together. They weren't really diaries, as I understand it; she wrote something only a couple of times a month. . . . To sort of sum up the situation; I don't really know."

"Did you talk about it often?"

"No."

"Have you ever read anything she wrote?"

"Never."

"But you've seen the diaries?"

"Yes," said Emmeline. "On the odd occasion. . . . We mentioned them every now and then, but it was her private business and had nothing to do with me."

"What do they look like?"

"Excuse me?"

"The diaries. How many do you think there are, and what do they look like?"

Emmeline thought for a moment.

"I don't know how many there are," she said, "but I think she kept them all. Ten or twelve, perhaps? They were the usual kind of spiral-bound notebooks with soft covers you can buy all over the place. Quite thick . . . black, soft covers. Or maybe blue, the ones I've seen at least. Maybe there were more. I don't think she showed them to her husband. But . . . I don't understand why you're asking about this. Is it important?"

"No, not really," said Jung reassuringly. "Just a detail, like I said. By the way, do you remember if she had one of those books with her when she was staying with you for a few days? In October?"

"No . . . no, I don't think so. I didn't see one, at least."

"Thank you, Fru von Post. That was all. I apologize for disturbing you."

"Not at all," said Emmeline. "No problem."

"Rooth, Maardam police," said Rooth.

"I haven't got time," said Mauritz Leverkuhn.

"Why did you answer, then?" said Rooth. "If you haven't got time?"

Silence for a few seconds.

"It could have been something important," said Mauritz.

"It is important," said Rooth. "Did your mother keep a diary?"

Mauritz sneezed directly into the receiver.

"Bless you," said Rooth, drying his ear.

"Diary!" snorted Mauritz. "What the hell has that got to do with you? And why the hell are you poking your nose into all this? We've had enough of you snooping around. Can't you leave people in peace? Besides, I'm sick."

"I've noticed," said Rooth. "Did she keep a diary?"

For a while there was no sound other than Mauritz's heavy breathing. Rooth realized he was wondering whether to hang up or not.

"Listen," he said in the end. "I've been in bed with the flu for two days now. A hundred and two temperature. I'll be fucked if I talk to you anymore. Both my father and my mother are dead. I don't understand why the police can't find something better to do instead of pestering us."

"You're taking medication, I hope?" asked Rooth in a friendly tone, but the only answer he received was a clear and dismissive click.

Rooth hung up. *Bastard,* he thought. *I hope you're bedridden for a few more weeks at least.*

"Do you really mean that?" asked Heinemann. "That the police have been treating you improperly?"

"What?" said Ruben Engel.

"That we've been bothering you unnecessarily," Heinemann explained. "If so, you should make a complaint."

"Yes . . . er?" said Engel.

"There's a special form you can fill out. If you'd like I can arrange to have one sent to you."

"Eh? That's not necessary," said Engel. "But for God's sake hurry up and get this business sorted out, so that we can get some peace and quiet."

"It's a bit tricky," said Heinemann, looking around the cluttered kitchen with his glasses perched on the end of his nose. "Murder investigations like this one are often more complicated than people can imagine. There's an awful lot of aspects to take into account. An awful lot. What are you drinking?"

"Eh?" said Engel. "Oh, just a drop of wine toddy—to raise my body temperature a bit. It's so damned drafty in this apartment."

"I see," said Heinemann. "Anyway, I shouldn't disturb you any longer. Do you know if Fröken Mathisen next door is at home?"

Engel looked at the clock.

"She usually comes home at about five," he said. "So with a bit of luck . . ."

"We'll see," said Heinemann. "Anyway, sorry to have disturbed you."

"No problem," said Engel. "The screwing machines are moving out, by the way."

"I beg your pardon?" said Heinemann.

"The couple downstairs. They must've found someplace better. They're moving out."

"Really?" said Heinemann. "We didn't know that. Thank you for telling us."

"You're welcome," said Engel.

Marie-Louise Leverkuhn's funeral took place in one of the side chapels in Keymerkyrkan, and apart from the vicar and the undertaker there were four people present, all of them women.

Closest to the coffin, a simple affair made of fiberboard and hardboard—draped with a green cloth that concealed the deficiencies—sat Ruth Leverkuhn in her capacity as next of kin. Behind her sat the other three: farthest to the left was Emmeline von Post; in the middle a pale woman of about the same age and, as far as Münster and Moreno could tell, identical to the Regine Svendsen who had supplied Heinemann with the information about the diaries; and on the right a tall, well-dressed woman about forty-five years old—Münster and Moreno had no idea who she was.

They had placed themselves strategically in the nave: they were sitting in an austere, light-colored pew, leafing furtively through their hymnals and keeping a discreet eye on the simple ritual taking place some fifteen feet away.

"Who is the younger woman?" whispered Münster.

Moreno shook her head.

"I don't know. Why isn't the son here?"

"He's sick," said Münster. "Or says he is, in any case. Rooth spoke to him on the phone this morning."

"Hmm," said Moreno. "So you won't be having a chat with him, then. Should I try to grab that woman afterward? She must have some sort of connection with the family."

"She could be one of those funeral hyenas, mind you," warned Münster. "It takes all sorts. . . . But by all means, see what she has to say. I'll see if I can get a word with the daughter."

He noticed that he was enjoying sitting here, squeezed up close to Ewa Moreno in the cramped pew, whispering. Whispering so closely to her ear that he could feel her hair brushing against his skin.

Keep on talking, Mr. Vicar, he thought. *Make sure you spin the service out for as long as possible—it doesn't matter if it takes all afternoon.*

What the hell am I doing? he then thought. Despite the fact that he was sitting in church with a hymnal in his hand.

"No problem," said the woman, whose name was Lene Bauer. "No problem at all—I meant to call you several times, but I never got around to it. . . . But then, perhaps I don't have all that much to tell you, when it comes to the nitty-gritty."

At Lene Bauer's suggestion they had ensconced themselves in a screened booth in Rüger's bar in Wiijsenweg, diagonally opposite the church. Moreno took an instant liking to the woman, who had apparently taken time off from her post at the library in Linzhuisen in order to attend the funeral. Her connection with Marie-Louise Leverkuhn was not especially strong: she and Lene's mother had been cousins, but there had been no contact at all during the last twenty to twenty-five years.

However, Lene had followed what had happened in the papers and on the television: they had socialized quite a bit in the sixties.

"Vacations by the sea," she explained. "A few weeks in Lejnice, Oosterbrügge, and similar places. I guess it was cheaper if we all went together. My mother and Marie-Louise and us children. Me and Ruth, Irene, and Mauritz . . . but I used to play mainly with Ruth; we are exactly the same age. Our fathers—my dad and Waldemar—only came to join us for an occasional evening or on the weekends. . . . That's about it, really."

"You haven't kept in touch with the children either?" asked Moreno.

"No," said Lene, looking a bit guilty. "A few letters to Ruth at the beginning of the seventies, but I got married quite early and had other things to think about. My own children and so on. And for several years we lived down at Borghem as well."

Moreno thought for a while. Sipped the wine they had ordered and tried to work out how best to continue. It certainly seemed as if this woman had something she wanted to say, but it might be something that wouldn't be mentioned unless she was asked the right questions.

Or was it just her imagination? Questionable female intuition? Hard to say.

"Did you enjoy those summer vacations?" she asked cautiously. "How many were there, incidentally?"

"Three or four," said Lene. "I can't remember, to be honest. Each of them several weeks. I was between ten and fifteen years old. We used to listen to the Beatles—Ruth had a tape recorder. Yes, I enjoyed it—apart from Mauritz."

"Really?" said Moreno, and waited.

"He was so terribly difficult to shake off," she said. "You had to feel sorry for him, of course—the only boy with three girls. And he was younger as well, but there seemed to be no limit to his determination to cling to his sisters, especially Irene. She didn't have a second's peace, and she never turned him away either. She coddled him and built sand castles with him, painted pictures and read him bedtime stories. For hours on end. Ruth and I kept well out of the way, as I recall, only too glad to off-load the responsibility; but I know I found it extremely difficult to put up with Mauritz. They never said anything to him, and he never showed the slightest bit of gratitude. A crybaby and a moaner, that's what he was."

"Hmm," said Moreno. "This is what you wanted to tell me, isn't it?"

Lene shrugged.

"I don't really know," she said. "I just started to think about them again when I heard about the terrible things that had happened. I couldn't believe it was true."

"No," said Moreno. "I suppose it must have been a shock for you."

"Two," said Lene. "First the murder. Then the fact that she'd done it. She must have hated him."

Moreno nodded.

"Presumably. Did you have any idea of what their relationship was like? Thirty years ago, I mean."

"No," said Lene. "I've been thinking about it now, in view of what's happened, but I was only a child in those days. I had no concept of things like that—and anyway, I hardly ever saw Waldemar. He turned up only occasionally. No, I really don't know."

"So it's the children you remember?"

Lene sighed and fished a cigarette out of her handbag.

"Yes. And then all that business of Irene's illness. I've somehow always felt that it was connected. Her illness and her being overprotective of Mauritz. There was something wrong, but I suppose it's easy to speculate. Darkness swallowed her up more or less all at once, as I understand it rightly. Just over twenty years ago, so it was a few years after our vacations together and I've no idea what it was all about. One can only guess, but it's so easy to be clever in hindsight."

She fell silent. Moreno watched her as she took out a lighter and lit her cigarette.

"You know that Ruth is lesbian, I take it?" Moreno asked, mainly because she didn't really know how to continue the conversation. Lene inhaled deeply and nodded slowly several times.

"Yes," she said. "But there are so many possible reasons for that. Don't you think?"

Moreno didn't know how to interpret that answer. Did this stylish woman have a similar bent? Had she had enough of men? She took another sip of wine and thought about it, then realized that she was beginning to drift a long way from the point.

What was the point?

That's certainly a good question, she thought. But she could think of nothing that might approximate an answer. Not for the moment. Just now.

It was nearly always like this. Sometimes in the middle of an investigation, it seemed impossible to see the forest for all the trees. She had thought about that lots of times, and of course the only thing that helped was to try to find a mountain or a hill that you could climb and get some sort of overview. See things in perspective.

She could see that Lene was waiting for a continuation, but it was difficult to find the right thread.

"What about your mother?" she asked for no particular reason. "Is she still alive?"

"No," said Lene. "She died in 1980. Cancer. But I don't think she had any contact with the Leverkuhns either in recent years. My father died last summer. But he knew them even less."

Moreno nodded and drank up the remains of her wine. Then

she decided that this was enough. She thanked Lene Bauer for being so helpful and asked if they could get in touch again if anything turned up she might be able to help with.

Lene handed over her business card and said that the police were welcome to phone her at any time.

How nice to meet somebody who at least displays an iota of willingness to cooperate in this case, Moreno thought as she left Rüger's. *Their kind were hard to come by. Not to say few and far between.*

But what Lene Bauer's contribution was actually worth in a wider context—well, she had difficulty in deciding that. For the time being, at least. They were in the middle of a thicket, and the brushwood was anything but uncommon.

I must improve my imagery, Moreno thought, somewhat confused.

But some other time, not now. She clambered into the car and thought that all she wanted to do for the moment was to discuss the matter with Intendent Münster. Preferably in a whisper, as they had found themselves doing in the church that morning, but perhaps that was asking too much.

More than a lot, in fact. She started the car. No doubt it would be best to postpone that conversation until tomorrow, she decided. To be on the safe side.

After these deliberations Inspector Moreno drove back to her temporary home, and spent all evening thinking about the concept of the battle of the sexes.

33

With the aid of Constables Klempje and Dillinger, Rooth and Jung searched the Leverkuhns' apartment in Kolderweg for four long hours on the Tuesday after Fru Leverkuhn's funeral.

It would have been quicker, Jung decided later, if they had done without the assistance of the constables altogether. Thanks to unbridled enthusiasm, Dillinger managed to demolish a bathroom cupboard that had no doubt been fixed to the wall for many a year (but since neither of the inhabitants of the apartment were any longer of this world, Rooth reckoned that they could lie low when it came to the question of damages), and Klempje's bulky frame tended to get in the way—until Jung had had enough and sent him packing to the attic space instead.

"Aye, aye, Captain," said Klempje. Saluted and disappeared up the stairs. When Jung went to check on how things were going not long after, it happened that with the aid of a bolt cutter, Klempje had broken into Fröken Mathisen's jam-packed storeroom and succeeded in removing most of the contents and piling them up in the narrow corridor outside. It was a considerable amount. Jung fetched Dillinger, gave still more detailed instructions to the pair of them, and half an hour later they came downstairs (Klempje looking suspiciously sleepy) to report: there were no diaries to be seen, neither in Mathisen's nor in the Leverkuhns' storeroom.

No doubt about it, as sure as the dawn—they hadn't found a single page.

Jung sighed and announced that unfortunately, the same applied to the apartment itself. Although he expressed it differently.

"What a heap of crap," said Rooth when he'd locked the door behind them. "I'm hungry."

"There's something wrong with your metabolism," said Jung.

"What does that mean?" asked Klempje, yawning so broadly that his neck muscles creaked. "I'm hungry, too."

Jung sighed again.

"But maybe it means something," he said. "If you look at it another way."

"What the hell are you talking about?" wondered Rooth.

"Don't you see?"

"No," said Rooth. "Don't keep me guessing like this. I can hardly contain myself."

Jung snorted.

"There are some cops you can bribe by offering them a bun," he said. "Anyway, look at it like this. If she really did keep diaries, this Leverkuhn woman, and then destroyed them, that must mean that they contained something of importance. Something she didn't want anyone else to read. Don't you think?"

Rooth thought about that as they walked back to the car.

"Crap," he said. "But that's just normal. Who the hell would want to leave a load of diaries to posterity? Regardless of what's in them? Not me. So that doesn't mean a thing."

Jung realized that there was probably something in that, but didn't think there was any reason to expand on it.

"I didn't know you could write," he said instead.

"Bullshit. Of course he can," said Klempje, picking his nose.

When they got back to the police station, Jung and Rooth went down to the prison cells for a chat with Inspector Fuller: it emerged more clearly than was desirable that Marie-Louise Leverkuhn had made no effort at all to keep a diary during the six weeks she had spent in cell number 12. Neither in notebooks with soft black covers nor anywhere else. Fuller could stake his bloody reputation on that, he claimed.

For safety's sake they checked with all the guards and the drowsy chaplain, and everybody agreed. Even if no more reputations were staked.

There were no diaries. It was as simple as that.

"Okay," said Rooth. "Now we know. It seems that everyone draws a blank in this goddamned lottery."

Shortly before Münster went home for the day he got a phone call from Reinhart.

"Do you have fifteen minutes to spare?"

"Yes, but not much more," said Münster. "Are you coming to my office?"

"Come to mine instead," said Reinhart. "Then I can smoke in peace. There are a few things I'm wondering about."

"I'll be there in two minutes," said Münster.

Reinhart was standing by the window, watching the sleet fall, when Münster arrived.

"I seem to recall that the chief inspector thought January was the worst month of the year," he said. "I must say I agree with him. It's only the sixth today, but it feels as if we've been at it for an eternity."

"It can't have anything to do with the fact that you've only just started work again, can it?" Münster wondered.

"I shouldn't think so," said Reinhart, lighting his pipe. "Anyway, I had just a few theoretical questions."

"Good," said Münster. "I'm tired of being practical all the time."

Reinhart sat down behind his desk, turned his chair, and put his feet up on the third shelf of the bookcase, where there was a space left for precisely this purpose.

"Do you think she's innocent?" he asked.

Münster watched the wet snow falling for five seconds before replying.

"Possibly," he said.

"Why would she confess if she didn't do it?"

"There are various possibilities."

"Such as?"

Münster thought. "Well, there's one at any rate."

"One possibility?" said Reinhart. "That's what I call a multiplicity."

"Who cares?" said Münster. "Perhaps it's simple, but it could be that she was protecting somebody . . . or that she thought she was. But that's just speculation, of course."

"Who was she protecting?"

The telephone rang, but Reinhart pressed a button and switched it off.

"It's obvious," said Münster, with irritation in his voice. "I've been wondering about it from the very start, but there's no evidence to support it. Nothing at all."

Reinhart nodded and chewed at the stem of his pipe.

"Then there's Fru Van Eck," Münster said. "And this damned Bonger. That complicates matters somewhat, don't you think?"

"Of course," said Reinhart. "Of course. I tried to talk to the poor widower at Majorna today. But there's not much of a spark left in him. . . . Ah well, what are you going to do now? In the way of positive action, I mean."

Münster leaned back in his chair.

"Follow up on that simplistic thought," he said after consulting himself for a few seconds. "See if it holds water, at least. I need to get out for a bit and chase things down. Only one of the siblings attended the funeral, so we didn't get very far then. And it wasn't exactly fun either, interrogating the mourners as soon as they left the church."

"No, it wouldn't be," said Reinhart. "When are you taking off?"

"Tomorrow," said Münster. "They live quite a long way up north, so it might be a two-day job."

Reinhart thought for a while. Then he removed his feet from the bookshelf and put down his pipe.

"It certainly is strange business, don't you think?" he said. "And unpleasant."

"Yes, indeed," said Münster. "I suppose they could be coincidences. It's over two months now since it all started, but it's only now that I'm beginning to sniff the possibility of a motive."

"Hmm," said Reinhart. "Does it include Else Van Eck?"

"I'm not really sure," said Münster. "It's only a faint whiff at the moment."

Reinhart's face suddenly lit up.

"Well, I'll be damned!" he said. "You're beginning to sound like the chief inspector. Are you starting to get old?"

"Ancient," said Münster. "My kids will start thinking I'm their granddad if I don't get a week off soon."

"Time off, oh yes . . . ," said Reinhart with a sigh, and his eyes began to look dreamy. "It's time to go home. I'll see you in a few days. Keep us informed."

"Of course," said Münster, opening the door for Intendent Reinhart.

34

He allowed himself an extra hour the next morning. Made the beds, washed up, took Marieke to nursery school, and left Maardam by ten o'clock. Driving rain came lashing in from the sea, and he was relieved to be sitting in a car with a roof over his head.

His main traveling companion was oppressive exhaustion, and it was not until he had drunk two cups of black coffee at a gas station by the motorway that he began to feel remotely awake and clear in the head. Van Veeteren used to say there was nothing like a long car journey—in solitary majesty—when it came to unraveling muddled thoughts, and when Münster set off he had cherished a vague hope that the same would apply to him as well.

For there was certainly a lot to come to grips with. And a lot of tangles to unravel.

First of all Synn. His lovely Synn. He had hoped that they would have been able to have a heart-to-heart the previous evening after the children had gone to sleep, but that's not how it had turned out. Quite the reverse, in fact. Synn had settled down on her side and turned out the light before he had even gotten ready for bed, and when he made tentative moves to try to make contact with her, she had already fallen asleep.

Or pretended to—he wasn't sure which. He lay awake until two o'clock and felt awful. When he finally fell asleep, he dreamed instead of Ewa Moreno. Nothing seemed to be going right.

Is this relationship coming to an end? Münster wondered as he came to the hills around Wissbork. *Is this what happens when two people start drifting away from each other?*

He didn't know. How the hell could he know?

All you can do is look after your own life, he thought. That is the only consideration. All comparisons are gratuitous and would-be-wise. Synn is unique, he is unique, and so is their family and their relationship. There are no guidelines, no pattern to follow. All you can do is rely on your feelings and intuition. Damn it all.

I don't want to know, he suddenly realized. *I don't want to know how it's going to turn out. It's better to be blind, and to hope.*

But Synn was right in one respect—even a worn-out detective intendent could understand that. Things couldn't go on like this— no way. Not their lives, or other people's lives. If they couldn't succeed in changing the conditions, making some radical changes to the way things were at present, well . . . it was like sitting in a train that was slowly but inexorably approaching a terminus where there was no alternative but to get off and go their different ways. Whether they wanted to or not.

Is her conscience as bad as mine? he wondered in a sudden flash of insight.

Or was that aspect also infected by gender roles? Was that perhaps another shield against a nagging conscience? he wondered, now that he was looking more closely at the situation—that calm, female sense of certainty, which could survive no matter the circumstances, but which he could never understand.

But which he loved.

The more I think about it, the less I understand.

He had driven more than sixty miles before he was able to concentrate his thoughts on his work and the investigation.

The Leverkuhn case.

Leverkuhn–Bonger–Van Eck.

He worked out that it was now more than ten weeks since the whole thing began. And they had been standing still for most of that time, if he were to be honest: November and half of December while Fru Leverkuhn had been on remand and they failed to find the slightest trace of Else Van Eck.

But then the investigation had exploded into action the week before Christmas. Marie-Louise Leverkuhn's suicide and the grisly discovery in Weyler's Woods.

It was as if everything had conspired to ruin his Christmas, he told himself glumly. To take away from him the opportunity to stop that train heading for ruin. For new incidents kept on cropping up afterward—tin after tin of red herrings, as Rooth had put it.

The information about the diaries, for instance. Did any diaries still exist? They had existed, that much was clear; but if he would ever be able to read what was in them (assuming there was something of importance)—well, that was probably a vain hope.

And that woman's report to Moreno. About family relationships by the seaside during a few summers in the sixties. What was the significance of that?

Or yesterday's discussion with Reinhart. Although he didn't know all that much about the investigation, Reinhart seemed to be thinking along the same lines as Münster himself. But perhaps that wasn't too surprising—Reinhart was generally more perceptive than most.

Then there was that conversation with Ruth Leverkuhn after the funeral. A woman difficult to make contact with. It hadn't yielded much, either. A pity he didn't know about what Lene Bauer had told him at the time. It would have been interesting to ask her to comment, if nothing else.

Yes, there were a few openings, no doubt about that.

Or pitfalls, if one preferred to adopt Rooth's pessimism.

Speaking of openings, he couldn't help wondering about the conversation with Van Veeteren yesterday evening. The chief inspector had rung shortly before nine to ask about the latest developments. Münster had failed to discover exactly what he wanted to know, or what he had in mind. He had hemmed and hawed and spoken in riddles, like he used to do when something special was brewing. Münster had met him halfway and told him about his plans, and Van Veeteren had urged him to be careful. Warned him to watch his step, in fact; but it was impossible to get him to be more precise or to give any positive advice.

Surely, this was remarkable? Was he on his way back? Had he grown tired of life as an antiquarian bookseller?

Impossible to say, Münster decided. As so often where Van Veeteren was concerned.

And in Kolderweg the Menakdise–de Booning couple were busy moving out. The screwing machines! Or *la Rouge et le Noir,* as Moreno had christened them, rather more romantically. Why? Why move out just now? It sometimes seemed as if everything depended on getting out of that building. The Leverkuhns were gone. The caretaker and his wife as well. And now this young couple. Only Fröken Mathisen and old Engel were left.

Very strange, Münster thought. *What's going on?*

At one o'clock he still had an hour's drive ahead of him, and decided it was time for lunch. Turned off the main road just north of Saaren and entered yet another of those postmodern rest bunkers for postmodern drivers. As he sat at his window table—with a view of the rain and the car park and four stunted larch trees—he made up his mind to inject his thoughts with more systematics. He turned to a new page in his notebook, which he had taken in with him, and started writing down all the things he had been thinking about during the last hour in the car. Telegram style. Then, as he sat chewing his healthful schnitzel, he had the list in front of him and tried to extract from it some new, bold conclusions. Or at any rate a few cautious old ones: there were five centimeters of blank page left at the bottom where he could note down these thoughts.

When he had finished eating, the centimeters were still blank; but nevertheless, for some abstruse reason, he felt sure of one thing. Just the one.

He was on the right track.

Fairly sure. The blind tortoise was approaching the snowball.

. . .

It was blowing at least half a gale in Frigge. When Münster had struggled out of his car in the circular open plaza in front of the railway station, he was forced to lean into the wind in order to make any progress at all. Inside the station he was given a map and a route description by an unusually helpful young woman in the ticket office. He thanked her for her efforts, and she explained with a smile that her husband was also a police officer, so she knew what it was like.

There, you see? Münster thought. *The world is full of understanding policemen's wives.*

Then he went out into the storm again, this time leaning backward. Clambered back into his car and studied the information he'd been given. It seemed that Mauritz Leverkuhn lived in a suburb. Detached houses and modern terraced houses, no doubt, and only an occasional apartment building, anything but a skyscraper. He checked his watch. It was only half past three, but as Mauritz Leverkuhn was supposed to be suffering from influenza, there was no reason to worry that he might not be at home.

He had no intention of calling in advance to arrange a meeting. *Certainly not,* Münster thought. *If you're going to take the bull by the horns, there's no point in asking for permission first.*

The suburb was called Gochtshuuis. It was on the western outskirts of the town. He started the car and drove off.

It took him a little more than fifteen minutes to find the place. A rather dull 1970s project with two-story terraced houses alongside a canal, and a somewhat sparse strip of trees pointing at the low marshland and the sea. A windbreak. All the trees were leaning eastward at the same angle. Mauritz Leverkuhn's house was farthest away, where the road petered out with a postbox, a recycling station, and a turning area for buses.

Concrete gray. Two low stories high, thirty feet wide, and with a pathetic swamp of a garden at the front. Probably a similar one at the back, facing the trees. Dusk was already in the air, and Münster noted that lights were on in two of the windows.

Here we go, he thought as he got out of his car.

If Intendent Münster had bothered to take his cell with him when he had lunch, he would certainly have had an opportunity to fill in the last empty lines of the page in his notebook.

Not with any conclusions, that's for sure, but with another point in the list of new developments in the case.

Shortly after one-thirty Inspector Rooth had tried to contact him—in vain, of course—in order to report the latest find in Weyler's Woods. The fact that nobody remembered to call again later in the day was partly because it was overlooked in the general excitement caused as a result of the find, and partly because—despite everything—it was still not clear how great a significance the discovery would have.

If any at all. The search party, a dozen strong, had finally found the remains of Else Van Eck's so-called intimate parts—a section of pelvis, a length of spine, and two appropriately large buttocks in comparatively good condition. As usual it was all carelessly stuffed into a pale yellow plastic bag, and just as carelessly concealed in an overgrown ditch. Organs, such as the intestines, liver, and kidneys, had been removed, but what made this find more interesting than all the others was that when it was all tipped out onto a workbench at the Forensic Medicine Department, they discovered a scrap of paper sticking out of one of the many folds that inevitably form on the body of a woman the size of Fru Van Eck.

It wasn't large, but still. . . . Dr. Meusse himself carefully lifted up a section of the rotting flesh and removed the strip of paper without tearing it.

Nothing to write home about, Meusse insisted, but quite a feat even so. A flimsy scrap of paper about the length and width of a banana stained by blood and other substances. There was no doubt that it was from a newspaper or magazine.

Naturally, Meusse appreciated the importance of the find and had it transported by courier to the Forensic Chemistry Laboratory on the same block. Rooth and Reinhart were informed immediately about the development, and spent most of the afternoon at the Forensic Chemistry Lab—if not to accelerate the results of the analysis then at least to keep themselves informed about them. Needless to say they could just as well have waited for information via the telephone, but neither Rooth nor Reinhart were of that bent. Not today, at least.

The results emerged bit by bit, reported with a degree of scientific pomp and ceremony by the boss himself, Intendent Mulder—the least jovial person Rooth had ever met.

After an hour, for instance, it was obvious that the object was indeed part of a page from a newspaper or magazine. *We know that already, you cockeyed jerk,* thought Rooth, but he didn't say so.

Forty-five minutes later it was established that the paper was high quality—not in the weekly magazine class, but nevertheless not from an ordinary daily newspaper such as *Neuwe Blatt* or *Gazett.*

Mulder pronounced the names of the two newspapers in such a way that it was obvious to Rooth that only in a state of dire emergency would he condescend to wipe his ass with either of them.

"Thank God for that," said Reinhart. "If it had been from the *Blatt,* we might just as well have thrown it in the stove without more ado."

At about the same time they received a photocopy of the strip of paper. Reinhart and Rooth—and Moreno, who had just arrived—crowded around it and established that the banana shape was unfortunately in a vertical plane, and that it was not possible to extract anything meaningful from the fragments of text. Not at the moment, at least—despite the fact that the technicians had managed to define individual letters with unexpected clarity. Ninety percent of the reverse side seemed to be covered by a murky black-and-white picture that was just as impossible to interpret. Rooth maintained that it was a cross-section of a liver in an advanced state of cirrhosis, but his opinion was not shared by his colleagues.

By shortly after three o'clock they had also started to draw cautious conclusions about the typeface—even if that was not something within the range of competence of the forensic chemistry technicians, as Mulder was careful to point out. It wasn't Times New Roman or Geneva or any of the usual faces, however, which enhanced the possibility of eventually establishing the origins of the scrap of paper.

At five o'clock Intendent Mulder closed up shop for the day, but expressed a degree of optimism—scientifically restrained—with regard to the continued analysis the following day.

"I'm sure you're right," said Reinhart. "But what are the odds?"

"The odds?" wondered Mulder, slowly raising one well-trimmed eyebrow.

"The probability of whether you will be able to tell me exactly what rag the bit of paper comes from before you go home tomorrow."

Mulder lowered his eyebrow.

"Eighty-six out of a hundred," he said.

"Eighty-six?" said Reinhart.

"I rounded it off," said Mulder.

"Wrapping paper," commented Reinhart later in the car, as he gave Moreno a lift home. "Just like at the butcher's."

"But surely they don't wrap meat up in newspaper?" said Moreno. "I've never come across that."

"They used to," said Reinhart. "You're too young, you're just a little girl."

I'm glad there are some people who still think that, Moreno thought as she thanked him for the lift.

35

He had to ring the bell three times before Mauritz Leverkuhn opened the door.

"Good afternoon," said Münster. "It's me again."

It took Mauritz a few seconds to remember who the visitor was, and perhaps it was that short space of time that put him out of step from the very start.

Or perhaps it was the flu. In any case, when it had registered with him that it was the police, he didn't react with his usual aggression. He simply stared at Münster with vacant, feverish eyes, shrugged his coat-hanger shoulders, and beckoned him in.

Münster hung his jacket on a hook in the hallway and followed him into the living room. Noted that it looked bare. It seemed temporary. A sofa and two easy chairs around a low pine table. A teak-veneered bookcase with a total of four books, a few DVDs, and a collection of various ornaments. A television set and a black stereo system. On the table was a porno mag and a few advertising leaflets, and the window ledge was livened up by a cactus two inches high and a porcelain bank in the shape of a naked woman.

"Do you live alone?" Münster asked.

Mauritz had flopped down into one of the easy chairs. Despite the fact that he was obviously still unwell, he was fully dressed. White shirt and neatly pressed blue trousers. Well-worn slippers.

He hesitated before answering, as if he still hadn't made up his mind what attitude to adopt.

"I've been living here for only six months," he said in the end. "We split up."

"Were you married?"

Mauritz shook his head with some difficulty and took a drink from the glass in front of him on the table. Something white and fizzy: Münster assumed it was some kind of vitamin drink, or something to reduce his temperature.

"No, we just lived together. But it didn't last."

"It's not easy," said Münster. "So you're on your own now?"

"Yes," said Mauritz. "But I'm used to that. What do you want?"

Münster took his notebook out of his briefcase. It wasn't necessary to sit taking notes in a situation like this, of course, but it was a habit, and he knew that it gave a sort of stability. And above all: an opportunity to think things over while he pretended to be reading or writing something.

"We have a bit of new evidence," he said.

"Really?" said Mauritz.

"It could well be that your mother is innocent."

"Innocent?"

There was nothing forced about the way he pronounced that word. Nothing, at least, that Münster could detect. Just the natural degree of surprise and doubt that one might have expected.

"Yes, we think she might have confessed in order to protect someone."

"Protect someone?" said Mauritz. "Who?"

"We don't know," said Münster. "Have any suggestions?"

Mauritz wiped his brow with his shirtsleeve.

"No," he said. "Why would she do something like that? I don't understand this."

"If this really is the case," said Münster, "she must have known who actually killed your father, and that must have been someone close to her, in one way or another."

"You don't say?" said Mauritz.

"Can you think of anyone who would fit the bill?"

Mauritz coughed for a few seconds, his flabby body making the chair shake.

"No," he said eventually. "I don't understand what you're getting at. She didn't have much of a social life, you know. . . . No, I can't believe this. Why would she do that?"

"We are by no means sure," said Münster.

"What's the new evidence you referred to? That would suggest this interpretation?"

Münster studied his notebook for a few seconds before replying.

"I can't go into that, I'm afraid," he said. "But there are a few other things I'd like to talk to you about."

Excessively phlegmatic, he thought. *Is it the flu, or is that his normal state? Or is he putting on a show?*

"What other things?"

"Your sister, for instance," said Münster. "Irene."

Mauritz put down his glass with an unintentional clang.

"What do you mean?" he said, and now, at last, there was a trace of irritation in his voice.

"They've sent us a letter from the home where she lives."

That was a barefaced lie, but it was the line he'd decided to take. Sometimes it was necessary to take a shortcut. He was reminded of Persian words of wisdom he'd picked up somewhere: *A good lie travels from Baghdad to Damascus while the truth is looking for its sandals.*

Not a bad thing to bear in mind, Münster thought. *With regard to short-term decisions, at least.*

"You have no right to drag her into this business," said Mauritz.

"Does she know what's happened?" Münster asked.

Mauritz shrugged, and his aggression crumbled away.

"I don't know," he said. "But you must leave her in peace."

"We've received a letter," Münster repeated.

"I don't understand why they would write to you. What do they say?"

Münster ignored the question.

"Do you have much contact with her?" he asked instead.

"You can't see Irene," said Mauritz. "She's ill. Very ill."

"We've gathered that," said Münster. "But that wouldn't prevent you from visiting her now and again, would it?"

Mauritz hesitated for a few seconds and took a drink from his glass.

"I don't want to see her. Not the way she's become."

"Wasn't she your favorite sister?"

"That's nothing to do with you," he said, and the irritation was returning. Münster decided to back off.

"I apologize," he said. "I realize that this must be difficult for you. It's not a lot of fun having to sit here and ask you such questions either. But that's my job."

No answer.

"When did you last visit her?"

Mauritz seemed to be considering whether or not to refuse to make any comment. He wiped his brow again and looked wearily at Münster.

"I'm running a temperature," he said.

"I know," said Münster.

"I haven't been there in a year."

Münster made a note and thought that over.

"Not for a year?"

"No."

"Did your parents use to visit her?"

"My mother did, I think."

"Your other sister?"

"I don't know."

Münster paused and studied the pale gray walls.

"When did you split up with that woman?" he asked eventually.

"What?" said Mauritz.

"The woman you used to live with. When did she move out?"

"I don't understand what that has to do with it."

"But would you kindly answer the question even so," said Münster.

Mauritz closed his eyes and breathed heavily.

"Joanna," he said, and opened his eyes. "She left me in October. She'd been living here for only a couple of weeks. We fell out, as I said."

October, Münster thought. *Everything happens in October.*

"These things happen," he said.

"Yes, they do," said Mauritz. "I'm tired. I need to take a pill and go to bed."

He sneezed twice, as if to stress the point. Fished out a crumpled handkerchief and blew his nose. Münster waited.

"I understand that you're not in good shape," he said. "I'll leave you in peace soon enough. But do you remember Lene Bauer?"

"Who?"

"Lene. She was called Gruijtsen in those days. You sometimes went on vacation together. In the sixties."

"Ah, Lene! Good Lord, I was only a kid then. She spent most of the time with Ruth."

"But that episode in the shed—no doubt you remember that?"

"What shed?" asked Mauritz Leverkuhn.

"You hid there instead of going to school."

Mauritz took two deep, wheezing breaths.

"I haven't a clue what you're talking about," he said. "Not a goddamn clue."

Münster checked into a hotel down by the harbor that seemed about as run-down as he felt. He showered, then dined in the restaurant in the company of two decrepit old ladies and a few members of a handball team from Oslo. Then he returned to his room and made two phone calls.

The first was to Synn and Marieke (Bart was not at home, as it was a Wednesday and hence film club at school). Marieke was being visited by a girlfriend who would be sleeping over, and hence had time only to ask him what time he'd be coming home. He spoke to his wife for one and a half minutes.

Then Moreno. That call lasted nearly half an hour, and of course that said quite a lot in itself. She informed him about the new plastic bag in Weyler's Woods and the ongoing investigation into the scrap of newspaper; but most of the time they talked about other things.

Afterward he couldn't really remember what. He spent an hour watching three different films on television, then showered again and went to bed. It was only eleven o'clock, but he was still awake when the clock struck two.

36

Thursday the eighth of January was a comparatively fine day in Maardam. No sun, but on the other hand no rain—apart from a couple of hesitant drops just before dawn. And a good five degrees above freezing.

Bearable, in other words; and there was also a feeling of cautious optimism and a belief in the future about continued efforts to throw light on the Leverkuhn case.

The Leverkuhn–Van Eck–Bonger case.

Reports from the Forensic Chemistry Lab were arriving in quick succession, but today both Reinhart and Rooth were content to follow developments by telephone. They didn't want to suck up too much to Intendent Mulder, and they did have other things to see to.

The first message arrived at ten o'clock. New analyses of the typeface and paper showed that in all probability the Van Eck strip of paper had come from one of two publications: *Finanzpoost* or *Breuwerblatt*.

It took Ewa Moreno five seconds to hit upon the possible link with the Leverkuhns.

Pixner. Waldemar Leverkuhn had worked—for how long was it? Ten years?—at the Pixner Brewery, and the *Breuwerblatt* must surely be a magazine for people connected with the beer industry. There was no reason to assume that a subscription would cease when a worker retired.

"Leverkuhn," said Moreno when she, Reinhart, Rooth, and Jung gathered for a run-through in Reinhart's office. "It comes from the Leverkuhns, I'll bet my reputation on it!"

"Steady," said Reinhart, enveloping her in a cloud of tobacco smoke. "We mustn't jump to conclusions, as they say in Hollywood."

"Your reputation?" said Jung.

"Metaphorically speaking," said Moreno.

After a few productive telephone calls they had discovered all they needed to know about both magazines. *Finanzpoost* was very much a business publication with financial analyses, stock exchange reports, tax advice, and speculation tips. Circulation 125,000. Came out once a week, and was sold to subscribers and also over the counter. Number of subscribers in Maardam: more than 10,000.

"Fucking bourgeois rag," said Reinhart.

"For the bastards who decide the fate of the world," said Rooth.

Breuwerblatt was a different kettle of fish. It was published only four times a year and was a sort of trade journal for brewery workers in the whole country. Print run last year: 16,500. No over-the-counter sales. Distribution in Maardam: 1,260. One of the subscribers was Waldemar Leverkuhn.

"One thousand two hundred and sixty!" said Rooth. "How the hell can there be so many brewery workers in Maardam?"

"How many beers do you drink a week?" wondered Jung.

"Ah, well, yes, if you look at it like that," said Rooth.

It was agreed unanimously to put the bankers on the shelf for now and concentrate instead on the much more respectable producers of beer; but before they could even start there was a knock on the door and an overweight linguist by the name of Winckelhübe—a specialist in semiotics and text analysis—entered the room. Reinhart recalled contacting Maardam University the previous evening, and welcomed Winckelhübe somewhat reluctantly. He explained the situation in broad outline and gave him a copy of the magazine extract, a room to himself, and a request to deliver a report as soon as he thought he had anything useful to say.

While Reinhart was busy doing this, Moreno contacted the editorial office of *Breuwerblatt*, which luckily was located in nearby Löhr, and after a typically efficient visit by young Krause, half an hour later they had two copies of each of the last three years' issues lying on the table.

"Good God!" said Rooth. "This is going like clockwork. We've barely got time to eat."

And it was Rooth who found the right page.

"Here we are!" he yelled. "Three cheers!"

"Altho' a poor blind boy . . . ," said Reinhart. He went over to Rooth to check.

No doubt about it. The little strip of paper sticking out of Else Van Eck's bottom in Weyler's Woods came from the September issue of the previous year's *Breuwerblatt*. Pages eleven and twelve. At the top on the left—a two-column announcement about a working environment conference in Oostwerdingen. The picture on the reverse side was part of a table and a suit belonging to the county governor who was officially opening a new brewery in Aarlach.

"This is pretty clear," said Reinhart.

"Crystal clear," said Moreno.

"It's obvious he has cirrhosis of the liver," said Rooth, examining the governor close up.

There followed a few seconds of silence.

"Did you say there were twelve hundred and sixty subscribers?" asked Jung. "So it doesn't necessarily . . ."

"Don't be such a prophet of doom!" said Rooth. "Of course it's from the Leverkuhns. So she's done in the old lady Van Eck as well, I'll stake my damned . . . house on it."

"Metaphorically speaking?" asked Moreno.

"Literally," said Rooth.

Reinhart cleared his throat.

"The evidence seems to suggest it might be from the Lever-kuhns," he said. "In any case, shouldn't we order some coffee and discuss the matter in somewhat more formal circumstances?"

"I'm with you there," said Rooth.

During the coffee session another report arrived from the Forensic Chemistry Lab, and Reinhart had the pleasant task of informing Intendent Mulder that they were already dealing with the matter.

Since it was rather urgent. In the unlikely event of there being other stuff to attend to at the lab, there was nothing now to prevent them from getting on with it.

"I understand," said Mulder, and hung up.

Reinhart did the same, lit his pipe, and smiled grimly.

"So, where were we?" he said, looking around the table.

"Oh, shit!" said Moreno.

"There speaks a real woman," said Rooth.

But Moreno made no attempt to comment.

"It's just dawned on me," she said instead.

"What has?" said Jung.

"I think I know how it happened," said Moreno.

Thursday the eighth of January was a relatively fine day in Frigge. Before setting off Münster noted that the gale had died down during the night and that the morning presented a pale blue non-threatening sky, and a temperature probably a few degrees above freezing.

He set out shortly after nine, weighed down by the same tiredness he had been feeling for the last few months. Like an old friend almost. *At least I have a faithful stalker,* he thought cynically.

According to the directions he had been given, the Gellner Home was situated just outside the town of Kielno, only a couple of miles from Kaalbringen, where he had spent a few weeks some years ago in connection with a notorious axe murder. As he sat driving through the flat countryside, he recalled those weeks in September. The idyllic little coastal town, and all the bizarre circumstances that eventually led to the capture of the killer.

And Inspector Moerk. Beate Moerk. Another female colleague he had gotten to know too well. Perhaps he ought to ask himself if this was a flaw in his character—being unable to keep certain female colleagues at the necessary professional distance?

He wondered what she was doing nowadays. Was she still in Kaalbringen? Was she still single?

And Bausen! What the hell was Chief Inspector Bausen doing now? He made up his mind to ask Van Veeteren the next time he saw him. If anyone would know, he would.

The drive took less than an hour. For some reason the Gellner Home was signposted from the motorway, and he had no trouble finding it. He parked in a lot with space for a hundred or so cars, but there was only a handful of vehicles there at the moment. He followed a series of discreet signs and entered the reception in a low, oblong building on top of a ridge. The whole complex seemed to be spread out over a considerable area. Yellow and pale green buildings two or three stories high. Lawns and plenty of flower beds and trees. Small copses and a strip of larches and mixed deciduous trees encircling the grounds. Irregular paths, paved with stone, and frequent groups of benches around small tables. The whole place seemed attractively peaceful, but he didn't see a single person in the open air.

I expect it's very different in the summer, he thought.

As agreed, he first met the woman he had spoken to twice on the telephone—the same confidence-inspiring welfare officer who had informed him about Irene Leverkuhn's illness during the first stages of the investigation in October.

Her name was Hedda deBuuijs, and she seemed to be about fifty-five. A short, powerfully built woman with dyed iron-gray hair and a warm smile that seemed unable to keep away from her face for more than a few seconds at a time. It was clear to Münster that the respect for her he had felt during the telephone calls was in no way precipitate or unfounded.

She gave him no new information in connection with his impending meeting with Irene Leverkuhn, and explained that he should not expect too much and that she would have time for a brief chat with him afterward, if he felt that would help.

Then she rang for a nurse, and Münster was led along several of the stone paths to one of the yellow buildings at the far end of the grounds.

He didn't really know what to expect from his meeting with Irene Leverkuhn—or indeed if he expected anything at all. In appearance she was nothing at all like her overweight brother and sister. More like her mother: slim and wiry, it seemed, under her loose-fitting pale blue hospital jacket. Slightly hunchbacked, with long, thin arms and a birdlike face. Narrow nose and pale eyes noticeably close together.

She was sitting at a table in quite a large room, painting in watercolors on a pad. Two other women were sitting at different tables busy with some kind of batik prints, as far as Münster could tell. The nurse left, and he sat down opposite Irene Leverkuhn. She glanced at him, then returned to her painting. Münster introduced himself.

"I don't know you," Irene said.

"No," said Münster. "But perhaps you'd like to have a little chat with me even so?"

"I don't know you," she repeated.

"Do you mind if I sit here for a while, and watch while you paint?"

"I don't know you. I know everybody here."

Münster looked at the painting. Blue and red in big, wavy shapes: she was using too much water and the paper was buckling.

It looked more or less like it did when his own daughter occupied herself with the same pastime. He noticed that the used pages in the pad looked roughly the same.

"Do you like living here at the Gellner Home?" he asked.

"I live in number twelve," Irene said. "Number twelve."

Her voice was low and totally without expression. As if she were speaking a language she didn't understand.

"Number twelve?"

"Number twelve. The other girl is called Rebecka. I'm also a girl."

"Do you often have visitors?" Münster asked.

"Liesen and Veronica live in number thirteen," said Irene. "Liesen and Veronica. Number thirteen. I live in number twelve. Rebecka also lives in number twelve. Twelve."

Münster swallowed.

"Do you often have visits from your family? Your mother and father, your brother and sister?"

"I'm painting," said Irene. "Only girls live here."

"Ruth?" said Münster. "Does she often come here?"

"I don't know you."

"Do you know who Mauritz is?"

Irene didn't reply.

"Mauritz Leverkuhn. Your brother."

"I know everybody here," said Irene.

"How long is it since you came here?" Münster asked.

"I live in number twelve," said Irene.

"Do you like sitting here, talking to me?"

"I don't know you."

"Can you tell me your mother's and father's names?"

"We get up at eight o'clock," said Irene. "But we can lie in until nine if we want. Rebecka always stays in bed until nine."

"What are you called?" Münster asked.

"I'm called Irene. Irene's my name."

"Have you any brothers and sisters?"

"I'm painting," said Irene. "I do that every day."

"Your painting is beautiful," said Münster.

"I paint in red and blue," said Irene.

Münster stayed for a while, until she finished the picture. She didn't even look at it, but simply turned to another page in the pad and started again. She never looked up to glance at him, and when he stood up to leave, she seemed unaware of his presence or his going.

Or even that he had ever been there.

"One of the problems," said deBuuijs when Münster returned to her office, "is that she is physically well. She might even be happy. She is forty-six years old, and frankly, I can't see her surviving in society, functioning as a normal citizen. Can you?"

"I don't really know," said Münster.

Fröken deBuuijs eyed him for a few seconds, smiling as usual.

"I know what you're thinking," she said eventually. "Cows and hens and pigs are also happy. Or contented, at least . . . until we slaughter them. But we demand a little bit more from life. Don't we?"

"Yes," said Münster. "I suppose we do."

"Irene hasn't always been like this," said deBuuijs. "Ever since she fell ill she has retired into her own little, familiar world, but she didn't feel secure before then either. In recent years, as long as she's been here in the Gellner Home, she's behaved as I assume she did when you spoke to her."

"Inside herself?" said Münster.

"You could put it like that. Never anywhere distant from her immediate surroundings. Neither in time nor space. But contented, as I said."

Münster thought for a moment.

"Is she on medication?"

DeBuuijs shook her head. "Not anymore. Or nothing to speak of, in any case."

"Any kind of . . . treatment?"

She smiled again. "I thought we'd get around to this eventually," she said. "We are expected to do *something*, after all—right? The least we can do is try to restore some kind of dignity. . . . Yes, of course Irene undergoes therapy—if she didn't, she would presumably come to a full stop one of these days."

Münster waited.

"We work partly on a traditional basis," explained deBuuijs, "but we also experiment to some extent. We don't take any risks, of course, but in Irene's case it has worked surprisingly well—or at least, that's what our therapist says."

"Really?" said Münster.

"We have a sort of conversational therapy every day. In small groups. We do that with all our patients. And then we have a few therapists who come here and work on an individual basis. Various schools of thought and methods, we don't want to exclude anything. Irene has been meeting a young woman by the name of Clara Vermieten for nearly a year now, and it seems to have gone well."

"In what way?" Münster asked.

"I don't really know," said Hedda deBuuijs. "They're taking a break at the moment because Clara has just had a baby; but she intends to continue the therapy in the spring."

Münster began to wonder if deBuuijs had something hidden up her sleeve, or if she was just making conversation out of pure politeness.

"If you would like to listen in, I can fix that," said deBuuijs after a short pause. "Seeing as you have come all that way."

"Partake?" wondered Münster.

"All the conversations are recorded on tape. I haven't heard them, but I called Clara when I heard that you were coming. She has nothing against your listening to the tapes. Assuming that you don't abuse them in any way, of course."

"Abuse them?" said Münster. "How would I be able to abuse them?"

DeBuuijs shrugged.

"I might have to switch off certain comments now and then," she said. "That's part of my job. Is that okay with you?"

"Yes," said Münster. "I understand."

DeBuuijs stood up.

"I think we are on the same wavelength," she said. "Come with me, I'll take you to her room. You can sit there for as long as you like. If you'd like a cup of coffee while you're listening, I'll bring you one."

"Yes, please," said Intendent Münster. "I could do with one."

37

"What do you mean?" said Jung. "How it happened?"

"It's an idea that struck me," said Moreno. She bit her lip and hesitated for a few seconds. "Do you remember that day—a Thursday, I think it was—when Arnold Van Eck reported that his wife had disappeared? We drove there. . . . Come to think of it, it was just Münster and I. Anyway, we arrived at Kolderweg to talk to Van Eck. We met Fru Leverkuhn in the entrance hall. She was clearing away stuff that had belonged to Waldemar, carrying out suitcases and sacks with his old clothes. She was going to take them to the charity shop in Windemeerstraat. She was busy doing that for most of the time we were there. But of course . . . of course, it wasn't just clothes she was carrying out."

Rooth froze, with his coffee cup halfway to his mouth.

"What the hell are you saying?" he exclaimed. "Are you suggesting . . . are you suggesting that she was carrying out the Van Eck woman before your very eyes? Butchered and packaged? That's the most . . . who was it who said something about a blind boy a few minutes ago?"

"It's not possible," said Reinhart. "Or maybe that's exactly what it is," he added after a few seconds. "Do you really believe this?"

"I don't know," said Moreno. "What do you all believe?"

"Believing is something you do in church," said Rooth. "You were the one there, watching. How the hell could *we* know what she had in the bags?"

"It's a bit steep," said Jung. "It sounds incredible."

Nobody spoke. Moreno stood up and started walking back and forth in front of the window. Reinhart watched her as he scraped out his pipe and waited. Rooth swallowed his Danish pastry and looked around for another. When he failed to find one, he sighed and shrugged.

"Okay," he said. "As you all seem to have been struck dumb, I'll take over the baton. Shall we go there again? For the seventy-fourth time? In any case we need to check if there's anything left of that magazine. And see if we can find any bloodstained suitcases. Although we ought to have found those already if they exist. If it is as Moreno says, it would be the most . . . Christ Almighty, the most . . ."

He couldn't think of what it would be. Reinhart put down his pipe and cleared his throat demonstratively.

"Jung and Moreno," he said. "You know the way?"

"Haven't you left yet?" said Rooth.

"There's just one thing I don't understand," said Moreno after they had established that there wasn't so much as a quarter of a square centimeter left of the *Breuwerblatt*'s September issue—nor any sign of bloodstained suitcases—in the Leverkuhns' apartment in Kolderweg. "If it really was her."

"What?" said Jung.

"Why?" said Moreno.

"Why?"

"Yes. Why on earth would she also want to kill Else Van Eck as well?"

Jung thought for a moment.

"Where do you think she did it?" he said. "The butchery, I mean. If we ignore why for the time being."

Moreno shook her head.

"How should I know? The bathtub, perhaps. Yes, she hit and killed her with a frying pan, then butchered her in the bathroom—

that sounds about right, don't you think? That's what I'd do. Afterward you only need to rinse everything down, maybe a bit of soap or scrubbing powder. But why? Tell me why! We can't just ignore the cause, there must be a reason."

"I don't know," said Jung. "I'm just one of the blind boys."

At a quarter to two—that same rain-free January day—there was a discreet knock on the door of Inspector Reinhart's room.

"Come in," said Reinhart.

The door opened slowly, and Winckelhübe the linguist popped his head around it.

"Ah, yes," said Reinhart, looking up from his pile of papers.

"Well, I've made a little analysis," said Winckelhübe, scratching his stomach. "I'm not a hundred percent certain, but I'm prepared to bet on it being about seals. The text, that is."

"Seals?" said Reinhart.

"Yes, seals," said Winckelhübe.

"Hmm," said Reinhart. "That's exactly what we suspected. Thank you very much. Send your invoice to the police authorities."

Winckelhübe remained standing there, looking slightly confused.

"Would you like a lollipop as well?" asked Reinhart. "I'm afraid we've run out."

It was obvious that the therapist Clara Vermieten treated several of the patients at the Gellner Home. In the bookcase of the cramped office deBuuijs showed Münster into, four of the shelves were marked with initials. It said I.L. on the top shelf, where there were several cassettes, neatly sorted into stacks of ten. Münster counted sixty-five of them. The lower shelves contained significantly fewer.

On the tiny desk was a portrait of a dark-haired man of about thirty, a telephone, and a cassette recorder.

Ah, Münster thought. *I'd better get to it, then.*

He lifted down one of the stacks. He noted that there was a date on the spine of each cassette: 3/4, 3/8, 3/11 . . . and so on. He took one out at random and inserted it into the cassette player. It seemed to have been rewound to the beginning, as it started with a voice he assumed was Clara Vermieten's, stating the date on which the recording was made.

Conversation with Irene Leverkuhn, the fifteenth of April, nineteen hundred and ninety-seven.

Then a short pause.

"Irene, it's Clara. How are you today?"

"I'm well today," said Irene in the same monotonous tone of voice that he had been listening to not long ago.

"It's good to see you again," said the therapist. *"I thought we could have a little chat, as we usually do."*

"As we usually do," said Irene.

"Has it been raining here today?"

"I don't know," said Irene. *"I haven't been out."*

"It was raining when I drove here. I like rain."

"I don't like rain," said Irene. *"It can make you wet."*

"Would you like to lie down, as usual?" Clara asked. *"Or would you prefer to sit?"*

"I'd like to lie down. I usually lie down when we talk."

"You can lie down, then," said Clara. *"Do you need a blanket? Perhaps it's a bit cold?"*

"It's not cold," said Irene.

Münster pressed fast forward, then pressed play again.

"Who is that?" he heard the therapist ask.

"I can't really remember," said Irene.

"But you know his name, do you?"

"I know his name," Irene confirmed.

"What's he called?" asked Clara.

"He's called Willie."

"And who's Willie?"

"Willie is a boy in my class."

"How old are you now, Irene?"

"*I'm ten. I've got a blue dress, but it has a stain on it.*"

"*A stain? How did that happen?*"

"*I got a stain when I had ice cream,*" said Irene.

"*Was that today?*" Clara asked.

"*It was this afternoon. Not long ago.*"

"*Is it summer?*"

"*It was summer. It's autumn now, school has started.*"

"*What class are you in?*"

"*I have started class four.*"

"*What's your class mistress called?*"

"*I don't have a class mistress. We have a man. He's strict.*"

"*What's he called?*"

"*He's called Töffel.*"

"*And where are you just now?*"

"*Just now I'm in our room, of course. I've come home from school.*"

"*What are you doing?*"

"*Nothing.*"

"*What are you going to do?*"

"*I've got a stain on my dress, I'm going to the kitchen to wash it off.*"

Münster switched off again. Looked at the stacks of cassettes on the shelf and rested his head on his right hand. *What on earth am I doing?* he thought.

He pressed fast forward and listened for another minute. Irene was talking about the kind of paper she used to make covers for her schoolbooks, and what they'd had for school lunches.

He rewound the cassette and put it back into the case. Leaned back in the chair and looked out the window. He suddenly shuddered as it dawned on him that what he had just listened to was a situation taking place—when exactly? At the very beginning of the 1960s, he guessed. The conversation was recorded less than a year ago, but in fact Irene Leverkuhn had traveled a long way back in her childhood— somewhere in that drab little house in Pampas that he had been looking at only a few weeks ago. That was pretty remarkable, for goodness' sake.

He began to respect this therapist and what she was doing. He hadn't managed to get a word of sense out of the woman who had sat at a desk painting, but here she was telling Clara Vermieten all kinds of things.

I must reassess psychoanalysis, Münster thought. *It's high time.*

He looked at the clock and wondered how best to continue. Just listening to cassettes at random, one after the other, didn't seem especially efficient, no matter how fascinating it might be. He stood up and examined the dates written on the cassette cases.

The first one was recorded just over a year ago, it seemed. On 11/25/1996. He took down the stack farthest to the right, comprising only four cassettes. The bottom one was dated 10/16, the top one 10/30.

He went back to the desk, picked up the telephone, and after various complications had Hedda deBuuijs on the other end of the line.

"Just a quick question," he said. "When did Clara Vermieten take maternity leave?"

"Just a moment," said deBuuijs, and he could hear her leafing through some ledger or other.

"The end of October," she said. "Yes, that's when it was. She had a little girl about a week later."

"Thank you," said Münster, and hung up.

He removed the top cassette from the stack and took out the one dated October 25. Saturday, October 25. Went back to the desk chair, sat down, and started listening.

It took about ten minutes before he got there, and while he was waiting he recalled something Van Veeteren had once said. At Adenaar's, as usual, probably one Friday afternoon, when he usually liked to speculate a bit more than usual.

"You've got to get to the right person," the chief inspector had asserted. "In every case there's one person who knows the truth— and the frustrating thing is, Intendent, that they usually don't realize it themselves. So we have to hunt them down. Search high and low for them, and keep persevering until we find them. That's our job, Münster!"

He recalled what Van Veeteren had said word for word. And now here he was, having found one of those people. One of those truths. If he had interpreted the evidence correctly.

"*Where are you now?*" asked Clara.

"*I'm at home,*" said Irene.

"*Whereabouts at home?*"

"*I'm in my bed,*" said Irene.

"*You're in your bed. In your room? Is it night?*"

"*It's evening.*"

"*Are you alone?*"

"*Ruth is in her bed. It's evening, but it's late.*"

"*But you're not asleep?*"

"*I'm not asleep, I'm waiting.*"

"*What are you waiting for?*"

"*I want it to go quickly.*"

"*What do you want to go quickly?*"

"*It must go quickly. Sometimes it goes quickly. It's best then.*"

"*You're waiting, you say?*"

"*It's my turn tonight.*"

"*Is there someone special you're waiting for?*"

"*His cock is so big. It's enormous.*"

"*His cock?*"

"*It's stiff and big. I can't get it into my mouth.*"

"*Who are you waiting for?*"

"*It hurts, but I have to be quiet.*"

"*How old are you, Irene?*"

"*Ruth couldn't keep quiet yesterday. He prefers me. He comes to me more often. It's my turn this evening, he'll be here soon.*"

"*Who's coming?*"

"*I've rubbed that ointment into myself, so that it won't hurt so much. I hope it will go quickly.*"

"*Where are you, Irene? How old are you?*"

"*I'm in bed. I'm trying to make my hole bigger so that there's room for his cock. It's so big, his cock. He's so heavy, and his cock is so big. I have to keep quiet.*"

"*Why do you have to keep quiet?*"

"*I have to be quiet so that Mauritz doesn't wake up. He's coming now, I can hear him. I have to try to be bigger still.*"

"*Who's coming? Who are you waiting for?*"

"*I can only get two fingers inside, I hope it goes quickly. His cock is terrible.*"

"*Who's coming?*"

"*. . .*"

"*Irene, who are you waiting for?*"

"*. . .*"

"*Who is it that has such a big cock?*"

"*. . .*"

"*Irene, tell me who's coming.*"

"*It's Dad. He's here now.*"

38

Jung was standing by Bertrandgraacht, staring at Bonger's boat for the hundred and nineteenth time.

It lay there, dark and inscrutable—but all of a sudden he had the impression that it was smiling at him. A friendly and confidential smile, of the kind that even an old canal boat can summon up in gratitude for unexpected and undeserved attention being paid to it.

What? You old boat bastard, Jung thought. *Are you telling me it was as simple as that? Was that really what happened?*

But Bonger's boat didn't reply. Its telepathic powers evidently didn't run to more than a discreet smile, so Jung turned his back on it and left. He pulled down his cap and dug his hands deeper into his coat pockets: a biting wind had blown up from the northwest, putting an end to the fraternization.

"I have an idea," he said when he bumped into Rooth in the canteen not long afterward.

"I have a thousand," said Rooth. "But none of them work."

"I know," said Jung. "Redheaded dwarfs and all that."

"I've dropped that one," said Rooth. "Nine hundred and ninety-nine, then. What are you trying to say?"

"Bonger," said Jung. "I think I know where he is."

Münster remained in the room with the cassette player for a quarter of an hour after switching it off. Stared out the window at the deserted grounds again while the jigsaw pieces inside his mind joined together, one after another. Before he stood up he tried to ring Synn, but she wasn't at home. Of course not. He let it ring ten or so times, hoping that the answering machine would kick in, but evidently she had switched it off.

"I love you, Synn," he whispered even so into the dead receiver; then he went back to Hedda deBuuijs's office.

She was dealing with a visitor, and he had to wait for another ten minutes.

"How did it go?" she asked when Münster eventually sat down on her visitor chair.

For one confused second he didn't know what to say. How *had* it gone?

Well? Exceedingly well? A disaster?

"Not bad," he said. "I discovered quite a bit. But there are a few things I need some help with."

"I'm at your service," said Hedda deBuuijs.

"Clara Vermieten," said Münster. "I need to speak to her. A telephone call would do."

"Let's see," said deBuuijs, leafing through a couple of lists. "Yes, here we are. There's something I need to follow up on, so you can talk undisturbed. I'll be back in fifteen minutes."

She left the room. Münster dialed the number, and as he waited he worried that Clara Vermieten might have gone away on an open-ended visit. To Tahiti or Bangkok. Or the north of Norway. That would be typical.

But when she answered he immediately recognized her silky voice and her slight Nordic accent from the cassette. It took a few moments for her to realize who he was, but then she recalled having given him permission to listen to the cassette recordings, via Hedda deBuuijs.

"Forgive me," she said. "I'm being pestered by a couple of children. They tend to wear you down."

"I know how it is," said Münster.

He had only two questions, and as he could hear the whining

and whimpering clearly in the background, he came straight to the point.

"Do you know about the murders of Waldemar Leverkuhn and Else Van Eck down in Maardam?" he asked.

"What?" said Clara. "No, I don't think so. . . . Maardam, did you say? There are so many. . . . What was the name again?"

"Leverkuhn," said Münster.

"Good Lord!" said Clara. "Is it . . . ?"

"Her father," said Münster.

Silence.

"I didn't know," said Clara after a while. "I don't know. . . . When did it happen?"

"October," said Münster. "The same week as you had your last conversation with Irene, in fact."

"I was in the maternity ward from the second of November," said Clara. "Gave birth on the fifth. Good Lord, does she know about it? No, of course she doesn't. Have you met her?"

"Yes," said Münster. "And I've listened to the tapes. Several of them. Toward the end."

Clara said nothing for a while again.

"I understand," she said eventually. "What you must have heard. But I don't really understand why it should be of any interest to you. Surely you don't mean it could have something to do with what happened? With the goings-on in Maardam? Did you say murder?"

"I'm afraid so," said Münster. "It's all very complicated. We won't go into that now, but I'd like to ask you something that's very important for our investigation. I hope you can make a correct judgment—but I'm sure you can," he added. "I must say I have the deepest respect for what you have managed to achieve with Irene Leverkuhn."

"Thank you," said Clara.

"Anyway," said Münster. "What I'm wondering is if she— Irene, that is—can remain in that state . . . in those childhood experiences . . . even after you've concluded your conversation. Or whether you have to return her to the present every time."

A few seconds passed.

"Do you understand what I'm getting at?" Münster asked.

"Of course," said Clara. "I was just wondering. . . . Yes, she could well recall it, what we were talking about. For a while, at least . . . if somebody were to strike the right chord, so to speak."

"You're sure about that?"

"As sure as one can be. The soul isn't a machine."

"Thank you," said Münster. "I have what I need to know. But I'd like to talk to you again at some point, if that's possible."

He could hear her smiling as she replied.

"You've got my number, Intendent. I have a brother in Maardam, incidentally."

"There's just one detail left now," said Münster when deBuuijs returned. "You said that you keep a record of all visits the patients in this home receive. Could you please give me access to that information? I know I'm being a nuisance, but I promise to leave you in peace after this."

"No problem," said Hedda deBuuijs with her usual enthusiasm. "Would you like to follow me?"

They went into the reception area, where deBuuijs knocked on a little glass window. Before long she was handed two red ring binders, which she passed on to the intendent.

"Last year," she said. "If you need to go further back than that, just knock on the glass window and tell one of the girls. There's something I must see to now, if you'll excuse me."

"Thank you," said Münster. "These two will be fine. You have been very hospitable and of great help."

"No problem," said Hedda deBuuijs, leaving him again.

Münster sat down at a table and started thumbing through them.

Now, he thought. *Now we shall see if everything falls into place. Or if it falls apart.*

Five minutes later he knocked on the window and returned the binders.

If somebody were to strike the right chord? he thought as he drove out of the car park. That is what Clara Vermieten had said. It couldn't be put any better.

"What the hell do you mean?" said Reinhart.

"Don't bother trying to comprehend what you don't under-stand anyway," said Van Veeteren. "Tell me the situation instead!"

"We're nearly there," said Reinhart.

"There?"

"Listen carefully, my dear ex–chief inspector," said Reinhart. "Münster is up north, and things are going according to plan, if not better. I spoke to him on the phone half an hour ago, and he'd unearthed evidence that points clearly in a certain direction."

"Go on," said Van Veeteren.

Reinhart sighed and explained patiently what had happened for another two or three minutes until Van Veeteren interrupted him.

"All right, that's enough," he said. "We'll drive there. You can tell me the rest in the car."

"Drive there? What the hell . . . ?" exclaimed Reinhart, but as he did so a warning light started blinking somewhere in the back of his mind. He thought for a moment. If there was a rule he had discovered that was worth following during the chief inspector's time—just one single rule—it was this one.

Never ask questions when Van Veeteren makes a sudden and apparently incomprehensible decision.

Reinhart had done that a few times. At first. Queried the deci-sion. He had always been proved wrong.

"You can pick me up outside Adenaar's five minutes from now," said Van Veeteren. "No, four minutes. Are you with me?"

"Yes," Reinhart said with a sigh. "I'm with you."

· · ·

When Münster had finished his dinner at a Chinese restaurant, he realized once again how tired he was. He drank his usual two cups of strong black coffee as an antidote, and wondered how many years it would be before he had stomach ulcers. Five? Two?

Then he paid, and tried to concentrate on work again.

On the case. The last act was looming now. About time too: he made a mental note to the effect that he would go to Hiller and demand a week off as soon as it was all over. Or on Monday. Make that two weeks.

Then he phoned Maardam from the car, to put them in the picture. He spent ten minutes relating the latest developments to Heinemann, the only person available. Heinemann concluded by urging him to be extremely careful, in his usual long-winded style.

When he had finished with Heinemann, Münster informed the local police authorities. Spoke to Inspector Malinowski, who had some difficulty in catching on at first: but he eventually seemed to have grasped the situation. He promised that everything would be on standby by the time he heard again from Intendent Müssner.

"Münster," said Münster. "Not Müssner."

"Okay," said Malinowski. "I've made a note."

He started the engine and set off. It was almost six o'clock, and darkness was beginning to settle over the deserted town. A strong wind had blown up again, but there still hadn't been a drop of rain this long Thursday.

He parked a few minutes later. Remained seated for a while, composing himself. Then he checked that he had both his gun and his cell phone with him and got out of the car.

39

"There's a film by Tarkovsky," said Van Veeteren. "His last one. *The Sacrifice*. That is what this is all about."

Reinhart nodded. Then he shook his head.

"Enlighten me," he said. "I've seen it, but it was several years ago."

"You should see Tarkovsky several times, if you have the opportunity," said Van Veeteren. "There are so many layers of meaning. You don't remember it?"

"Not off the top of my head."

"He poses a fundamental question in that film. We could put it like this: If you meet God in a dream and make him a promise, what do you do when you wake up?"

Reinhart stuck his pipe in his mouth.

"I do recall that," he said. "He's going to sacrifice his son in order to make the reality that is threatening everybody merely an illusion, isn't that right? A world war becomes only a nightmare if he carries out that deed?"

"Something like that," said Van Veeteren. "The question, of course, is whether we really do receive signs like that. And what happens if we ignore them. Break the agreement."

Reinhart sat in silence for a while.

"I never stood on the lid of a well during the whole of my childhood," he said.

"That's presumably why you're still alive," said Van Veeteren. "How long to go?"

"An hour," said Reinhart. "I have to say I'm still not at all sure what the heck Tarkovsky has to do with this trip. But I suspect you are not going to tell me?"

"You suspect correctly," said Van Veeteren, lighting a newly rolled cigarette. "That's also part of the agreement."

The taxi driver's name was Paul Holt. It was Krause who had tracked him down, and Moreno met him in his yellow car outside the Hotel Kraus. A slim man in his thirties. White shirt, tie, and a neat ponytail. Moreno sat down in the front passenger seat, and when he shook her hand and introduced himself she detected the distinct smell of marijuana on his breath.

Ah well, she thought. *He's not going to be driving me anywhere.*

"It's about that fare of yours a few months ago," she said. "Fru Leverkuhn in Kolderweg. How well do you remember it?"

"Quite well," said Holt.

"It wasn't exactly yesterday," said Moreno.

"No," said Holt.

"You must have had hundreds of fares since then, surely?"

"Thousands," said Holt. "But you remember the special ones. I can tell you in detail about an old man in spotted trousers I drove eight years ago, if you want me to. In detail."

"I understand," said Moreno. "And that trip with Fru Leverkuhn—that was special, was it?"

Holt nodded.

"Why?"

Holt adjusted his hair ribbon and clasped his hands over the steering wheel.

"You know why just as well as I do," he said. "I mean, there were articles in all the newspapers about them. Mind you, I'd have remembered that trip in any case."

"Really?"

"It was a bit unusual, and that's the kind of thing you remember."

"So I gather," said Moreno. "Can you tell me where you drove
to, and what she did?"

Holt wound down the side window about four inches and lit an
ordinary cigarette.

"Well, it was more of a goods delivery than anything else. Both
the backseat and the trunk were full of suitcases and bags. I think
I pointed out to her that there were delivery firms for jobs like
that, but I'm not sure. I took it on, anyway. You do what you have
to do."

"Where did you go?"

"First to the charity shop in Windemeer," said Holt. "Dropped
off a few of the bags. I waited outside while she sorted things out
in the shop. Then we continued to Central Station."

"The railway station?"

"Yes, Central Station. We carried in the rest of the stuff. I think
there was a suitcase and two other bags—those big, soft-sided bags,
you know the kind. Yes, there were three of them. Heavy, too. She
locked them away in luggage lockers, and then we drove back to
Kolderweg. She got out at the shopping center. It was pouring."

Moreno thought for a while.

"You must have a good memory for details," she said.

He nodded, and drew on his cigarette.

"I suppose so," he said. "But as I said, it's not the first time I've
thought about that trip. Once you've recalled something, it's there.
Sort of like a photo album. Don't you think?"

Yes, Ewa Moreno thought after she had left the yellow taxi. He
was right about that. There were things you never forgot, no matter how much you wished you could. That early morning four
years ago, for instance, when she and Jung broke into a flat in
Rozerplejn, and found a twenty-four-year-old immigrant woman
with two small children in a large pool of blood on the kitchen

floor. The letter informing her that she would be deported was lying on the table. She recalled that all right. . . .

That remained in the photo album of her memory. And other scenes as well.

She checked her watch and wondered if there was any point in driving back to the police station. Or in calling and informing them about what Paul Holt had said. In the end she decided that it could wait until tomorrow. After all, everything seemed to confirm what they had guessed must be the facts. Marie-Louise Leverkuhn had used Central Station as a storage depot for a few days, or a day or so at least, before finally disposing of the butchered caretaker's wife in Weyler's Woods. Simple and painless. A neat solution.

On the way home she stopped to check the buses leaving Central Station. It fit. There was a bus. Number sixteen. It ran every twenty minutes during working hours. Once an hour if you preferred to work under the cover of darkness. Nothing could have been simpler.

But she would wait until tomorrow before reporting this. Unless Intendent Münster got in touch during the evening: that would obviously present an opportunity to report then.

It could well be an advantage to have something concrete to talk about. She had started to feel like she was standing with at least one foot on the wrong side of the border. That border you had to stake everything on not crossing—not least because all the roads over it were one way only. Once over it, there was no going back.

In my next life I'm going to be a lioness, Moreno thought, and made up her mind to sublimate all her desires and indeed the whole of the world by jumping into the bath and having a long soak in jujuba oil and lavender.

"You again?" said Mauritz Leverkuhn.

"Me again," said Münster.

"I don't get the point of all this," said Mauritz. "I've got nothing more to talk to you about."

"But I have quite a lot to talk to you about," said Münster. "Are you going to let me in?"

Mauritz hesitated for a moment, then shrugged and went into the living room. Münster closed the door behind him and followed. It looked the same as it had that morning. The same advertising leaflets were lying in the same place on the table, and the same glass was standing beside the easy chair on which Mauritz was now sitting.

But the television was on. A program in which four colorfully dressed women were sitting on two sofas, laughing. Mauritz pressed a button on the remote control and switched it off.

"Yes, indeed," said Münster, "I have a lot to talk to you about. I've been talking to your sister this afternoon."

"Ruth?"

"No, Irene."

Mauritz made no reply, didn't react.

"I spent several hours at the Gellner Home, in fact," said Münster. "You've been lying to me."

"Lying?" said Mauritz.

"Did you not say this morning that you hadn't been to see her for over a year?"

Mauritz emptied his glass.

"I forgot about that," he said. "I went to see her last autumn, I'm not sure when."

"Forgot?" said Münster. "You were there on Saturday, October twenty-fifth, the same day your father was murdered."

"What the hell has that got to do with it?"

He still didn't seem to have made up his mind what attitude to adopt, and Münster realized that his head must be spinning now. But surely he must have been expecting another visit? He must have known that Münster would return sooner or later. Or had the flu and the fever stopped his mind from working?

"Can you tell me what you and Irene talked about last October?"

Mauritz snorted.

"It's not possible to talk to Irene about anything sensible. You must surely have noticed that if you've been visiting her?"

"Maybe not in normal circumstances," said Münster. "But I don't think she was in her normal state that Saturday."

"What the hell do you mean by that?"

"Do you want me to spell out what she told you?"

Mauritz shrugged. "Go on," he said. "You seem to have a screw loose. Have had all this time, come to that."

Münster cleared his throat.

"When you arrived at the home, she had just finished a therapy session, isn't that right? With a certain Clara Vermieten. You saw her immediately afterward, and then . . . then she began talking about things from your childhood, things you had no idea about. Concerning your father."

Mauritz didn't move a muscle.

"Is it not the case," said Münster, "that on that Saturday afternoon you discovered circumstances you knew nothing about? Circumstances which, to some extent at least, explain the occurrence of Irene's illness? Why she became the way she is now."

"You're out of your mind," said Mauritz.

"And isn't it a fact that this news affected you so deeply that to a large extent you took leave of your senses?"

"What the hell are you sitting there babbling on about?" said Mauritz.

Münster paused.

"What I am talking about," he said eventually, as slowly and emphatically as he could, "is that you discovered that your father had been abusing both your sisters sexually throughout the whole of their childhood, and that as a result you got into your car, drove down to Maardam, and killed him. That's what I'm talking about."

Mauritz was still sitting there motionless, with his hands clasped in his lap.

"I can understand your reaction," Münster added. "I might have done the same if I'd been in your shoes."

It's possible that those were the words that made Mauritz change his tune. Or at least, to give way slightly. He sighed deeply, wiped the sweat off his brow, and seemed to relax.

"You can never prove this," he said. "You're being ridiculous. My mother has admitted to doing it. If it's true what you say about my father, she had just as good a reason for doing it as I had. Don't you think?"

"Could be," said Münster. "But it wasn't her that did it. It was you."

"It was her," said Mauritz.

Münster shook his head.

"Incidentally, why did you visit your sister on that particular Saturday?" he asked. "Was it because your girlfriend had just left you? The time scale seems to fit."

Mauritz didn't reply, but Münster could see from his reaction that the guess was probably spot-on. It was the same old story. Just as when a game of patience is about to be resolved, and the cards seem to turn up in a predictable order.

"Shall I tell you what happened next?" he asked.

Mauritz stood up with difficulty.

"No thank you," he said. "I want you to leave immediately. You are coming out with a mass of sick fantasies, and I have no intention of listening to you any longer."

"I thought you had just agreed that Irene really did tell you this?" Münster said.

Mauritz stood there for a few seconds, swaying back and forth indecisively.

"Your mother caught you in the act, didn't she?"

He didn't answer.

"Did she come home while you were stabbing him, or did you meet her on the way out?"

I'd give a fortune for his thoughts right now, Münster thought. *Surely he'll give up?*

"I suspect there are a few other things you don't know about," said Münster. "About what happened next, that is."

Mauritz stared at him for a few blank seconds again. Then he sat down.

"Such as what?" he said.

"Fru Van Eck," said Münster. "Did you see her that night, or was it just she who saw you?"

Mauritz said nothing.

"Have you any explanation for the murder of Else Van Eck? Did your mother tell you what happened? I'm asking because I don't know."

"You know nothing," said Mauritz.

"Then I'll have to speculate," said Münster. "But it's only of academic interest. Fru Van Eck saw you when you came to Kolderweg to kill your father. She told your mother she'd seen you a few days later. I'm not certain, but I assume she tried to use that knowledge to her own advantage. To earn money. Your mother reacted in a way she had never expected. She killed Fru Van Eck."

He paused for a few seconds, but Mauritz had no comment to make. *He knew about it,* Münster thought.

"She killed the caretaker's wife. Then she needed a few days to butcher the body and get rid of it. Then, when all was done, she confessed to the murder of your father, so that we would stop investigating and you would go free. A cold-blooded woman, your mother. Very cold-blooded."

"You're out of your mind," said Mauritz for the second time.

"Obviously she couldn't confess to the murder of Else Van Eck as well because she wouldn't have been able to give a motive. It all fits together, you see—I think you have to admit that. She commits one murder, but confesses to another one: perhaps there is some kind of moral balance there. I think that's the way she thought about it."

Mauritz muttered something and scrutinized his hands. Münster watched him for a while without saying anything. *He'll crack any minute,* he thought. *I don't have the strength to sit through all this again at the police station. I simply don't have the strength.*

"I'm not sure either why she committed suicide in her cell," he said. "But it's not difficult to sympathize with her. Perhaps it's not difficult to understand anything of what she did. She was protecting you from being discovered as the murderer of your father, and she murdered another person in order to continue protecting you. She did a lot for your sake, Herr Leverkuhn."

"She owed a debt," Mauritz said.

Münster waited, but there was no continuation.

"A debt for what your father did to your sisters, do you mean? For allowing it to happen?"

Mauritz suddenly clenched his fists and thumped them down on the arms of the chair.

"Hell and damnation!" he said. "He made Irene go mad and she didn't do anything to stop him! Can't you understand that he didn't deserve a natural death? The bastard! I'd do it again if I could. I was prepared to accept responsibility for it. I was going to do so, and that's why . . ."

He fell silent.

"Why she committed suicide?" asked Münster. "Because you were thinking of confessing?"

Mauritz stiffened, then seemed to crumble, and nodded weakly. Münster took a deep breath and closed his eyes. Opened them again and looked at the figure slumped in the chair opposite him: he tried to decide what he really felt about him.

One of those losers, he thought. *Yet another one.*

He must have been damaged by his childhood, even if it didn't make itself felt as dreadfully as in his beloved sister.

Those accursed, inescapable birthmarks that could never be operated away. That could never be glossed over or come to terms with.

And that accursed, pointless evil that kept on asserting itself, over and over again. Yes, he felt sorry for him. He would never have believed it an hour ago, but he did now.

"Are you going to arrest me now?" said Mauritz.

"They're waiting for us at the police station," said Münster.

"I don't regret a thing. I'd do it again, can you understand that?"

Münster nodded. He wanted comfort and understanding now. Münster recognized the situation. Oftentimes, it wasn't confirmation of a justified crime that would provide the release the perpetrator was longing for, but words. Being able to talk about it afterward. The ability to explain his actions face-to-face with another person. A person who understood, and a face that could tolerate the reflection of his desperation.

Oh yes, it had happened before.

"It would be wrong for a bastard like him to complete his life without being punished. . . . To get away with something like that."

"Let's go now," said Münster. "We'll talk about the rest at the station."

Mauritz stood up. Wiped the sweat off his brow again and breathed deeply.

"Can I just go to the kitchen and take another pill?"

Münster nodded.

He left the room, and Münster heard him dropping a tablet into a glass and then filling it with water. *Thank God,* he thought. *It's all over now. I can wash my hands of this awful business.*

It was too late when Münster realized that the passive resignation displayed by Mauritz Leverkuhn for the last few minutes was not quite what it had seemed. And too late when he realized that the carving knife they had spent so much time looking for in October and the beginning of November had not in fact been thrown into a canal or a trash can. It was in Mauritz Leverkuhn's hand now, just as it had been during the night between the twenty-fifth and the twenty-sixth of October. He discovered that fact out of the corner of his eye, looking over his right shoulder, felt for his pistol in its holster, but that was as far as he got. The knife blade entered his midriff from behind: he felt an agonizing stab of pain, then he fell headfirst onto the floor without taking the strain with his hands.

The pain was so acute that it paralyzed him. Penetrated the whole of his body like a white-hot iron drill of agony. Neutralized his ability to move. Annihilated time and space. When it eventually began to ease, he heard Mauritz Leverkuhn leave and slam the front door.

He turned his head and thought the cool parquet floor felt pleasant against his cheek. Gentle and conciliatory. *I'm tired,* he thought. *This would never have happened if I hadn't been so tired.*

Before a black wave of oblivion flowed over his consciousness, he thought two more thoughts.

The first was of Synn: *Good, I don't need to know how things would have turned out.*

The second was just one word:

No.

40

The police station in Frigge had moved since Van Veeteren served his apprenticeship in that northern coastal town. Or rather, they had squeezed a new building into the same block and rehoused the forces of law and order in almost the same place as before. Van Veeteren didn't think the move had improved anything. The new police station was built mainly of gray concrete and bulletproof glass, and the duty officer was a young red-haired man with prominent ears. Not a bit like old Borkmann.

Ah well, Van Veeteren thought. *At least his hearing ought to be sharp.*

"Reinhart and Van Veeteren from Maardam," said Reinhart. "What's your name?"

"Inspector Liebling," said the redhead, shaking hands.

"Chief Inspector Van Veeteren used to work up here actually," said Reinhart. "But that was probably before you were born."

"Really?" said Liebling.

"At the dawn of recorded time," said Van Veeteren. "Late nineteenth century. Have you heard anything?"

"You mean . . . ?" said Liebling, feeling a little nervously for his thin mustache.

"He ought to be here now, for Christ's sake," said Reinhart. "It's nearly eight o'clock."

"Intendent Münster from Maardam," Van Veeteren explained.

"Yes, I know," said Liebling. "Malinowski filled me in when I relieved him. I have the details here."

He tapped away at the computer keyboard and nodded his head in acknowledgment.

"Intendent Münster, yes. Expected to come in with a suspect . . . but there hasn't been one yet. He hasn't turned up yet, I mean."

"When did he contact you?" Van Veeteren asked.

Liebling checked.

"Five fifty-five," he said. "Inspector Malinowski took the call. I came on duty at six-thirty."

"And he hasn't called again?" asked Reinhart.

"No," said Liebling. "We haven't heard anything more since then."

"Did he give you any instructions?"

Liebling shook his head. "Only that we should stand by for when he arrived with this . . . person. We've got his number, of course. His cell."

"So have we," said Reinhart. "But he's not answering."

"Damn it!" said Van Veeteren. "Give us the address, and we'll go there! This is taking too long."

Liebling printed it out.

"Krautzweg 28," he said. "It's out at Gochtshuuis. Would you like me to come with you? To show you the way."

"Yes, come with us," said Van Veeteren.

"There's a light on," said Reinhart ten minutes later. "And that's his car."

Van Veeteren thought for a moment.

"Call one more time, to make sure we don't barge in at a vital moment," he said.

Reinhart took out his cell phone and dialed the number. Waited for half a minute.

"Nothing," he said. "He might have switched it off. Or forgot to charge the batteries."

"Batteries?" said Van Veeteren. "Do you need batteries in those bloody things as well?"

Inspector Liebling cleared his throat in the backseat.

"There's no other car standing outside," he pointed out. "And there doesn't seem to be a garage. . . . Assuming the Audi belongs to your man."

"Hmm," said Van Veeteren. "That's right. Okay, let's go in. Liebling, stay here in the car, in case something happens."

"Got you," said Liebling.

Reinhart and Van Veeteren approached the front door cautiously and listened.

"Can't hear a thing," said Reinhart. "Apart from the bloody wind. Nothing to be seen through the window either. What should we do? Ring the bell?"

"Try the door first," said Van Veeteren.

Reinhart did as told. It was locked.

"Okay, we'll ring the bell," said Van Veeteren. "Do you have your gun?"

Reinhart nodded and took out his Grossmann. He pressed himself as close to the wall as he could and Van Veeteren rang the bell.

Nothing happened. Van Veeteren waited for ten seconds, then rang again.

Nothing.

"Go around the house and check," said Van Veeteren. "I'll stay here."

It took less than half a minute for Reinhart to go around to the back and then return.

"It's not possible to get around the whole building," he explained. "This house is joined onto the next one. I couldn't see anything through the windows. I don't think there's anybody in."

"Then what the hell is Münster's car doing here?" asked Van Veeteren. "We have to go in."

"I suppose we do," said Reinhart.

Van Veeteren muttered a stream of curses while looking for a suitable means of assistance. He eventually found a stone the size of a clenched fist in the soaking-wet flower bed next to the drive. He dried it, weighed it in his hand for a second or two, then threw it at the living room window.

"Bull's-eye," said Reinhart. He went up to the broken pane, removed a few pieces of glass, put his hand through the hole, and opened it.

It was Van Veeteren who climbed in first, and Van Veeteren who saw him first.

"Oh fuck!" he said. "Fuck, fuck, fuck!"

Intendent Münster was lying on his stomach on the light-colored parquet floor, halfway out into the hall, as if he had been on his way out when he fell. His arms were stretched along the sides of his body, and on the back of his light green sweater, about an inch above the waistband of his trousers and to the right of his spine, was a dark red stain, slightly bigger than the palm of a man's hand.

"Ambulance, Reinhart! Like greased lightning!" roared Van Veeteren. Then he leaned down over Münster and started checking his pulse.

Good God, he thought. *This wasn't part of my leave-of-absence agreement.*

When Mauritz Leverkuhn left his home in Frigge, he drove due south for an hour and a half. When he came to Karpatz he changed direction and continued eastward until he came to Tilsenberg, just a few miles from the border. He filled his tank and turned off toward the north.

The nationwide alert was set in motion at 8:45, and when a police patrol car found his white Volvo at a rest stop off the motorway just outside Kossenaar, it was half past six in the morning.

Mauritz Leverkuhn was lying asleep under a blanket on the backseat, shivering, with a sky-high temperature and in a state of total exhaustion. On the floor in front of the passenger seat was a carving knife with a handle of mahogany and a blade about eight inches long, covered in blood.

Leverkuhn was taken to the police station in Kossenaar, but his condition was such that he was not subjected to questioning.

Given the circumstances, it was not considered necessary for him to say anything at all.

V

41

It took the two divers dressed in green and black less than a quarter of an hour to find Felix Bonger.

Jung stood in the rain in the middle of the little group of on-lookers in Bertrandgraacht, and tried to benefit from the scant shelter provided by Rooth's battered umbrella. When the swollen body was lifted up onto the quay and put inside a black body bag, he noticed that the woman on his left, the mannish Barga, was sniffling.

"It's so sad," she said. "He was such a fine fellow, Bonger."

"He was indeed," said Jung.

"They should really have left him there. Buried under his own boat—that would have been stylish."

Maybe, Jung thought. *That wasn't such a bad idea. Although perhaps it would have been more stylish if they had never found him. Let's face it, he had nothing to do with that other business. Absolutely nothing.*

He had slipped on the gangplank, that's all, when he came home that Saturday night. Drunk and unsteady on his feet. *It could have happened to anybody,* Jung thought. *It could have happened to me.* Presumably he had hit his head and fell into the water. Sunk a few feet, and later floated up against the bottom of his own canal boat.

And stayed there. Under his own floor. Yes, Barga had a point.

"Poor bastard," said Rooth. "Lying in the water doesn't make you any prettier. But I should congratulate you. You were right after all. . . . There was nothing more mysterious to it than that. I wonder how many other missing persons are lying in canals."

"Let's not worry about that just now," said Jung. "I think we ought to try to get a roof over our heads instead."

"Another good idea," said Rooth, shaking the umbrella so that Jung became even wetter than he was already. "But there's one thing you can clear up for me first, before I forget."

"What's that?" said Jung.

"That pair of screwing machines . . . de Booning and whatever the other bugger is called—why did they move out?"

"Menakdise," said Jung. "Tobose Menakdise. Guess."

"I haven't a clue," said Rooth.

"Okay. They need a bigger flat. She's expecting a child."

"How odd," said Rooth.

Jung was just about to turn around and leave when he felt a hand on his shoulder. It was Fru Jümpers, who was standing under another dripping umbrella.

"I was just wondering," she said. "Would you gentlemen like to come in for a glass of something? In my boat that is. Barga and I think we ought to drink a toast to the dearly departed."

"I don't know about that," said Jung. "I think we ought to—"

"Yes, of course," said Rooth. "We'll be there in two flicks of a donkey's tail."

At first Ulrike Fremdli thought the antiquarian bookshop was closed, but then she saw Van Veeteren sitting back in a wing chair in the middle of all the shelves.

"You won't sell much if you sit there all the time," she said.

Van Veeteren looked up from the little leather-bound volume he had in his hand.

"You have to become acquainted with the stock," he said. "Nice to see you."

"The same to you," said Ulrike Fremdli with a smile. Then she became serious. Looked at him with a slightly doubtful expression, shaking her head slowly.

"You are a remarkable fellow," she said. "I can't get over that. Do you mean . . . are you saying that your *Macbeth* dream came true?"

"True and true," muttered Van Veeteren.

"How is he?"

"Better," said Van Veeteren. "I was there an hour ago. He'll pull through, but they'll have to remove that kidney. And he's bound to be off work for several months—maybe that's just what he needs. He was foolish to go in on his own like he did."

Ulrike nodded.

"He's been worn-out," said Van Veeteren. "At least, that's what his wife, Synn, said. She was there at the hospital with the children. And Inspector Moreno as well. . . . It was good we turned up when we did—he couldn't have coped with lying there for much longer."

"But what about that dream?" said Ulrike again.

Van Veeteren didn't answer. Instead he leafed back through a few pages of the book he was reading.

" 'There are more things in heaven and earth, Horatio, than are dreamt of in your philosophy,' " he quoted. "*Hamlet*. A lovely little edition. Printed in Oxford in 1836. Just came in."

He held it up.

"I thought it was *Macbeth* we were talking about?" said Ulrike.

Van Veeteren stood up and replaced the volume in a bookcase with glass doors.

"It doesn't matter," he said. "There's something about Shakespeare. I think he's said more or less all that needs saying. He covers everything, you could say. . . . He'd even have been able to make something of that Leverkuhn family, no doubt."

"What do you mean?"

"Listen to this. The father rapes both his daughters. . . . One goes out of her mind, the other becomes a lesbian. The son murders his father and stabs a police officer. The mother takes all the guilt upon herself, butchers a witness, and hangs herself. Just the stuff to turn into a tragedy, don't you think?"

Ulrike eyed him skeptically.

"Is that what it's all about?" she said. "This case?"

"In a nutshell," said Van Veeteren. "And you should bear in mind that until three months ago they were regarded as a perfectly normal family—until somebody happened to lift the lid on them."

Ulrike thought that over for a while.

"How do you put up with it?" she said in the end.

"I don't put up with it," said Van Veeteren. "I work in a bookshop."

She nodded.

"I've heard it said. But you put your oar in, nevertheless, don't you?"

"I become involved," said Van Veeteren. "There's a difference. Anyway, it's . . ."

"It's time for lunch," said Ulrike. "I'm free until two o'clock. Are you coming?"

"Of course," said Van Veeteren, stretching his arms above his head. Adjusted his back gingerly and suddenly looked worried.

"What's the matter?"

Van Veeteren cleared his throat. "Nothing. I just can't help wondering, that's all."

"Wondering?"

"If this really was the way the tragedy happened. If life is a novel or a play, as some people suggest, it wouldn't be all that difficult to write another chapter, or another scene—or what do you think?"

"I don't know what you're talking about," said Ulrike Fremdli. "I'm hungry."

He took hold of her hand and squeezed it slightly awkwardly.

"I'm sorry," he said. "It's just that I sometimes find it a bit hard to keep my thoughts in check. Let's go."

42

Elaine Vorgus stared first at the tarot cards, and then at her lover.

"It's remarkable," she said. "I don't think it's ever happened to me before. All sixteen cards the wrong way around—no, I've never seen the likes of it before. I'll have to look it up in the books."

"What does it mean?" asked Ruth Leverkuhn, sipping her wine at the same time as she leaned forward over the table and stroked her girlfriend's bare arm. "What does it mean when they're back to front?"

It was not the first time they'd been sitting there like this, and even if it was Ruth's fate lying on the table in front of them, she knew that it meant more to her girlfriend than it did to herself. Elaine responded to her caress and looked up from the cards.

"The significance is the opposite of what the cards say," she said. "The message is reversed. Wealth means poverty, strength means weakness, love means hatred. . . . It's as simple as that. But all sixteen cards, that must mean something very special. As if . . ."

"As if what?" said Ruth, with loving patience.

"As if it referred to somebody quite different from you. As if the whole of you were back to front in some way. . . . But I'm only guessing. I've never come across sixteen cards the wrong way around before."

"Let's write it all down and leave it until later," said Ruth. "I want to drink more wine and then make love instead."

Elaine smiled and thought for a while. Then she raised her glass and ran her tongue over her lips a few times.

"Your wish is my command," she said with a smile. "Where would you like to start? In the bath, perhaps? I think I'd like that. I just need to make that phone call first."

"The bath's a good idea," Ruth decided. "Yes, I'd like to have you with me in the bath. Write down what's on the cards and then make that call. I'll get in the bath first, and be waiting for you."

Once in the bathroom she stood and contemplated her sizable body in the mirror. Lifted up her heavy breasts and sucked at each nipple for a few seconds. Stroked herself carefully between her legs with a finger in order to get confirmation of her desire.

Then her brother cropped up in her thoughts again, and she moved her hands to more neutral regions.

Poor Mauritz, she thought. *Fool!* She sighed and wrapped a bath towel around her. Continued thinking while she somewhat mechanically and absentmindedly rearranged the perfume bottles on the shelf under the mirror and selected her favorite foam bath scents.

What is the point of confessing to something you haven't done?

The question had been buzzing around in her mind for some days now. Nagging at her, making her worry. Why couldn't Mauritz simply have admitted to being a weakling instead? A cowardly and confused person who would never have been able to carry off anything like that? Not in any circumstances.

Twenty-eight stabs! Mauritz?

It was ridiculous. Anybody who knew anything at all about him could have explained that it was absolutely impossible.

But of course there wasn't anybody who knew anything about him. Apart from her.

So perhaps it wasn't all that odd after all. She had begun to realize that was the case after a few days. That he wanted to take the blame, and that people believed him. There was a sort of logic. A twisted and back-to-front logic, but it made sense even so.

But why had he gone to the trouble of buying an identical knife when they had already disposed of the real one—that was a genuine mystery. When she thought about it, she realized that this was the only thing she didn't understand. Couldn't make head or tail of it. He could never have planned to use it. To stab that police officer? The fact that he actually did so could hardly be explained in any other way than his being possessed by a sudden ability to act. Sudden and unexpected. Like a will-o'-the-wisp. Nothing else.

That was presumably how things were. The knife was an idée fixe. The stabbing of the police officer a coincidence: an act on the spur of the moment. Something to show her—or Irene, in some obscure way—that he did have it inside him. . . . But no, it was too far-fetched. Too logical. Mauritz could never plan and carry out anything like that. He could work something similar out in hindsight, perhaps, but he could never plan it in advance and then do it. He had never been able to think and act like that. That was the root of his weakness.

When he came to visit her in a state of near nervous collapse that Saturday in October, he had declared that he was going to do it—he had just discovered all the horrors that had happened in the past and was on his way to Maardam to give his father what he deserved. To take horrific revenge for their ruined youth and kill him without mercy. She had asked him why on earth he had come to her first, and then it was only a few minutes before he had collapsed in a heap on her sofa. Lay there, sniffling and shaking.

It was when she saw that pitiable performance that she made up her own mind. Decided to carry out the deed herself. He didn't even try to protest. Simply gaped at her with eyes shining in gratitude. Gratitude and desperate, desperate weakness.

That was also the image she had in her mind's eye when she did the deed. That damp-eyed, naked helplessness on the face of her brother. That pent-up hatred of their father.

And now he was in prison. For a number of crimes. It was remarkable, no doubt about it. When she spoke to him a few hours ago, he had seemed just as calm and collected as he had been for the last few days.

Reconciled, perhaps. Ready to take his punishment for the crime it had been his duty to commit, but which he didn't dare do. And for what he had done on the spur of the moment when in a confused state. Come to think of it, she couldn't recall ever having heard him sounding as secure and harmonious as he did now. Not as a child, or as a youth, or as an adult. That was the fact of the matter.

Perhaps there was a sort of meaning after all, Ruth thought. *A point to it all.* If her mother hadn't managed to protect her daughter as she had intended—simply because Mauritz hadn't been able to go through with the pretense—then perhaps there was no reason to prevent him from doing it. To take the blame as the vicarious murderer. If that's what he wanted to do.

Poor little Mauritz. Poor little brother.

She shook her head. That was the fact of the matter. And there was a lot in what Elaine had said. All the cards were the wrong way around.

Now she appeared in the doorway. Ruth observed her slim, naked body in the mirror. Her hot, slightly intoxicated gaze. Her black, almost bluish hair.

I love her, she thought. *Love, love, love. At least there is one member of the family left who is capable of doing that.*

In her own way.

She smiled. Let the bath towel fall to the floor.

BORKMANN'S POINT

Chief Inspector Van Veeteren is called to the sleepy coastal town of Kaalbringen to assist the local police in the investigation of two recent ax murders. Soon the case turns from bad to worse when another body turns up and one of Van Veeteren's colleagues, a young female detective, disappears without a trace. Now Van Veeteren must find the killer, and, he hopes, his colleague, before anyone else comes to harm. Riveting and intellectually satisfying, *Borkmann's Point* unfolds like a chess match where each move could prove deadly.

Crime Fiction

THE INSPECTOR AND SILENCE

When one of the Pure Life's members is found raped and strangled in the forest near the group's camp, the chief inspector is called to investigate. The Pure Life has chosen to remain silent about the incident rather than defend itself, so Van Veeteren's only lead is the anonymous caller who reported the body. As the unidentified woman continues to assist the authorities, her knowledge suggests she's more than just a passing Good Samaritan, but her tips become doubly perplexing as a new string of increasingly horrifying crimes defy everything Van Veeteren and his team thought they knew about the case.

Crime Fiction

MIND'S EYE

The swift conviction left Van Veeteren uneasy: Janek Mitter woke one morning with a brutal hangover and his wife dead in the bathtub. With only the flimsiest defense, he is found guilty and committed to a mental institution. But when Mitter is murdered in his cell, Van Veeteren regrets not following his gut and launches an investigation into the two murders. As the chief inspector delves deeper, the twisted root of these violent murders will shock even him.

Crime Fiction

WOMAN WITH BIRTHMARK

Van Veeteren and his associates are left bewildered by the curious murder of a man shot twice in the heart and twice below the belt. An utterly dull man, the only suspicious activity his surviving wife can report is a series of peculiar phone calls. Repeatedly the telephone would ring, offering no answer but an obscure pop song from the 1960s. This siren song would be linked to an identical murder, but the true connection remains unknown. Van Veeteren pursues his subject across the country, wading through outrageous leads and fruitless tips in this chilling mystery.

Crime Fiction

THE RETURN

On a rainy April day, a body—or what is left of it—is found by a young girl. Wrapped in a blanket with no hands, feet, or head, it signals the work of a brutal, methodical killer. The victim, Leopold Verhaven, was a track star before he was convicted for killing two of his ex-lovers. He consistently proclaimed his innocence, however, and was killed on the day of his return to society. This latest murder is more than a little perplexing, and Chief Inspector Van Veeteren is determined to discover the truth, even if it means taking the law into his own hands.

Crime Fiction

VINTAGE CRIME/BLACK LIZARD BOOKS
Available wherever books are sold.
www.randomhouse.com

READ THE LATEST—BREAKING MYSTERY, CRIME, SUSPENSE, AND THRILLER NEWS—VISIT THE NEW WEEKLY LIZARD DESKTOP AND MOBILE WEBSITE

www.WeeklyLizard.com

- Features the latest in the mystery, crime, noir, and thriller genres
- Content-driven site, drawing material from a wide variety of sources into interactive posts that invite visitors to share their own comments
- Frequent new and timely features ranging from author essays and original stories to author and character profiles, as well as film posts, witty wiseguy quotes, and much more

---

MORE MYSTERY, CRIME, SUSPENSE AND THRILLER READS